# Hemingway Cutthroat

Also by Michael Atkinson

*Blue Velvet*
*Ghosts in the Machine*
*One Hundred Children Waiting for a Train*
*Flickipedia*
*Exile Cinema: Filmmakers at Work Beyond Hollywood*
*Hemingway Deadlights*

# Hemingway
# Cutthroat

## MICHAEL ATKINSON

Minotaur Books

*A Thomas Dunne Book*
New York

A THOMAS DUNNE BOOK FOR MINOTAUR BOOKS.
An imprint of St. Martin's Publishing Company.

HEMINGWAY CUTTHROAT. Copyright © 2010 by Michael Atkinson. All rights reserved. Printed in the United States of America. For information, address St. Martin's Press, 175 Fifth Avenue, New York, N.Y. 10010.

www.thomasdunnebooks.com
www.minotaurbooks.com

Library of Congress Cataloging-in-Publication Data

Atkinson, Michael, 1962–
  Hemingway cutthroat / Michael Atkinson.—1st ed.
        p. cm.
  "Thomas Dunne Books."
  ISBN 978-0-312-37972-8
  1. Hemingway, Ernest, 1899–1961—Fiction.   2. Journalists—Spain—Fiction.   3. Americans—Spain—Fiction.   4. Spain—History—Civil War, 1936–1939—Fiction.   I. Title.
  PS3601.T496H45  2010
  813'.6—dc22

                                                          2009047484

First Edition: August 2010

10  9  8  7  6  5  4  3  2  1

For my mother

# Acknowledgments

A thankful tipple to the following friends and accomplices for help technical, linguistic, and otherwise: Michael Magee, Sharon McCreary, Mario Diaz, Margaret Smith, Stephen Koch (whose book *The Breaking Point* was an invaluable timeline and almanac for me, never mind that in matters other than chronology and geography it was largely as much a fiction as the book you're holding), my devil-may-care editor Peter Joseph, my intrepid agent Barbara Braun, and Laurel, my first reader and voluptuous confederate.

# Hemingway Cutthroat

# 1

At about the same moment José Robles Pazos was murdered, Ernest Hemingway was drunk on sangria. He would soon become a hunted man, and of course it was the sangria's fault.

Earlier, just as Robles was being led down a mountainside cut with runoff trenches now dusty in the early spring, led down by a rope tied to his wrists, blindfolded with the torn sleeve from his own shirt, Hemingway was 174 miles away in Madrid, riding in the backseat of an old, roofless Fiat Zero. The car was issuing backfire blasts so loud it occurred to him that the locals might think the Fascists had marched on the city again and were lobbing grenades into the street. It belonged to a flabby, unemployed Spanish journalist named Albarran, whom Hemingway had met the night before at a smoky basement game of *Mus*, several blocks from the Hotel Florida. Hemingway, in Spain only three days and looking for old-fashioned trouble, lost almost all of his pocket money because he never quite fathomed the game, which smelled like poker but kept involving bridge-style partnerships, and Albarran promised the American he'd take him to see a bullfight in the morning.

But there were of course no bullfights in Spain in 1937, because of the war. Albarran insisted he would make good on his claim, and so before lunch the next day Hemingway found himself horrifyingly sober and tortured by a migraine, driving northeast through the cloudy, bomb-pocked city. In the front seat next to Albarran was another fat Spaniard, older, who only whispered to Albarran in guttural hisses even when spoken to in ordinary tones.

The longer the drive, the more Hemingway began to seethe.

"C'mon, Albarran, tell me."

"No, no, señor, you will see when we get there, I tell the truth."

"I shoulda seen this coming."

Martha was shopping. Until lunch.

The Fiat parked in front of a broad, seemingly abandoned expanse of bombed-out apartment buildings. The three men got out, instinctively hunching and hustling over to the building's facade. Shells were known to sometimes fall. Albarran knocked on the door, traded a few Catalan obscurities with another man through the crack, and the door opened wide. They walked down a hallway, down a staircase that stank of mold.

"What the," Hemingway said.

Another door, and then the basement. They walked down a worn set of wooden steps into a vast cellar, its low ceiling supported by massive pine joists and columns that looked positively medieval. The space was empty, save for some rusty petroleum barrels and stacks of empty egg crates. And for the bull, who was tethered to a central column with a thick barge rope.

Hemingway could see immediately, even in the low light from the strung-out wire of bulbs lining the ceiling, that the bull was old, twenty years if it was a day, emaciated, and probably sick. Its ribs were visible and heaving from its breath, and its coat was shaggy. Its eyeballs were milky with cataracts.

How'd they even get the animal down here? he wondered. There were twelve or so other men in the basement standing around, drinking rum from unmarked bottles. Hemingway looked around—there were no seats, no area to watch. If you were in the basement, you were part of the show.

"*Una gran corrida!*" Albarran chortled.

"You've got to be shitting me."

"It is *course libre*, señor."

"I'm out of here," he said, turning just as a boy ran over to the daydreaming bull and with a quick gesture untied the rope from the column. As the boy dove back into the perimeter shadows, another man raised a pellet rifle and shot the wheezing bull in the flanks.

The bull instantly bellowed and launched into a furious, confused charge, foam flying from his parched nostrils, coming right at Hemingway and Albarran before hooking its whitened horn on another column and tripping, crashing onto its side. Hemingway had to dive away from the stairs, and every man on the room was on the balls of his feet as the bull stood up again, pissed and aching and half blind, and came at them in a vicious gallop, horns out, crushing the egg crates and bumping into the rough stone walls with a startled yelp. Hemingway and the other men ran around the perimeter or sometimes across the open middle, and the bull tried to chase them, always coming faster and sooner than you'd think, so the diving, sprinting, laughing Spaniards were often enough caught on its head, ripped by its horns, and thrown into the air.

"Jesus Christ," Hemingway growled, keeping one eye on the staircase and trying to dash in inconspicuous bursts clockwise around the room, as the weathered old animal ran more or less also clockwise but intersected the room haphazardly in a homicidal rage, hitting the columns at random and shaking the rafters, looking for the nearest man to gore.

Hemingway didn't get far at first, spending a long minute huddling in the shadows behind the other men. If anyone is going to catch a horn in the ribs, he thought, it's going to be one of these nutless scamps.

But then Hemingway pushed Spaniards out of his way, which the men took to be part of the game, pushing each other as well into the line of fire. Crouching down behind a column, he took a rum bottle offered by a shirtless teenager covered in sweat, but before he could bring it to his lips the bull hit the opposite side of the column with the full force of his skull. The bottle shot out of Hemingway's hand, and the column gave way in a thunderous shredding of old, dry wood. It crumbled in half. Hemingway bolted and leaped for the retaining wall, and the ceiling above the column shuddered and gave off plumes of dust and bowed down some two feet with epic structural screaming.

The Spaniards just whooped it up and kept running, taunting the bull. All Hemingway could focus on was the stairs.

But then the bull took them out—the boy who'd untied the rope ran scrambling up the steps, and the bull came at him and hit the staircase with its crown, and as the boy flew over the last step, up and through the doorway, the whole apparatus splintered around the bull, the beam joints falling over his neck and tripping up his front hooves, so he bucked and crashed, and broke the joints and planks up into kindling in just a few jerks of his massive body.

Hemingway couldn't believe it. Now what? Edging close to the shattered wood now, Hemingway recalculated—could he move the old barrel over and jump up on it? But how, without getting nailed? Maybe I'll just have to kill that bull, he thought, with a pipe or something, but he didn't remember seeing anything like that in the semidarkness. Only bottles. A pike or something, a blade, that's all it would take, I've seen it done enough times. Of course, I've seen men die trying, too.

If that fucking beast takes out one more column, we're all dead.

All of those things I should be doing. This is a new low. I won't be even able to tell Joe Russell about it.

He stepped toward the broken stairs—he reached up to the

fractured wood step under the doorway, but it came off in his hand.

The Spaniards leaped around and hooted. The bull caught one of them on its head, the drunken fellow was lucky to avoid the horns, but then the bull heaved and threw the guy up and behind him, and before the flying man hit a low joist and broke his jawbone on it, his body snagged and ripped the wire that juiced the lightbulbs, and in a snap the room was pitch-black.

Except for the doorway at the top of the erstwhile steps, from which light flowed onto Hemingway, the bull turned.

*Fuck*, he dove again into the darkness, and the bull hurtled by him with a hairbreadth to spare, the horn brushing his jacket. Then the animal's brow hit the stone wall full-on, and fell to its knees. The sound of it must've been as audible on the street as an underground tremor.

In the half-light, Hemingway could see the animal's bulk slowly get to its feet and turn, like a losing boxer in the tenth round, unsure of where he is. Maybe it'll just have a heart attack, he thought, but it turned again, and the goddamn Spaniards started laughing and yelling, the bull remembered it was enraged and out for blood, and charged again. Tiptoeing out of the bull's vicinity, Hemingway was some distance from the stairs now, and the bull sought out the few men in his direction. As it did he could see across the way the rest of the Spaniards boosting each other up and out the doorway on their shoulders. They were quiet suddenly, not laughing, and the bull paused, puzzled, facing Hemingway, who also didn't make a sound.

It's smelling now, he thought. It began to pace toward him.

Hemingway panicked and looked for cover. There was an iron drum to his left and in a scramble he grabbed it by its rim, pulled it over on its side, and shot inside.

It stank so badly of petrol it stung the back of his throat to breathe. He could hear the bull: It snorted and charged and hit the barrel with its horns, knocking it into the wall. It rolled back a little, and the bull wound back a few steps and ran and hit it again. Hemingway would've thrown up had he eaten anything that day, but his migraine, which he'd forgotten about the moment he saw the bull, began echoing back on itself now, booming, and he felt as if he were strapped to the clapper of a giant cathedral bell at high noon. He began to dry heave. After a few pregnant moments, the bull hit the lying barrel again, hard, and it bounced off the wall and rolled, over and over, clattering, past the bull and about twenty feet out into the open cellar, Hemingway bracing his body inside with his knees and hands. He was growing delirious, and remembered being tricked as a kid to crawl into an old pickle barrel and then being rolled down an embankment, and throwing up his breakfast of oatmeal all over himself. He remembered washing chunks of it out of his hair afterward. Those bastards. But then he remembered it was his cousin Kit who rolled him, and he felt bad because Kit didn't make it out of Reims in 1918.

It was quiet. Hemingway was on his back, which made him feel vulnerable. He listened: nothing. It was two whole minutes before he dared to crawl, inch by silent inch, out of the barrel, squinting into the darkness.

The men were all gone, even the one with the broken jaw. Presumably the last was pulled up by his friends. Hemingway looked for the bull, and did not see it standing anywhere near the shafts of light coming from the doorway. He let his eyes acclimate to the shadows, and saw it, prone and on its side, only ten or so feet away. Hemingway stood up and walked over to it: The animal was sprawled out dead. Maybe it had that coronary after all. Long overdue, the crazy old fucker.

He rolled the barrel over, set it upright but bottom up, climbed onto it, and boosted himself up. Outside, Albarran's Fiat sat at the curb, empty. Without thinking, really, that he was stealing, Hemingway bounded into the driver's seat, pushed the ignition button, and drove it back south through the wet streets, toward the Hotel Florida.

He had only the desire for drinks, and pulled over to the disheveled cantina where he was to meet Martha for lunch. The waiters had dared to put tables out on the sidewalk.

So, as José Robles, a colonel in the Popular Front and the Spanish government's adjutant to the Comintern, was yanked along through the wild gorse and heather by a cadre of silent men with heavy footfalls and carbines that bounced dully against their backs with every step down the slope, Hemingway sat down in the sun that had just cut its way from the clouds, and ordered sangria, which came in a pitcher with large wedges of chipped ice. Sooner rather than later, a journalist from Boston noticed him and shook his hand, then an American woman did the same, asking him to autograph her *Farewell* hardcover. Then, after sangria was reordered and the migraine dissipated like released pipe steam, a Spanish girl of nineteen who'd been sitting alone with a lemonade accepted his invitation to sit with him and share his wine. She was Ana, a Zaragoza señorita in her second year at the university, a nurse in the making and a virgin still but perhaps not for long. He knew he smelled badly of gasoline, but she never mentioned it. Who couldn't love this hazel-eyed angel, he thought. When she asked him if he was married, he had to think about it for a moment.

"Yes. But in America, being married is sort of like a hobby. I don't treat it very seriously these days."

"Here, marriage is like a job."

"With no pay."

"*Si!* And you can't quit! I want to go to America. I want that hobby—marriage only on Sundays, if I'm bored and it's raining!"

"You'd fit right in."

While Hemingway spoke with and to this Zaragoza girl, watching her dimples deepen with the wine and flattery and telling her about Italy during the Great War, and Robles was pulled like a mule down a Sierra de Gúdar foothill, John Dos Passos was in Paris. He'd taken the aging German ocean liner, now the HMS *Berengaria,* from New York. That afternoon, Dos Passos had interviewed, for *Fortune* magazine's series on the Popular Front, Minister of the Interior Marx Dormoy. That morning Dormoy had successfully mustered a vote of confidence from Parliament after being pilloried up and down the boulevards for allowing the anti-Semitic cavemen of the Croix-de-Feu to march, and therein precipitating a riot of protesters, several of whom were shot by nervous policemen. The minister was visibly relieved he hadn't annihilated either his career or the French Popular Front, and tucked into a quiche the size of a volume of Balzac as he spoke with Dos Passos, and he spoke in large, lovely—if cheese-spittled—paragraphs. So, Dos Passos left the offices beside the Jardin de Luxembourg with a large and vital article in his pocket that he would barely have to write, and treated himself to a cognac somewhere in a heavily shaded side street in Saint-Germain-des-Prés. Women walked in and out of the sunlight across the street, and none looked at Dos Passos, who rather resembled a portly, balding supporting character in *Blondie,* but with watery, slightly crossed eyes. Sitting there, letting his mind wander too far from fiction, Dos Passos thought ahead to Spain, where the revolution was finally happening—the rocky ground he'd loved since his school days was finally being sown with modernity and fellowship and hope.

José Robles walked as he was pulled on a rope, John Dos Passos drank cognac alone, Ernest Hemingway drank sangria with a teenage girl. Ana was getting woozy, but she was perky and fast-thinking, and Hemingway could see why she was probably the first person ever in her family to go to university.

"Señor, is that what American newspapers have told you?"

"What? The Radical Republican Party wasn't leftist?"

"No! Centrist at best. Lerroux is a snake."

"And the CEDA?"

"Crazed monarchist jackals."

"So who was on the left in '33?"

"Azana, and the socialist parties, same as today."

"But there was no Popular Front."

"Not until '35."

"It's all hard to keep straight."

"Perhaps for you."

Ana gulped, burped with a smile, and pulled her cardigan around her. Fucking politics, he thought. Why is it always so complicated? On the other hand, this girl was at that stage, with her eyelids at half-mast and her legs widening slowly under the table, that made Hemingway think rampaging filthy thoughts and made his scrotum tingle. After all he'd been through already that day. Fucking bull. Get her number, he thought, get something. That's the thing about getting women drunk—if it doesn't have a chance of working out, next time you start all over again at square one.

"Ana, tell me, how many boys have you known? I bet a girl like you, with eyes like yours, has known a good many."

"So you think I am a farm whore. Because I have green eyes."

"No! Green? No, no—I meant that you may have entertained, no, endured a few boys, who wanted you to compromise yourself, right? I bet they're always scouting you, like wolves."

"Well, yes, a few. They do scout. So?"

"So you have not allowed them." More wine. "You have not lost your flower."

Ana blushed but would not allow herself to appear embarrassed. "No, I haven't, señor, and I won't lose it today."

Perhaps not. Ana began to sway, her eyelids fluttering. Hemingway, at thirty-seven a robust and red-cheeked soldier of experience and ego and lovemaking and writing hard-won sentences, decided finally that this young girl was not fair game by any standard, not even a drunkard's.

Ana began to grow pale, and looked as if she was suddenly, yet halfheartedly, afraid of throwing up. Hemingway looked around the café—many eyes were naturally on him, the loud-voiced celebrity writer from *los Estados Unidos*, stinking of gasoline, sitting not with the flashy blonde with whom he came to Spain but some soused, raven-haired señorita nearly young enough to be his daughter. He began to panic. What if there was a photographer in the crowd? The area was thick with Brigadesmen and reporters and Russians and students.

Ana abruptly moved her chair out, and bent down, her head between her knees. Getting ready to vomit.

"Ana, should we aim for the curb, huh?"

Dos Passos had another cognac, and thought ahead to Spain some more, dreaming of attaining a proper Communism in *that* country, a country where the food is good, and he missed Katy, and he knew he'd see Hemingway there again, and sighed when he thought of what an electrifying pleasure and a tortuous ordeal that would simultaneously be. He began writing on napkins. He hoped the cognac would cure his constipation, because it sometimes had that effect, and kept downing cognacs through the next hour until they gave him the runs. Later, he made it back to his cheap hotel room in Paris just in time to avoid an accident, and sat on the toilet with a rhythmic cognac headache. Then, recovered, he typed up his Dormoy article in no time flat on his trusty portable, and took a nap.

But earlier, during the moment, or moments, we're talking about, half past 2 PM or so, a zone ahead of Greenwich Mean Time, March 23, 1937, at the café with the nauseous Ana, Hemingway began to squirrel the napkins he'd scribbled on into his pockets, a few notes for his dispatches about "the café with fresh girls from Zaragoza," and the brooding dusk and the way the waiters stood together under the awning talking in whispers. He didn't want to leave the notes behind should he have to bolt, which he'd do if she began throwing up under the table. Bent over, Ana began to quietly retch toward the sidewalk, but nothing came of it.

Hemingway contemplated just getting up and leaving anyway, avoiding eye contact all the way around the corner, when three tall, ropey-armed young men and a high-cheeked young woman came quickly slaloming between the tables to Ana's side.

"There you are!" one said. "Ana! What's going—"

Ana began to slur something unintelligible. The young woman looked around, saw the eyes of the crowd around them. The sternest of the young men lowered his face to Hemingway's.

"What did you do to her? How do you know her? She's a good Catholic girl, her father thought she could be a nun!"

Ana snorted.

Hemingway put his hands up defensively. "We were just having some sangria! Honestly, I don't know her!"

Another young man came down from his standing height. "You're American?! What's your name?"

"Hemingway."

"That novelist?! *Santa Maria!* You've defiled this girl. She'll be lucky if her father doesn't kick her out like trash! He saved a machinist's wages for years to send her to college!"

"She's just drunk—"

"Just drunk!" the boy barked. "What kind of girl do you think she is? You're endangering her—did you know we're at war?"

"Yes, *gracias,* I know."

Martha appeared on the sidewalk a few feet away, holding large white bags, her mouth gaping. Hemingway shook with a double take between her sudden appearance and the assault of the students.

"Señor Hemingway," the sternest young man growled, bending into the older man's face, "Ana's father will find you. You've shamed his only daughter. He will come for you and he will cut your throat. This is *not* America!"

"What the fuck," Martha said. Everyone looked to her, if only for an instant. "Who's this?"

"This is Ana, she's in school—" Hemingway offered, as the young men struggled to get Ana to her feet.

"Ernest, she's pie-eyed. What were you planning on doing with her, now that she can't walk."

"Nothing. We were just talking, fer Chrissake—" Hemingway stood up, ready to go. "About politics."

"Uh-huh."

"What, I'm lying? Politics."

"That so. Christ, you reek like a grease monkey. What the hell have you been doing?"

Ana was shuttled away through the tables by the young men. The young woman took two steps up to Hemingway.

"He will, he will come after you," she said. "He's almost killed strangers for just talking to her. His name is Señor Teodoro Fajardo, of Zaragoza. He has nothing now but his family's honor."

"Something to look forward to." Martha.

"Jesus Christ," Hemingway said mostly to himself, watching the students go. It wasn't even 1 PM yet, and Hemingway was ready to give the rest of the day away to whomever would have it.

Martha and Hemingway walked back to the Florida, stewing and bickering. They plowed through the usual crowd of acolytes and hangers-on in the lobby. Upstairs, Hemingway gave a hungry Josephine Herbst some dried sausage and water crackers, and then shut the door.

"You were angling toward fucking her—"

"No, I wasn't—"

"C'mon, she was gorgeous, you got her skunked, don't give me that crap—"

"Goddammit, the sangria just got away from me, that's all—"

"I shouldn't even be here with you. I should've known better than to believe you, everyone told me—"

"Everyone!"

"Yes, every last person on Earth told me, don't get swayed by him, he's a serial husband, he's a lost ship trying out different ports—"

"Us meeting in Spain was supposed to be a secret, I thought."

"Oh sure. In a hotel full of American journalists. A lot you care. And why should you? What do you have to lose? Your wife is waiting in Key West for you, right? Darning your socks."

"Shut up."

It went on like that for another forty-five minutes, until they had talked around the concept of illicit sex so much that they had to do some of it, so they stripped, opened a bottle of inexpensive but good *cava,* and got down to it. As Martha screwed and drank wine and said things Pauline never would with her legs over Hemingway's shoulders, she got louder, and as she got louder the obligatory knocks on the door of room 108, and the traffic in the hallway, dwindled to nothing.

Neither one gave another thought to Ana or her father Teodoro Fajardo, though they might well have.

By then Robles was dead. He had been led by rope into a grassy dale somewhere in the rocky perimeter hills of Valencia and made to kneel. They fired a bullet through the front of his skull and out the back. It would be over three weeks before anyone found him.

# 2

A Hershey's bar?"
John Dos Passos stood in the middle of 108, holding chocolate. It was all he had. Almost three weeks after the cognac runs, April 11. He looked like a schoolboy without his homework.

Madrid was still cold, still gray and sad and beset with icy rains, as if the weather itself knew the woeful outcome of the war and was trying to tell everyone before it was too late.

Hemingway sat in a thick robe, writing in bed, polishing his dispatch for the North American Newspaper Alliance about the recent shelling that *killed an old woman returning home from market, dropping her in a huddled black heap of clothing, with one leg suddenly detached,* and so on. But it was two o'clock, and he'd bought a bottle of old port while out the day before, and it was almost gone. It was time to get up and rouse the sleeping hordes, find a battle, collect an experience. More than a little bleary, he'd just decided to let Martha polish the story, insofar as it needed to be polished, or whatever, when Dos Passos finally arrived in Madrid. Stepping through the door. Empty-handed, except for a piece of candy.

The month in Madrid had been war-worried. Small shells would rain down into the city on occasion, and even hit the Florida, to little avail as yet. The war was in its ninth month, and almost five months had passed since the triumphant November defense of Madrid by its own citizens and a handful of Brigades against divisions of Moroccan troops, Italian light-armor battalions, and German panzers. The Battle of Guadalajara, far northeast, was won decisively by the Republicans in March. The Fascists still tried to encircle the city, town by outlying town, and any effort for the Republican forces to burst forth beyond the hinterlands invariably resulted in massive losses. Most of 1937 was stalemates and frustration and blood-saturated soil.

Hemingway was suffering a familiar state of conflict—not about the war or the Republicans, God knows, no matter how many Russian apparatchiks showed up with fake Spanish names, no matter how many conscripted Italian soldiers got killed at Franco's behest (he still liked Italians, he couldn't help it), no matter how much the entire Popular Front government seemed to be controlled by Stalin, who doubtless had agendas that took little consideration of Spaniards per se. You draw sides against Hitler and Mussolini, or you stay out of the fight. No, he was torn about his own role in the mess—he, as always, wanted to get down to the authentic, to experience the war as the peasants did. But then once he was in Spain, and the best intact hotel in Madrid was offered to him, and he had decided it'd be best to bring lots of food and drink and, why not, Sidney Franklin the sheep-doggy only-Brooklyn-boy-to-be-an-ex-bullfighter to run errands—well, it became far from authentic. Once he landed in a zone of true human desperation, looking for truth, Hemingway always, because he could, sought out the best his money could buy, indulged himself, lived it up. He'd share, of course, that was part of the fun. Where else could you live high and fast if not in a war zone? But then he'd begin to hate himself for it, and ride the undulating carnival ride between hollowed-out depression and the efforts at drunken bliss he'd make in reply. He was a fraud, a three-dollar bill, a charlatan everyone treated like a messiah. There was never a respite, a definitive arrival, a sense of *thereness*. God*damn* it.

"Dos, for the love of God, you didn't bring any food?"

"Oh, shit."

"You forgot food."

"Yes, I forgot, but I just came from Valencia—"

"Dos, there's nothing to eat here. Not much, anyway, that's edible."

"I know, I know—hey, the car that picked me up is loaded—"

"Sure it is, that's from Largo, from the government, to supply the whole hotel."

"Whatever, Ernest—"

"No whatever, Dos, you're just going to bilk off other people while you're here?"

Dos Passos felt his bowels fist up. Here we go.

"Some fucking Republican," he growled.

"I never said I was a fucking *Communist*!" Hemingway flipped his pen angrily across the room, hitting the bathroom door.

"Still in here!" Martha chirped from inside.

"You've got a good snootful in you already, don't you," Dos Passos said, taking his coat off. Sidney Franklin lumbered in with the last of Dos Passos's bags, felt the percolating hostility in the air like humidity, and left without a noise.

"Oh, piss up a rope," Hemingway grunted, pouring some more port. He was getting hungry, but didn't dare break out the closet larder after hollering about starvation to Dos Passos, the most guileless and righteous American Communist he knew.

"I won't eat, OK? I'll drop a few pounds." Dos Passos stuck his belly out a little, as a mock peace offering. Hemingway cracked a smile into his glass.

"OK."

"I'll live on your leftovers. On the scraps you leave in your beard."

"You're a riot."

"You and food. Honestly. 'We ate bread, and it was good.' "

"Alright, that's enough."

"Good thing I brought the dozen cases of Chambolle-Musigny with me."

"Really?"

"No."

"I need you like I need another mother-in-law."

"Yes. Look, I'm staying at the hotel, I'll buy from the hotel, I'm not so fucking worried about what I'm eating."

"Fine."

"But look, Ernest, something's really wrong. Pepe Robles is missing."

Throwing his legs over the side of the bed, Hemingway looked up. Both men had known José Robles for years, as medical volunteers in Italy during the war in 1917 and 1918, and later when Robles taught Spanish at Johns Hopkins in Baltimore. But Dos Passos knew him better, met him earlier, and matched his idealisms to Robles's—crazy Marxist utopianism. Hemingway remembered a fiercely smart, buoyant young Spaniard talking up Lenin, dazzling any Italian girl he laid eyes on, and regurgitating a mouthful of Antonio Machado poems, watery-eyed, whenever he'd had even one drink. Hemingway had liked him well enough, and drank with him several times, and knew his Republican heart was pure. Robles had even visited Key West once, and the two had gone fishing and caught a sixteen-pound bigeye thresher, which they brought home and grilled over wood. He remembered that weekend because Robles, still a bachelor, recited poetry to Pauline (who knew no Spanish), and the two generally became swoony over each other until Hemingway, lubricated with Scotch, got good and poleaxed about it and challenged Robles to fisticuffs. The Spaniard, laughing, suggested they make it a swordfight, which they did, on the veranda with two dress Spanish army blades Hemingway had bought in Mexico City. Pauline ran for cover. Only after Hemingway got cut on the shoulder and Robles caught a slash on his pant leg that nearly exposed his scrotum did the two give into giggles and resumed drinking. Pauline dressed the wounds.

So Robles was a good egg, not cracked or rotten, he thought, a man of confidence and humor. But Hemingway also had always thought Robles was ambitious and naïve, and Hemingway never warmed to ambition or naïveté, especially in combination.

"Whatta you mean, 'missing'?"

"Arrested."

"What for?"

"No one will say. No one has any record of it. But his wife said they arrested him."

"Who's 'they'?"

"No one knows."

"When?"

"Over three weeks ago."

"What?"

Christ, this is all I need, Hemingway thought. He had a war to cover, one wife to disentangle, another (hopefully) to lock in, a food cache he had to practically guard with his life, *The Spanish Earth* to finish with Joris Ivens—except where Ivens and the footage was, no one seemed to know—another novel to begin (he'd begun fishing for characters in Spain the moment he climbed off the boat), and, if the fates were with him, genuine combat situations to find that he could run into and which might finally put him out of his misery altogether.

On top of all that, a missing *camarada*? Spain was one vast shallow grave; assassinations and disappearances were as common as Sabbaths.

"I don't have room in my head for this."

"Sorry for the inconvenience."

"He's the adjutant to the Comintern, for God's sake. No one's looked into it?"

"Not as far as I can find. They shrug, as if he just went off on a bender." Having made himself a crucial intermediary figure between the Popular Front and the Soviets, Robles was not a minor character in Spain since the war began. Everybody knew him, he'd been to every function, meeting, and ceremony, he was a phone call away, when the phones were working, from every bigwig in Madrid and Valencia. How could he just vanish?

Martha came out of the toilet wearing only a chemise, but neither man glanced her way.

"Dos, what do you want me to do?"

It was a fair question, but one that dripped trouble like nitroglycerin. Hemingway knew what Dos Passos would be thinking and wanting to say the minute the question came out of his mouth—that Hemingway was, relatively speaking, an opportunist and an egomaniac who didn't really give a rat's ass about Spain or the peasants or democracy. That the fate of an actual friend, in wartime, wasn't quite as important to him as his newspaper dispatches or his next novel or the money earned from the last novel, or even the food in the closet. That he was only interested in turning the civil war into a place where he can drink, screw, eat, and make a public spectacle of himself. That actually fighting Franco's Nationalists, doing what was moral and brave, wasn't something for which he was willing to make the sacrifices. And so on.

It wasn't true. Not entirely.

But Hemingway knew also it was true, too much of it. He'd heard Dos Passos grumble to this effect before, in Italy, in Florida, and after he'd returned from Russia. And it echoed what was already hailing down in Hemingway's own head. The emptiness of acquiring things, the maddening ephemerality of sex and drunkenness, the addictive irritations of fame, the absence of something in his life he could hold and look at and declare meaningful. Writing did the job often enough, but only while it was happening, not after. What was already written felt like a product, something for someone else to buy. It wasn't happiness or peace, on the page, it was just craft. There was a disconnect he couldn't escape between making something and then the thing made. Still under forty, still looking forward, he couldn't help thinking that there should be, what?, an attainment of glory and satisfaction somewhere in his strivings. But for unfathomable reasons he couldn't find it anywhere. He'd run to Spain hoping to find *it* here, whatever it was, fulfillment maybe, but instead he found drinks to buy, favors to grant, dispatches to knock off. Political manure to sink his foot into and then try to extract it from.

"Ernest, you could try to do the right thing." Dos Passos said it slowly, deliberately without righteousness or bile, so his old friend, of whom he was frankly a little tired, would not get defensive.

Hemingway didn't. He'd always had the emotional armor of a bull, and could usually only admit he was wrong about anything, for example, to a woman he was hoping to either bed or marry. That is, unless he was caught on a dark day, when looking in the mirror was verboten and the drinking started before noon. When his resources were desperately low, and he was likely to agree were someone to call him a pansy coward libertine and pretentious fool.

"But Dos . . . we're scheduled to go to the front—"

Dos Passos didn't say a thing. The front will still be there, he could've said, what's more important, et cetera. Silence did it.

Twisting up inside like a wrung bath towel, Hemingway didn't decide anything, and wouldn't have let Dos Passos know if he had.

"Let's go see Gorev about it, at the Embassy," Hemingway said. "See what he says."

He took a last sip of port and felt as it warmed him chest to cheek that this war zone wouldn't be the war zone he'd hoped for in his various dreams. Not this week.

"I could go alone," Dos Passos, shuffling a little.

"No, we'll go."

"You trust Gorev?"

"Not to give me change of a quarter."

# 3

Everyone knew the Russians ran the show, ever since the January 1936 elections, which swept the Front's leftist coalition to power, and particularly after Franco's coup d'état campaign ignited the war in July. Once the war began, Stalin fed and fueled the Front in opposition to Franco's alliance with Mussolini and Hitler. But he was, of course, doing more than just aiding the Spanish; he was establishing an imperialistic foothold, controlling the government's decisions (the postwar issues would be ceded to the know-it-all Soviets, just as wartime power had been), covertly molding a potential satellite, one *this* close to France and England.

Vladimir Gorev—"Sancho," as he instructed every Spaniard he met to call him—may have been the most powerful man on the Iberian peninsula in April 1937, a leading Red Army general sent to direct the Republican forces and, indeed, the entire wartime apparatus of Spanish government, a regal, six-foot-three Muscovite lightly carrying five languages (including Tatar, but not including Spanish), a memorized devotion to Pushkin, a reputation as a peerless battlefield tactician, and the intimate trust of Stalin, which alone gave him the air of a demigod. It was Gorev who'd led the hodgepodge defense of Madrid in November, after the Caballero government had abandoned the city for Valencia. If there was a single individual responsible for the ease and definitiveness with which Stalin's apparatchiks pulled the strings of the Second Spanish Republic, it was Gorev.

It was also Gorev for whom the Popular Front hired Robles as adjutant and translator, making the almond-eyed egghead professor an army colonel so he could take the job. So, it would seem confronting Gorev with the question of Robles's disappearance— his presumed detainment or death—was a little like walking into gunfire. Wouldn't Gorev have realized something was wrong once a single weekday had passed without word from Robles? Or not? Perhaps at first Gorev thought Robles was simply stuck without a ride in Valencia, where he kept his family and where he took infrequent weekend trips. But after a week, two weeks, three? If he did nothing, does it mean he knew about it, on some level, and wasn't surprised? Which would mean he was complicitous?

Or, maybe the assassins were NKVD, Soviet internal affairs, which Gorev wouldn't know about by definition, Hemingway thought in the back of the Front-chauffeured car driving to the Soviet Embassy, Dos Passos next to him picking at his cuticles, looking out the far window at the cold, sad city.

But maybe it was the splintering Trotskyites in *el Partido Obrero de Unificación Marxista* making a rash political point, and Gorev just didn't think one Spaniard more or less was worth the worry. Or maybe it was lingering anarchist militia members, avenging any number of executions by the Communists. Maybe it was just Cordoban lowlifes to whom Robles owed card money. Perhaps it *was* Nationalist *espías*, and Gorev was too busy with the fate of Spain and the terrifying weight of Stalin's voice in his ear to care. Christ, could be anyone. Spain was a viper pit of cross-purposes and vendettas and power grabs, and even sussing out who was on whose side was like untangling clumped fishing line.

"I've had too much booze." Hemingway rubbed his temples in circles.

"Have the driver pull over and pick you up an orange juice." Which Dos Passos did himself, leaning up over the front seat, pointing out in his smooth Spanish a café on the left side of the road.

"These posters!" Hemingway said, looking out at the buildings and walls plastered with vibrantly colored, graphically muscular Popular Front art. The car waited at the curb, engine running. "They're so beautiful. Where'd they come from?"

"Russia," Dos Passos answered. "Russian artists. Just like in Moscow. State-approved. Unmistakable."

Hemingway sat back, massaging his eyes.

". . . I'm stuck on what I'm doing, Dos. That last book is a lemon."

"Which one?"

"It's probably coming in the fall. *To Have and Have Not*."

"What's wrong with it?"

"It's spiteful, and it's a mess."

The two men had been competing like mountain gorillas for years, and Hemingway always won, grandly, in fame and royalties and accolades and even Hollywood paychecks. So he could afford, by this late date, to show his bruises to Dos Passos, who could always be trusted to do the civil thing and not call him a pompous blowbag. Even if that's what he was to some. Hemingway could do it, too, because he knew that Dos Passos was running out of fresh ideas, stylistically, that he couldn't do that nutty *U.S.A.* thing for much longer, that it was likely he would begin to fade as a prominent figure as the years rolled onward, in ways Hemingway had no intention of doing. Max Perkins might've demanded that damn Morgan book too soon, but "The Snows of Kilimanjaro" was proof enough to everyone, or at least to plenty of people, that Hemingway still had the marksmanship and the grace required for the long haul. Dos Passos was a canvasser, a mural painter, a collagist, only as good as his source materials. His innovation was a novelty, not a precision tool.

"Don't see how it could be that bad."

". . ."

"Wait and see. Start again. Right?"

"Sure, I am, I'm trying. Maybe something here."

"Shouldn't be difficult to find a story here."

"You'd think."

"Ernest, in Valencia . . ."

"Yes."

". . . I saw Julio Alvarez del Vayo."

"Of course you did. Whatta cocksucker."

The juice came, in a tall glass, the waiter waiting and watching as Hemingway drank it.

"Del Vayo said nothing, would barely acknowledge me. All I did was ask where Robles was, and he stammered around, and said something about him being 'alright,' as if I'd asked about the man's health. Why would he say that?"

"Because he's not a good liar on the balls of his feet, that's why."

The car went into gear and continued.

"Hmmm."

"But they're pretty busy in Valencia, Dos, there's a war going on. He's the foreign minister, he could've been thinking about a hundred other things."

"Yes . . . But so far it's all we have to go on. Del Vayo is also the government's main propaganda honcho—administering to us, the journalists, that's his job, too. He doesn't do it, the Comintern would drop him like a dead clam."

"Maybe he's overwhelmed. Who the fuck knows. He's just a journalist, too, you know, he's really only a magazine writer at heart. Maybe he's so in over his head he let something slip."

"So you think del Vayo knows. About Pepe."

"I have no idea. But we'll see if Gorev knows—if we play it

right. No demonstrations, no explaining things. Let him fill the silences."

"You're not writing this, you know, this is for real."

"I oughtta slug you."

They pulled in in front of the embassy on Velasquez, which occupied one of the oldest, grandest buildings in the city, sprawling along the block like the medieval palace it might actually have been, its wide front steps choked with the flow, up and down, of dozens of nascent bureaucrats and apparatchiks and soldiers, heaving office furniture, shuttling in and out of black cars with dispatches under their arms, dashing to and waiting for and emerging from meetings and more meetings. The two writers had no problem with the first set of guards, showing their press passes. Their appointment was at four, and it was 3:45 PM. And yet they waited, not saying anything to each other, on a bench in the vast tile-paved hallway outside Gorev's office for a solid fifty minutes. The sun came down on hazy legs through a high arched window, reminding Hemingway of church, a particular Episcopal church in Oak Park, but also of any number of churches in Spain and Italy, and in fact, come to think of it, virtually any Mediterranean building he'd ever been in that was over 200 years old. They were all like churches. They were all beautiful, places in which you could get lost dreaming.

When a secretary finally escorted them in, through two successive offices and into Gorev's huge, marble-walled central space, the distances between the broad mahogany desk and the chairs in the room too far by several feet, Gorev stood up and merely leaned over his desk to shake hands. His bearing was monarchal, his uniform unbuttoned only at the throat, his face bony and lipless, his eyes large and blue and half-lidded, revealing less than a rhinoceros's. His hand was larger than Hemingway's, and Hemingway had a jolt of remembered teenage insecurity, shaking the hand of a mountain of a man at his father's hunting club, a dark-haired man who mocked the boy for his youth and slightness.

"Gentlemen." Gorev's voice rang deep like an iron bell in a cave and in English with an accent so Europeanized it could suggest almost any nationality east of the Rhine. "I'm happy to give you a few moments, Mr. Hemingway, always a pleasure, and this is Mr. Dos Passos? Call me Sancho!"

"Sancho, *rat teebya veedet.*"

Hemingway groaned a little inside—was this going to be an impress-the-Russkie pissing match?

"You speak Russian, Mr. Dos Passos? Good to know!"

"Not fluently."

"Good to know!"

Hemingway filled his cheeks with air.

"I must tell you," Gorev tossed to Dos Passos, "I love *Orient Express.*"

"You're the only one." They both laughed. Hemingway sat down first, and then the others did.

"So, two great American writers—two great *Illinois* writers!— here to see me. What can I do for you?"

*Illinois?* Nose out of joint, Hemingway felt his dehydration headache come on just in time.

"Sancho, we were wondering what you could tell us about where José Robles is."

Dos Passos chimed in. "He's been missing for three weeks, according to Margara Robles, you know, his wife."

Gorev furrowed his brow in melodramatic concern.

"Robles? Haven't seen him!" The Russian gazed unblinking at the men, and then, after a moment, shrugged a little, saying, "well?"

"Yes," Hemingway said. Did he not understand? "Neither have we. Because he's missing. His wife says he was arrested."

"In the middle of the night." Dos Passos.

Gorev's eyebrows shot up like they were on curtain cords. But they shot up, it seemed to both of the writers, a quarter of a second too late.

"Arrested? By whom?" His attention dropped to his desk, and he began rummaging through drawers. Hemingway and Dos Passos looked at each other.

"We don't know. That's why we're here." Hemingway shifted in his seat.

Gorev did not look up from his open drawers.

Hemingway took a breath. "Sancho!" Gorev sat up like a fire alarm had gone off. Hemingway continued, in a loud and slow manner that demanded attention, and gave no indication of being aware that speaking to Gorev in this patronizing manner could perhaps get him killed, dumped in a ditch, by morning. "General, José was your translator, yes? We are interested in finding out what has happened to him. He was an integral member of your team here, yes? Then please tell us what you can about why he has been missing for three weeks. Surely you noticed." So much for not filling in the silences.

"Noticed?"

"Surely you noticed when he didn't come to work, day after day. You know José, you know he loved the Republic."

"No, Comrade Hemingway, I can't say I did notice. He had a number of duties, and sometimes days would go by. This is a war, you understand that."

"Yes,—"

"And I'm running it. You understand that." Gorev was trying to command the situation, but he trembled. His breathing was loud.

"Yes."

"And you expect me to keep track of every *chernozhopyi* that walks through this office—"

"What the hell does that mean?" Hemingway looked at Dos

Passos, whose eyes were wide. "What'd he just call Pepe?" Dos Passos didn't say a word.

"Robles is a free man," Gorev croaked, his hand in the air gesturing thoughtlessly like he was tossing seed to pigeons. "Maybe he quit. Went back to America."

"He was arrested, General." Dos Passos was getting red in his cheeks and on his forehead.

"And you think *I* had him arrested?!" Gorev hissed this, his eyes bulging. Hemingway could see that his shirt collar was dark with sweat.

"No, Sancho, we're just trying to find out—"

Gorev slumped his head into his two hands on the desk, exhaling. Hemingway and Dos Passos glanced at each other. The Russian sighed heavily. It was clear to the two men that Robles was not the subject of the presumably frantic conversation Gorev was having in his own head. When Gorev slowly raised his head, his hands held thin clumps of dry hair. His eyes were wet.

He tried to steady himself. "You use the word 'arrested' and that implies that it was official, no? You don't say 'kidnapped.' You imply we of the Popular Front absconded with one of our own bureaucrats and are, what, holding him somewhere? Don't you see what a foolish thing that is to suggest? You know the Moscow Trials are still going on, comrades. I know it. Everyone knows it. Everyone should be aware . . ."—his voice slowed, tired, as if an elephant sat on his chest—"that everything you say can . . . be heard."

He rubbed his eyes.

"Perhaps," he continued, brightening, "it seemed like an arrest to his wife, or maybe she was dreaming. Maybe she's lying, cheated on her husband, ha!, and drove him to catch the next boat to New York! I like that one!"

Gorev laughed, and then stopped, and the two writers looked at each other again. He swallowed hard. He looked at his watch.

"But Sancho—"

The Russian looked up again at Hemingway, but wearily, as if he was wondering why these Salvation Army nuns were still begging him for loose change. "Yes?"

Hemingway didn't know what was passing through the Russian's skull, and knew only that he had to tread firmly but gently and fearlessly, as you would around a rabid dog before you shot it.

"We're journalists, you understand," Hemingway said, "and we might be given cause to file a story, for American newspapers, about this, about Robles and his so-called arrest and how no one will tell us or his widow where he is or what the charges are, or if anyone has any record of it, and how in fact his disappearance seemed to have evaded you and your office completely. You understand that. Now, we're here as guests of the Popular Front, and I'm sure the people in Valencia or in Moscow wouldn't like it if we were compelled to start filing stories about the Communists, what, feigning ignorance or avoiding questions about an army colonel's disappearance. You know how famous we are, many other papers and journals would pick up a story like that. You know, those big muckety-mucks in Valencia and Moscow might decide that we're trash after that, but their real problem would be with whomever gave us that story, and whoever let us file it."

Now Gorev was surprised. His eyes froze. "Look, my friends, my Americans, you're making a mountain out of an anthill. I'll tell you what is going on with Robles, but it is not for print. It is top secret. I tell you as comrades."

"OK."

"José is on assignment. He is undercover, infiltrating a Trotskyite contingent that's been giving us trouble."

"Really. He's a spy. That's what you're telling us. Anti-Stalinists."

"Yes! Exactly. It's not my operation, but that's probably what the arrest scenario was for, to give his wife a story."

"But—" Dos Passos couldn't get around his own tongue.

"That's not much of a cover story," Hemingway said. "Why wouldn't they have blamed the arrest on the Trotskyites?"

"Maybe that was their intention, but she didn't understand."

"Maybe?"

"Horseshit," Dos Passos blurted, wiping sweat from his head.

The phone on the desk rang, and Gorev jerked and instantly went pale. He looked intently toward the door to the secretary's office, and waited for her to take the call. When the ringing stopped, he closed his eyes.

"Sancho," Hemingway continued, and began to sweat himself, "if everyone's supposed to think POUM or some anarchist party kidnapped Robles, why wouldn't they expect your forces to be tracking him down? Why wouldn't've anyone in the last three weeks even admitted to noticing that Robles was gone? Dos went to Valencia, and if what you say is true that means every petty bureaucrat in the government knows Robles is a spy inside an anarchist faction, and is covering it up—how's that secret being kept, when from what I hear you can't keep news of a fart in Valencia from ending up as a dispatch on Franco's nightstand?"

Gorev's eyes were reddening, but he didn't move a muscle. He seemed to be staring through the men's heads and at the back wall. Hemingway couldn't keep his mouth shut.

"Why would you need to infiltrate the anarchists, anyway, when you've got more than enough to wrestle with from the Nationalists? Only the Comintern would be interested, and only in the interests of purges, which José wouldn't have anything to do with. He may be a good Communist, but he's no Trotskyite hunter."

"This is smelling more like a news story every second," Dos Passos composed himself enough to say.

Gorev jumped up. "I don't give a dead rat's mother's maggot guts about Robles! *Blyadskii* Robles! You write a word about

Robles anywhere"—he was ranting now, a huge hand and its index finger thrust out over the desk—"and I promise you you'll end up in a Spanish pit under a stack of Italians! One more word about him *right now,* and you're both officially deported, sent out on the first tramp steamer to Panama! Now go back to your fucking hotel and drink yourself silly, content and relieved with yourselves that today, just today, your names didn't fall darkly into Comrade Stalin's ear!"

Heaving like a last-place racehorse, Gorev stomped away to the left, his head down, his hands wiping sweat from his neck, and disappeared out the far door, opposite to the one Hemingway and Dos Passos had come through, with a crashing slam.

The writers stood up slowly, passed through the other door, into the secretary's office, retrieved their coats from the coat rack, said nothing, and glumly headed down the stairs and out of the building.

"I've never been witness to a performance like that in my life," Hemingway finally said in the car, "and I've drunk absinthe with Ezra Pound."

"I can't imagine what we're supposed to think."

"That Russian word . . ."

" 'Black ass.' 'Nigger.' "

"Jeez."

"What was wrong with him, you think?"

"The Trials, I would imagine. The big Bolsheviks are getting tried, but I keep hearing how others down the ladder are simply being purged by Big Joe. That seems to be the point of it, that no one ever knows if it'll happen to them. By the looks of him, Sancho just got a bad message this morning, and he's headed for a collapse."

"But why, after all he's done—"

"Trotsky got criminalized. No one's impervious."

"Christ . . . So now what?"

"What? I'm doing exactly what Gorev told me to do. Going

back to the hotel. Getting snockered. Don't tell me you don't understand what just happened. We just walked a minefield, Dos.
We just got away with our hides."

"I know very well. But Pepe's still missing."

"Yes he is. I'm still going back to the Florida."

"You're kidding me. You're going to let it drop. You're going
to forget about Pepe. You're going to let whoever took him just
take him, and that's that."

"Um . . . That's right."

The conversation ended there. The ride through the city was
silent, one man looking east, the other looking west.

# 4

The Florida was a busy hive with three general breeds of bee: journalists from all corners, International Brigadesmen on leave, and whores. The social laws that might've sent these three contingents to different hotels and different neighborhoods were obliterated by the war; they fell together like dice shaken in a cup. "The greatest and most varied collection of ladies of the evening I have ever seen," Hemingway would later write, which meant that the women varied in weight from 89 pounds to 320, in race from alabaster-cheeked Muscovites to black Rhodesians, in beauty from horse-faced products of farm rape to several of the most luminous faces Hemingway'd ever confronted. If he could resist most of them individually, he could hardly resist appreciating them in toto and sauntering among them as if he were shopping, dizzied and delighted and spoiled by the sheer multiplicity of choices available to him. As it happened, he couldn't quite resist all of them individually, and he'd come back from the second floor after having just finished making love with a long-limbed, nonpareil-colored, cheekbones-like-zoot-suit-lapels Senegalese goddess named Maimouna with eyes the shape and color of almonds when Martha came back from interviewing a Republican widower for *Colliers* and sniffed at him in the bathroom of 108.

"What's that?"

"What?"

"You smell like . . . shea butter."

"What's that?"

"African women use it, it's in their soap."

"Really?" Hemingway sniffed his own arm desultorily. "Hmmm. Don't smell anything. Shall we crack the Armagnac?"

"You go ahead. I'm going back to New York. You come and get me when you decide you can keep your hands off the livestock."

Just like that, Martha packed and left. Hemingway denied any tomfoolery and pleaded with her, but she just smiled occasionally and ignored him, which made him furious, and after the door slammed shut he broke out the Armagnac by himself. Some distance into the bottle, Hemingway remembered Martha was supposed to go to New York anyway sometime soon to meet with Joris Ivens about that film, and he realized she'd probably finished researching the magazine piece she was sent to write, and missed Manhattan and her mother. So the odor of shea butter and the suspicion of whoring gave her an excuse and a convenient launching pad.

Or maybe she was genuinely upset, genuinely on the outski.

Huffing, drinking the afternoon away, taking notes about a Brigadesman, a Yank, come to the hills as a bomber? an assassin? a strategist? and having frank, moist sex with a Spanish girl? . . . in a tent? Maybe. Wouldn't it be too cold, out there in the mountains? He'd never written a sex scene before, and had no idea how he'd go about it. Would the bullshit-free, no-adjectives approach kill its power, and would a free-associative run-on sound too much like an anonymous Victorian sheet-soiler? And all the dialogue would have to be Spanish but read as English, right?

He'd get Martha back, in good time. He didn't need to chase

her. He hoped he didn't need to. Should he, even? He wouldn't be able to even try to pursue her, at least, until tomorrow, because he'd already had far too much very fine Armagnac to make sensible travel decisions. Who'd she go to now, anyway? What writer, what man in New York stands a chance of measuring up? James Thurber?!

Anyway, worse came to worst, Pauline waited in Key West, as always. The marriage wasn't scotched yet. Meeting Martha in Spain was supposed to be a secret, but Hemingway knew even if he'd fucked Martha on the dinner table on Whitehead Street while Pauline tried to cut a roast, Pauline would still accept an apology and take him back.

For now, the warm, syrupy wolverine bite of the brandy gave him a lordly view of the world from his provisioned station in 108, shells landing with crackling thuds miles away, gunfire spitting into the far distance, the spare and desolated and noble web of city sounds from what was left of a saddened Madrid rising to his windows like the tentative birdsong after a heavy rain.

But soon the sugary booze in his system made him pace, made him sense that the day was meant for something better than solitary brooding, and so Hemingway went back up to the second floor, a second bottle of Armagnac in his fist, to bask in the fake adoration of the Florida's prostitute population, and perhaps, free as a soldier on leave, engage with them in a fashion appropriate to wartime, recklessly, three at a time, drunk as a skunk and not giving a single spare thought to tomorrow.

"Señor!" four of them crooned in unison—a pretty red-haired Corsican, a middle-aged Basque woman with loop earrings, a worn Burgundian with eyes still as bright as Marlene Dietrich's, and a Ukrainian teenager with disproportionately heavy breasts under a lacy blouse and shawl that hid nothing—as others poked their heads out of the open doorways that weren't closed with business, as Hemingway welcomed them at the top of the stairs into his gesturing embrace, and suddenly realized that they could all drink his bottle in moments flat if he let them, and warmly kissed each as he did in fact choose three to follow him to the room at the end of the hall to which the first woman, the Corsican, led him. The other two were the Ukrainian girl and a Cordoban maiden with skin like café con leche, a mole smack in the middle of her cleavage, and a relaxing tendency to grin when life got chaotic around her.

In short order Hemingway was done. But because he said he'd pay them, the women continued with each other, and drank enough brandy to laugh about it and even have orgasms, and then Hemingway, the four of them loaded and naked and smelly on the large bed, told them the story about Agnes and the Great War, and the Corsican was moved to silent tears.

The Corsican girl then told her own story, about a boy she loved who foolishly went to Greece as a rather inexperienced soldier of fortune and was rumored to have been killed by a Thessaloníki pimp, and his twin brother, whom the girl quite naturally and effortlessly gravitated toward back home and feel in deeper love with, only to have the lad fall into a well and die. The woman from Cordoba then told the story of her husband, who enlisted with the French army and was killed at the Marne but not before he fathered a daughter with a farm girl in Nantes, to whom the Cordoban whore sends money every month, and a gift of a French book, Balzac or Hugo or Dumas, every June birthday.

The tale the Ukrainian girl had to tell, her large breasts resting on the mattress, was more mundane but somehow possessed a blacker shade of tragic: She recounted in detail how when she was twelve someone, soldiers or policemen of some type, very official and formidable, kicked down her family's front door in the middle of the night, tied her father to a kitchen chair, and beat him across the back of the head with blackjacks until he was unconscious. "Who?!" and "Where?!" they'd screamed at the girl's father, but the man only said he didn't know, pleaded with them to believe him, until he'd passed out. They then ransacked the house, breaking virtually every piece of furniture, untied the man, and spirited him out of the house, leaving his family behind crying. The Ukrainian girl never saw her father again, and though her mother stayed in the Ukraine devoted to finding out where they took her husband and what they did to him, the girl left when she could at eighteen, and never held much hope that her father would ever be found alive. Why would he be, after all that?

And Hemingway thought: Robles. He thought of how he'd heard this new kind of story come out of Moscow and Minsk and Berlin and Rome and Lisbon for years now, of how Robles was apparently ripped from his bed in the darkness in just that same way, of how much was happening to Europe in the dead middle of the night, without documentation or the rule of law. The continent was going insane, each nation, like caged possums left days without food. Turning glum and headachy in a bed-top whorl of compliant bodies, Hemingway was hearing the shouting, the screaming, the batons hitting muscle and scalp, the car ride in the blackness. Was Robles a Fascist spy? Or a spy against Franco who'd been caught up? Or was he lumped in with the Trotskyites and simply purged?

But what to think? Hemingway couldn't possibly have come to a reasoned conclusion, even if he weren't drunk and surrounded by naked prostitutes kissing and drinking, about the Popular Front or Stalin or Trotsky or POUM or the Valencia government or even Roosevelt's noninterventionist stance, because everyone had political motives that were hidden like the underwear of an unfaithful husband, or like the card-cheat's extra ace. The ideals of the Republic, as much as he wanted to believe in them, always seem to come with shadows, or compromises, or residual hypocrisies. There was no honor left, if there ever were any, behind the lines. He knew in his heart that fighting the Fascists was right, and that was an easy decision to make; unfortunately, the enemy of his enemy could not be relied upon to be his friend. It wasn't a ballfield or schoolyard. Spain was more like a poverty row barroom, in which despair and hunger brings everybody together, and then deranges them with booze and worry until old vengeances and spites and greed blossom into bloodshed.

Robles, blindfolded, in the back of a car. Hemingway had the image caught in his thoughts like a jig hook. He couldn't get it out. The women long gone, hours later, he couldn't get it out.

# 5

This is how it became known amongst the Americans in Spain in 1937 that José Robles had in fact been abducted and executed in March, outside Valencia. The word trickled down from Alvarez del Vayo, the notoriously soulless and duplicitous foreign minister, to Josephine Herbst, the mousy and diminutive American journalist, when Herbst had met with him upon first arriving in Spain. She'd obtained her unlikely letter of introduction from the Comintern's public relations office in Paris, which didn't make her a Red so much as an opportunist, and had mentioned, over coffee with del Vayo, the names of both Dos Passos and Robles, and del Vayo very quickly said that he'd heard that Robles was not merely missing but already dead. He'd heard that the deceased had been accused of being a spy for the Nationalists in some capacity, but del Vayo did not offer up any further details, and in fact acted as if he had none. He'd shrugged. A lot of powerful men in Spain in 1937 did a lot of shrugging. Herbst knew not to press the matter, because she'd been lucky to get into that office, in the middle of the war, to begin with.

Then she told Hemingway. The wee hours of the morning

following Hemingway's trio-of-whores idyll, 5 AM or so, saw a series of small cannon shells hit the Florida. The building shook, windows broke, and blood pressures shot up like rockets. Herbst practically wet her bed, Dos Passos got up to put earplugs in, Sidney Franklin gave up on sleep and got dressed, Antoine de Saint-Exupéry came out in his nightgown distributing black-market grapefruits he'd hoarded to panicky journalists in the hallway, a slumming Errol Flynn could be heard baying like a wolf up in the prostitutes' rooms, *Daily Express* reporter Sefton Delmer scrambled for the stairs wearing only his pin-striped boxers, Comintern lackey Gustav Regler emerged running with a much-dented doughboy helmet on his head, and Hemingway took to the halls breathlessly, instinctively eager to run toward the blast area, not away.

But soon it was over, and the bleary-eyed and nerve-thrummed Americans, Brits, Russians, and Frenchmen took to wandering the lobby or heading back upstairs to put on clothes. Herbst found herself standing beside Hemingway by the lobby's front door, looking out at a night sky long into giving way to sunrise rosiness, and as she was still shaking he invited her up to 108 for a belt. She'd never had a drink before three in the afternoon in her life and her stomach didn't want one now, but such invitations were not to be declined, regardless of the hour or the situation.

There, as they were sitting in Hemingway's chairs sipping a single malt with a five-syllable name, the subject of Dos came up, how Hemingway was beginning to think Dos might get him and all of them in trouble if he kept carping on this Robles business, and then Herbst told Hemingway, syllable for syllable, what del Vayo had told her just days before.

"Dead? When? A spy? For Franco?" Hemingway slurped. Herbst shrugged, like a titmouse with a twitch. "Robles was as much a spy as my Aunt Patootie. He was a goddamn Cub Scout. You bought that crap?"

Herbst shrugged again. "Ernest, I never met the man. I was not in a position to accuse del Vayo of lying, anyway."

"He *was* lying, like a fucking rug. Pepe was no Fascist, fer Chrissake. Pepe was an angel, an irritating fucking clean-shirted hero. He wouldn't've pissed on Franco if Franco were burning alive. You know what this means."

Herbst clearly didn't care; she was only concerned with writing some pieces and selling them to various magazines and then getting the hell out of that nightmarish landscape as quickly as she could toss her suitcases aboard a bus.

"No, I don't have any idea."

"It means Robles was murdered for sure, that somebody had it out for him, *something* happened. And they're thinking it'll vanish in the artillery smoke, because there's a war on."

"So?"

"So. It means, goddammit, that Dos is right. It means someone has to at least try to find out the truth."

"Oh, my," Herbst moaned. "You're out of my league, Ernest."

"Josie, so am I."

Sitting there on the edge of his bed, a touch drunk way too early and with a woman he had absolutely no designs upon, Hemingway felt the worm turn—he knew from there he would be compelled, was already being compelled, by his own worst instincts, to seek out the dark and presumably blood-sticky center of Robles's story, to stick a flag up the ass of the mercenary bottom-feeder that thought he could get away with killing such an innocent man and then lie about it, lie to *them*, to American journalists putting themselves at risk here in Spain because they wanted to help the Republic and fight Fascism. What careless bile, what goddamn *nerve*. Hemingway liked to feign manly disinterest in the bad fortune of others most of the time, but sometimes he simply couldn't. This was the story of Harold Dolsch back in Kansas City, this was the story of Lombardy during the war, this was the story of Scott in Paris, this was Chicago and

Paris, stretches of writing and drinking and adventure-seeking interrupted, shockingly, by gouts of injustice, which had a way of stealing his sleep. For Hemingway, this compulsion didn't feel like righteousness, nor did it look that way from the outside, ever. Rather, it was cosmic pride and ego, or the painful lack thereof, leaving a vacuum he had to fill. Perhaps it was both, vacillating back and forth in a maddening ricochet.

Robles seemed to be a classic example of this. But Hemingway was already thinking of ways out of it, ways to come at it halfway. Maybe I'll just ask around a little, he reasoned, and that'll be that. Maybe it'll end up being an unknowable, maybe it'll have to remain a mystery. It wouldn't be the first time in a civil war, right?

But he'd test the waters, see what's to be caught out there. After all, maybe there'd be a book in it. Or a story. At least, a few dispatches and maybe a feature for *Look*. Maybe it would finally get him killed, in a heroic way he'd welcome in the last seconds. That'd be a relief. But maybe he'd survive, and, unlikely as it was, maybe plumbing Robles's fate would give his life from there on a sense of completion and substance. Hemingway had a hard time picturing that humdinger, but maybe anything was possible.

But whatever the eventual upshot, Hemingway could feel the slope steepen beneath him and the unanswered questions' gravity grab him by the ankles.

But first, Dos.

"I'll tell Dos," Hemingway said.

"Good." Herbst was woozy with alcohol and anxiety.

Hemingway couldn't stand spending all day with a fuming, outraged, grieving Dos, so he didn't look for him that morning; he napped. That afternoon all of the international journalists were shipped out to a government castle outside of Madrid for a gala lunch, to fete the newly mustered XV Brigade— including the Lincoln contingent, fresh from beatings at Jarama and Teruel—being officially brought under the Republic's command, and to toast the Republic's sixth anniversary. It was so much happy horseshit, speeches and marching band trumpetings and exaltive backslappings, though the castle itself was spectacularly, decayingly gorgeous, lit up on the inside by oil lamps and heated by roaring fireplaces and laden with the best open bar and limitless buffet Hemingway had ever seen in or out of Europe. Suffering a walking hangover already by two, he got a drink at the bar first, a double tequila-and-lime, drank it, got another, and while the mayor of Madrid babbled on the bandstand he found Dos Passos moping around the crowd's fringes, shrugging off a few sycophantic petty bureaucrats along the way.

"Dos, about Pepe—"

Dos Passos gave only a minuscule glance of indignation, the two men's last conversation in the car still hot in his ears. But then it passed, and Dos listened in earnestness.

"The word is, Dos, that Robles is dead."

Dos Passos froze, breathing deeply and slowly through his nose, taking a moment.

"Where'd you hear this?"

"A friend of a friend of a friend. But it came from del Vayo."

"That turd. Lied to my face."

"No surprise."

"But that's official, then?"

"I wouldn't say that. It was off the record, I guess. And del Vayo claimed to just be retelling what he's heard."

"It's like a game of Chinese whispers. Who knows what the truth is."

"Maybe. Look, Dos, gossip and news gets fucked into knots all the time in this place, but when the foreign minister says he heard a man is dead, it's probably true. Especially given the arrest and Gorev's meltdown."

"But you see that it's not quite good enough."

"Yes."

"Is it good enough for you?" Dos Passos was being gentle but forceful, yet again. Hemingway would only allow himself to be cowed and shamed by his friend a few more times that year.

"No. It's not, Dos. But what can we do."

"Find out."

"Find out . . ."

"Yes. It's still a crime. It still requires justice."

Justice. Hemingway didn't think, in that moment, that Dos had any notion of how to investigate the matter, or what such an investigation could cost him in the end. All Hemingway saw in the man was fiery righteousness, which was all well and good as long as Hemingway didn't get sucked into just bull-heading around, squandering his celebrity goodwill and pissing people off in a city where the primary question seemed to be not whether a troublemaking loudmouth would get disappeared in the middle of the night, but which faction or covert force would get the payout to do it.

That night, Juan Posada, the Republic's amiable police chief in Madrid and who knows what other position of eminence in the constantly shifting, constantly retitled Popular Front bureaucracy, held yet another invitation-only shindig in his astonishingly lavish penthouse suite. Hemingway went for the drinks and what promised, finally, to be good Spanish food, and to nose around amidst the politicos and Russians.

For what reason Dos Passos went he couldn't say. But Posada himself met him on the balcony, under the moon turned yellow like a smoker's tooth. He told him flat-out that yes Robles was dead, yes the Republic has compelled everyone all to do some horrible things and overlook others, yes but don't keep asking, no one knows exactly who did it but no one wants to know, either, from this moment on just be goddamn quiet about it.

Dos Passos listened, and was not satisfied. Posada soon threw up his hands, as that was his best gesture and symbolic of how he managed the war and the Comintern and the anarchists and the unnecessary killings and his own survival. Throw up your hands, a variation on a shrug. Posada would survive this, Dos Passos thought. He was the roach that bombs and pesticides and stomping feet could not kill.

Dos Passos left in a huff soon thereafter, and Hemingway didn't know it for an hour, involved as he was in talking up a reporter for *Le Temps* whose bustline outmeasured her hips by a margin you could see from across the room, and whose flirtatious eyes reminded Hemingway of Clara Bow. As much as he'd wanted to seduce her, right there on Posada's penthouse bed, he kept probing her for her knowledge of the Popular Front's middlemen, the ones that might have been secretly commissioned by the bureaucrats to complete an assassination and who would delegate the job to subordinates or mercenaries. This squelched her ardor in good order, but not before she mentioned the name "Quintinilla," apropos of a general uptick in mysterious disappearances and the increasing influence of the Comintern in Spain. The woman was clearly not a Communist—a beautiful French journalist who wasn't a Marxist?!, if only he could focus on her *sans chemisier* and not on what she might know!—and so, as she probably wasn't closely connected to the Front, her opinions probably came from whatever lucky devil, probably a politician, shared her wartime bed. But what had she heard? Quintinilla was a notorious name one would only mention to Ernest Hemingway at a government party if one wanted to nudge a mountaintop rock into an avalanche. The "executioner of Madrid," and a commissar of some security detail or another given license by the Soviets, Pepe Quintinilla was an infamous and much-feared secret cop in the Second Republic, but also a seasoned European sophisticate, and Hemingway was one of the few civilian big shots that Quintinilla seemed to respect. Plus, he had a deep thirst for *porto.* When Hemingway met him, Quintinilla had just returned from Moscow, and glowed with secret power and purpose, like a man personally anointed by God to lead a crusade. He was an icy customer, quite capable of making the average oblivious tourist suddenly shudder in fear for his or her life without Quintinilla having said a word, but Hemingway also knew he could outdrink the Spaniard with whatever libation was on hand, grain or grape. And like so many Spaniards, a drunk Quintinilla was a brick-stupid, embarrassingly inept Quintinilla.

Two weeks before, Hemingway caught a glimpse of this Quintinilla, when after a long afternoon of brandy at the Gran Via a half block from the Florida the long-limbed, heavy-lidded secret agent tried to light a cigarette from a fat candle at table's end, and lit his sideburn on fire instead. The cigarette dropped, Quintinilla howled and smacked himself in the side of the face with the force of a duelist's challenge, and essentially knocked himself over a long bench, sending him to the floor. Across the restaurant, you could see the man's expensive English shoes, with his feet still in them, swoop up toward the ceiling, and then vanish in the shadows. You could hear as well what sounded like a 200-pound bag of golf balls and chicken legs hit the floorboards. And you could faintly smell the bitter smoke that comes from burning human hair. Quintinilla showed up at the Gran Via the next day with a new haircut and not a twinge of visible self-knowledge about the incident. No one reminded him.

Hemingway smelled trouble on this French woman. She'd only give her first name, Pascaline, which made him lean in close, and plant his fat hand on the penthouse wall beside her head.

"Oh, you know," she burbled, far from sober herself, "Quintinilla, the 'executioner,' they say he takes work like that. And likes it."

"Who say?"

"*Monsieur* Hemingway, everybody say, nobody say. C'mon."

"But I need to know, I need to talk to somebody that knows how those things are happening, who gives the orders."

"*Mon dieu, pourquoi?* You're writing about assassinations some-where?"

"Well, no—"

"Who'd want to hear that? Except the Germans?"

"Yes—"

"Then you're a crusader? Or what, one of those 'fifth colum-nists'?"

"Please—"

"I know, I know, you're Ernest Hemingway. You're writing a new book, and the war is just your new little story." She paused to burp. *"Mazel tov!"* She said it with a flip of her hand.

Then she was gone, an *excusez moi*, a skirt flutter at the nearest door, and Hemingway stood alone, swaying. Mazel tov? He stood, suddenly seriously inebriated, realizing he'd have to find Quintinilla. But then he'd be mixing in a real way, not in a slumming-American-celebrity way, with Soviet spies and war-time collateral. If he was lucky, he'd come to know who was re-sponsible for Robles's death, but then what? What did he intend to do? If his luck held out, what would it come to?

If he was unlucky, the questions he didn't want to entertain—they slid right off his brainpan, and into the abyss like the math lessons he didn't want to remember from the seventh grade—were irrelevant. Lucklessness meant the questions never get asked.

# 6

That night he dreamed about Robles, about Italy during the war, and a moment at the front by the Isonzo River when Hemingway had seen Robles pick up a dying man's hands and shin bones after a shell had hit and place them with the man on his stretcher, knowing the man wouldn't survive to triage but doing it so the man would feel better, that he believed there was a chance he'd be reassembled like an unstrung marionette. Hemingway dreamt that as he watched he felt how he'd always remembered feeling: disquieted, because he knew he wouldn't have bothered to do the same. He would've quickly told the dying man a bullshit story, made something up. He was a writer. Robles was not.

Hemingway awoke in 108 not remembering the dream or the ride home in the state car with Josie, and not caring much—he mixed orange juice with a little gin, ate pickled herring out of a jar, and knocked out two 800-word dispatches to NANA about "fifth columnists" and the disappearance of Robles, neither of which were ever published anywhere. The syndicate loved the fact that they had Hemingway's name on a byline, but the Alliance editors were never very delighted with the articles, which poetically described the impacts of the war and didn't actually involve very much reporting. Hemingway knew how to write straight-on reportage, God knows, but it didn't interest him now, and he was contracted, and he did what he liked, New York desk jockeys be damned.

Sidney Franklin knocked and came in, pointed questioningly to the single piece of wet herring left in the jar on the front table, and waited until Hemingway slowly looked up, let several seconds pass, and then gave a single disapproving nod with his chin. Franklin slurped and sat down.

"Don't sit down. Go get Dos."

"Can't, boss, he left. Josie mentioned it, we found coffee—"

"Where'd he go?"

"Valencia."

*Christ.* Dos running ahead like a faithful dog after his master fell off a cliff. He didn't, Hemingway knew, have the slightest idea what he was doing. He never reported on crime for a big city newspaper; he was, instead, a rich boy who spent time in the Sorbonne and had tutors and escorts, and never worked a low-paying job in his young life. Dos Passos still trusted people. He still believed in good and evil.

Hemingway sent Franklin into the streets to look for whatever chardonnay he could find, and worked for a while on the story he was thinking of, about the *Americano,* the one that the NANA contract and the trip itself was supposed to fuel. But of course he just doodled. He'd need to get out into the war more, ride up the mountains, put his hands into the hands of the Spaniards fighting miles away from their own farms before the imperative dynamics of the book would present themselves. Some writers could just sit on their asses in the same room every year and conjure all kinds of nonsense right out of the air, like Dos, kinda. Like Joyce—the bulge-headed homunculus. Like Gertrude, God knows. But Hemingway never had that knack. He had to go see it himself, and then write about what he saw, use his friends and women and acquaints as models, install himself often enough as a character, and then make sure the character was flawed and unlikable—somewhat. Tragically flawed. Or unable to be noble, maybe, in a lousy modern world that has strangled nobility. The man in "Hills Like White Elephants," that was him, that was virtually a transcription of a conversation he'd had with a *London Times* reporter named Undine in 1919, as they sat in Victoria Station. Scramble a few details, make himself look like a right cold creep, and there it was. But the point is, you can't really make that stuff up. Did Fitzgerald ever write a short story like that? Did Joyce, did anyone? If you want the thing to weigh a certain amount in your hand, you have to go out and find it in the world, you can't make it up like a children's story.

But so far, Hemingway's book would be about drinking to kidney-aching excess in a hotel room, not terribly close to the war. His grandmother wouldn't even buy that book.

The moment he relinquished his pencil, he began thinking about Robles, about meeting up with Quintinilla, about how Dos might himself end up under some loose soil, righteously and cluelessly nosing around and allowing himself to be branded a "problem" by the Comintern.

It also occurred to Hemingway that he didn't know Robles that well—maybe ten meetings in all, from Italy in 1917 to New York in 1930, all of them generously lubricated. Most of what he *thought* he knew about Robles was from Dos Passos. Could Robles have been a Fascist spy, as del Vayo had said? It seemed preposterous—but then, who were these crazy Fascists, and why did they think the way they did? Were they all just indignant reactionaries? Or puppets? Hemingway didn't have a clue.

Use the morning, he thought. He knew of one man in Madrid who knew Robles better than Dos Passos knew him, a high school chemistry professor–turned-Marxist-bombmaker, working with POUM, named Obdulio Pilas. Dos Passos had mentioned him as a lifelong cohort of Robles's, from when he was Robles's teacher in Barcelona until the two split in the early '30s over politics. Robles went with the Soviet Communist path, and Pilas believed instead in Trotsky, in "permanent revolution," and in the transparency of the USSR's brutal totalitarianism. As far as Hemingway was concerned, the Popular Front and POUM seemed like equal opponents that differed only in tactic and in how pure they judged each other's intentions to be. Whomever won the power struggle in the end, the Soviets would be there to resume puppeteering.

In the meantime, Hemingway didn't know how to find Pilas. All he knew was that the man remained in Madrid after the battle in November, and Robles met him on occasion for drinks and argument. Bomb-expert anarchists could not be found in the phone book.

"Sidney, who do you know in POUM?" Hemingway used his polite voice since Franklin had actually returned with five bottles of 1928 Alsace Willm pinot gris, for which he traded the desperate wine seller a small case of peasant-grade goose paté.

"Nobody. They're headquartered in Barcelona." Franklin was always sweating, even when it was cold, due to the labor it took to even get his bulk out of a chair.

"I know where they are. But there's got to be some loud-mouthed Trotskyites around here somewhere."

"Don't know. But I think Flynn is a sympathizer."

"Errol Flynn? He's POUM?"

"No, he's a movie star. But I think I read in a Hollywood magazine that he likes POUM and doesn't hold with the Stalinists."

"Who would've thought he'd have an opinion either way."

"No, apparently he's a very bright guy."

"Bullcrap. What the hell is he doing here, anyway?"

"Don't know."

"Hollywood rubbernecker."

"Why do you want a Trotskyite, anyway?"

"Because I'm looking for one in particular. Who knew Robles."

Franklin didn't quite understand, but didn't expend the energy to inquire further. Buttoning his shirt, Hemingway was up and out, and headed upstairs to the whores' rooms on the second floor with two of the Alsace Willms. Everything was still quiet this early in the morning, but the sound of a man's heavy footfall in the hallway eventually caused a sleepy head to poke through her door—the fortyish Basque woman, who croaked *"Hemingway!"* and planted an odiferous kiss on his lips and a hand on his crotch.

*"No, mi chica,* I cannot, no time. *Por favor,* take some wine, and also, do you know where Señor Flynn is?"

The Basque woman's eyes lit up, her fist around the bottle neck. "Oh, Señor Flynn! *¡Él es como un dios venido a la tierra! ¡Ese hermoso pinga!"*

"Yes. I'm sure it is. His room?"

She pointed up. "302."

With the second bottle, Hemingway loped up the stairs as quietly as he could. He'd probably be waking a hungover Flynn and rousing him from a tangle of female bodies—and why? To ask him about who he knows in Madrid that in turn might know a certain POUM-affiliated bomb maker. It sounded just insane enough to make Flynn laugh, because Flynn was, among other things, Hemingway knew, always very aware of how the scenes in his preposterous life could be turned into drinking stories he could tell later. The men had only met once before, in Key West the previous August, when Flynn, having wrapped *The Charge of the Light Brigade,* went on a fishing tour to Cuba and back, courtesy of Warner Brothers. The skipper was one of Hemingway's Sloppy Joe's cronies, Eldon Peark, and so Hemingway met them and bought the whole party a round the evening before they launched. Four hours later, not quite satisfied with boisterous old salt banter and tropical Gulf air and tequila at a table with Ernest Hemingway, Flynn began looking for trouble—something had to *happen*—and he jovially struck up a conversation with a huddle of shrimp men at the bar he knew very well were already extremely drunk and, by the looks of them, grumpy bar brawlers from boots to broken nose bridge. Flynn was of course the model of congeniality, and cut an awe-inspiring figure in any public place, but he also knew how his fame and persona often inspired "real men" to start taunting the matinee hero after a few dozen cocktails, and he loved to provoke them. Other stars, Clark Gable for instance, famously knew how to talk around a booze-muscled tough-talker in public and escape without an incident, but Flynn reveled in it, launching in swinging, savoring the opportunity to prove he wasn't just a pampered Hollywood pansy. Hemingway didn't know what triggered the shrimp men, but in a moment they were off their stools, and one came at Flynn, and Flynn expertly dodged him, and swung a right hook into the man's ear that sounded like somebody dropped an iron pan in the kitchen. The shrimp man fell to his knees and threw up on the floor. His pal, standing behind him, let out a panicky sob and cried. Flynn apologized to the standing shrimp men, patting the weeper on the back. An ambulance came and brought the nauseous shrimp man to the local doctor's office, with a concussion. Flynn had his story.

Hemingway stood in front of 302 and knocked firmly but with no urgency. It was nine-thirty. The door was opened by a beautiful black-haired woman Hemingway had never seen before. Flynn was standing in the center of the room, suave and straight-backed, fully dressed completely in white, tying a kerchief loosely around his throat, not hungover nor even caught slightly off guard.

"Ernest! I've only been in town a few days, haven't had time to come and say hi, come in, come in!"

Hemingway didn't like feeling sheepish, which he was for some reason, so he boomed a little, walking in, trading greetings, handing Flynn the wine, which he was glad to see Flynn recognized and appreciated, swapping a little gossip about Marlene Dietrich and Lupe Vélez, sitting down, bandying about what evening later in the week would be good to meet up at the Gran Via and do some serious tippling.

But Hemingway had this thing, this problem, and he explained it briefly.

"A murder, in the middle of a civil war? Sport, you're really writing a story, aren't you!" His affected, sable-soft English accent clicked gently, just as it did when a microphone was near.

"No, no, not yet anyway, I'm serious about this. And I need to find a man in Madrid, a certain man, who knew my friend from childhood. And he's with POUM."

Flynn's grin gently tightened to a reserved smile. "Why would you ask me about that?"

"I heard you knew some of those crazy Marxists. Here in town."

"Heard from who?"

". . . My man heard it around, I don't know. Errol, does it matter?"

"Probably not." Flynn brightened a touch. He screwed a cigarette into a holder and lit it. "Who's this fellow?"

"Pilas? Obdulio Pilas."

"Obdulio Pilas!" Flynn said it like it was the name of a vaudeville clown he fondly remembered from his youth. "Of all the radicals in Spain, that aborigine is the one you're looking for? Yes, I know of him. What in the blazes could you want with him?"

"Information. He knew Robles."

"Is that so." Flynn was beginning to enjoy the espionage flavor of the moment, and the fact that he was telling Ernest Hemingway something Hemingway didn't know about the underground in Madrid and not vice versa. "OK, Ernest, well, I don't know where he is, but last time I heard him mentioned, he was hunkered down south of the Casa de Campo. On Calle de Sepulveda."

"The number?"

"There's no number."

"No?"

"Uh-uh. He was living in the basement of an old synagogue, only the rabbis don't know he lives there. Can you imagine? Honestly, if he's still there, it shouldn't be hard to find, there aren't many left that haven't either been burned down or converted into churches. It had a name like Bet Aria. Or Bet something. Bet Elea. I forget."

"You forget?"

"What do you want, old man? I've been in town three days and haven't had a single sober moment untroubled by loose women." Of course he smiled.

"How do you know about Pilas, anyway?"

" 'Don't know, my man heard . . .' Kidding you! No, it was Trotsky. I met him in the spring. Warners went to Mexico to shoot the scenes for the *Light Brigade,* you remember, the scenes that required killing horses. Hundreds of them. They couldn't do it in California because I raised a stink. So they went to Mexico, and once my close-ups were finished shooting David Niven and I went down and tried to get the Mexican government to stop it. Of course they wouldn't. I don't hold with just killing animals for a movie. But while we were down there, we stayed with Trotsky, who's in exile there you know, staying with Diego Rivera, and his wife, that painter Frida Kahlo, Lord that woman was ugly, Ernest. Had a terrific time, and when I told

Leon I was planning on coming to Madrid, he told me who to look up. All his old party cronies. I haven't looked up anyone yet! They're all hiding out, but not many in the cellars of synagogues. Trotsky did talk. Obdulio Pilas was one he told me to avoid."

"Avoid?"

"Apparently, he's insane."

It was only 10 AM or so when Hemingway stepped out onto the Calle Floridablanca. The city was quiet and the sky was opening its cloud cover in fissures, allowing morning sun to stretch through. He and Flynn had tentatively agreed to meet in a few evenings at El Patio, and Hemingway was half hoping it wouldn't happen—Flynn was too much the ballbuster, too much the center of attention and ego-prover. Too much, in fact, like an exaggerated version of Hemingway himself, but without the perhaps dubious saving grace of being an artist, of being devoted to perfection and truth and whatever else it was to which Hemingway considered himself, after drinks, devoted. But now the city was genuinely peaceful, and so Hemingway had no trouble getting a cab and angling southwest across the city toward Casa de Campo.

On Calle de Sepulveda, Hemingway walked for thirty minutes west-southwest until he stopped at a cantina and had what he couldn't quite believe was only his first drink of the day, a tequila mojito. Then another, and the bartender didn't understand his question because he didn't know the Spanish word for synagogue, and then he walked back east-northeast up the boulevard, passing old apartment blocks and churches and restaurants, most seemingly abandoned, all cratered by bombshells and blackened with the fire of the November fighting.

He walked past the synagogue once without seeing it, but doubled back. No name was attached to the slim, worn Gothic building with a large wooden front door, but there was a splintered rectangular bare spot on the door jamb where a mezuzah must've been, apparently hit and sent flying by bullet fire along with a good amount of the facade's trim and stone ornamentation. It was dark and locked. There was an alley.

An alley a slim girl could've shuffled down, but Hemingway got stuck five feet in, his belly tight against the synagogue, the back of his wool jacket getting shredded on the weather-frayed brick of the adjoining building. He reached his hand back out to the corner on the street, but found himself several inches too far in. Sucked in his gut, but still felt his jacket rip. And then a man appeared at the alley's mouth, and all Hemingway saw was shadow.

A rifle was brought up to eye level and steadily pushed into Hemingway's face, so he could smell old powder on its barrel.

"*¿Quién eres tú?*" The man's voice was distant in his throat, and calm. Hemingway couldn't see his features, but could only tell that he was skinny and muscular, like an African.

"*Estoy* . . . Oh fuck. I'm here about José Robles Pazos."

The gun didn't lower. Instead, the man raised the barrel up, just past Hemingway's scalp, and pulled the trigger. Hemingway felt the hot breeze of the bullet go through his hair. The city didn't react. In the narrow chasm the sound made Hemingway's teeth shake in their gums, and then he couldn't hear anything at all.

Crazy as an alehouse rat, he thought, this bastard, must be Pilas.

Then the man with the rifle stepped into the dark notch of the alley, which he could sidle into without much difficulty, and just pushed Hemingway farther in. The less Hemingway budged and the more he shouted, the harder the man with the rifle pushed, ripping Hemingway's jacket good, inching him deeper in with rough shoves until Hemingway came to a widening in the brick walls he couldn't see before, and stumbled into the space.

"You crazy fucker—" Hemingway blurted, and in an instant the rifle was up at eye level again.

But then it lowered, and the man squeezed past Hemingway toward the back of the alley to a small wooden door with a new bullet mark on it and a padlock that might've dated to the 1700s. Both men had to duck through the door. Hemingway followed the man, feeling with aggravation the tattered back of his jacket, down stone steps into a medieval basement lit up only by a single oil lamp on a box. The corners of the room were dark with large, fearless rats. When Hemingway's eyesight grew accustomed to the murk, he saw what looked like munitions crates in the far corner.

"I'm looking for Obdulio Pilas," Hemingway said. "You must be Obdulio Pilas."

The man, filthy and middle-aged but wired and decisive like an Asian hand fighter, just looked at him with wide eyes. It was hard to imagine that some years earlier he'd been a schoolteacher.

Hemingway was getting tired and dry. "Do you have a drink? *Vino?*"

Pilas's eyebrows shrugged, and dug out a bottle of unlabeled homemade brandy from a pile of sundries, all of the man's spare and pitiful belongings blending together with the vermin and the crates and the refuse and dirt that more or less filled the subcellar. Hemingway had no hard time believing that no one else knew or cared about the place.

But they drank. Hemingway sat on a box, winded, but Pilas stood.

"You're a friend of Pepe's." Pilas said this in perfect English, croaking as if turning a rusted gear.

"Yes, Señor Pilas. I've known him since the Great War. In Italy. And . . . I'm here to tell you he is dead."

Pilas shrugged with his heavy eyelids.

"Many people have died. Many people will die. I will die, I'm sure of it."

"Sooner or later, right?" Hemingway, glass in face, trying for a smile.

"Sooner," Pilas said, no smile.

"OK, look, señor, I've come for help. Pepe was apparently murdered—no one's even found the body yet—"

"Popular Front cocksuckers," Pilas spit.

"Maybe. But we don't know who did it yet."

"We?"

"John Dos Passos and I."

"Who?"

"The writer? Do you have any idea who I am? Hemingway?"

Pilas shrugged with his shoulders this time. "I don't read American books, Henryway."

"Hemingway."

"So, Pepe was killed."

"Yes, I've come to ask you about Pepe. I knew him well, medium well I guess, but I did not know him so well, as well as you did, I hear."

Pilas shrugged with his bottom lip. "I knew him since he was fourteen, and not such a great chemistry student, I can tell you. He was constantly lighting smelly chemical fires to impress the girls. But he was a very smart fellow, especially for someone who fell for the Stalinist line."

"Since he was fourteen! Then you know him well, like a son or a brother."

"Yes, *Americano.*"

Hemingway took a breath. "What we've been hearing, unofficially, is that Pepe was arrested and killed because he was a spy for Franco. Or they think he was."

Pilas's face creased like a hung sheet hit by a falling branch. "And you, Henryway, you think this might be true."

"No, I do not think so. But like I said, I didn't know Pepe that well—"

"Then stop calling him Pepe! If you don't know him well enough to laugh until you retched at the accusation of Pepe being a Fascist, or even merely a traitor, then you don't have the right to call him anything but Señor Robles!" Pilas's voice ripped and rang in the closed space, and Hemingway felt flying spittle land.

"Señor," Hemingway tried to communicate gravitas, "the Robles you speak of, that's the Robles I knew."

"There is no other. You insult his memory and his family suggesting anything else."

"I'm not suggesting anything or insulting anyone, you old maniac. I needed to know from someone who knew him a long time whether it was possible he was a Fascist or anything like it because frankly I don't understand the Fascists. I don't understand what moves them, what makes them fight."

"That's easy, Henryway. Two things."

"Hemingway."

"Two things: money and fear. Many are simply paid, including most of the spies. Pepe gave up a rich teacher's life to work for the Front. What money could they have paid him? But many are also afraid. Afraid of losing their country, afraid of losing power, afraid of anything new."

"And Pepe was not afraid."

"Don't be an idiot, Pepe was afraid of many things, he was a man. But he was not afraid of the future."

# 7

Hemingway escaped Pilas's cellar just as the wild-eyed freedom fighter was getting sufficiently agitated by the wine to start talking about his own history, his own abandonment of a teaching profession in '35 and his apprenticeship in bomb making, and the loss of his wife to a bullet wound during a workers' riot not long thereafter. Hemingway escaped by simply finishing his drink and striding quickly to the miniature door, which closed behind him with Pilas still talking in the darkness. He sucked in his gut and inched through the alley quickly, like a Mark Twain brat shimmying through a fence slat.

He walked for an hour before he found a working cab that could take him the rest of the way to the Florida. He'd been gone almost four hours.

The afternoon over the city grew dusky dark with storm clouds that never rained. But the shells did begin to fall.

Hemingway went next door at the Gran Via. Sidney Franklin had told him he'd seen Quintinilla there near the back terrace, leisurely picking over a stew and a brandy. Hemingway also found a note for him at the desk from Josie, who said she was treating another new-to-Spain American journalist, one Virginia Cowles, to lunch, and that he should come by if he could. Hemingway also hadn't had a drink since he left that dynamite-packed cellar on the south side of the city, over an hour and a half earlier, and his teeth began to ache.

Striding through the Gran Via not unlike an archduke through his own coronation, wearing a long wool coat and black sailor's cap he'd grabbed off Franklin's skull minutes before, Hemingway spotted Josie with her guest out on the back terrace, literally three tables away from the table where Quintinilla sat, his face buried in a French newspaper. He walked by Quintinilla, came around Josie's broad back, and aimed right for the redhead.

"Miss Cowles," Hemingway said with a seductive smile, making to kiss her hand once he held it in his own. But Cowles snapped it away first, laughing.

"Don't give me that, Hemingway, I heard all about you, you are some kind of crazy springtime lurcher dog, aren't you?"

Eyebrows up, Hemingway quickly sat down, making eye contact with the waiter, who would bring port and sangria without being told.

"And you, Miss Cowles, are a rash judgment-maker," is all he could come out with, thinking, Shit, I'm either going to die at this brilliant, cynical woman's feet right here, or hear enough in the next hour to wish she'd fall under a truck.

It came to be the latter, as it happened, as Cowles continued to insult Hemingway to his face with lovely gusts of laughter—gaily calling him "Lieutenant Irish Toothache" at one point—and Josie grew redder and redder.

But Hemingway didn't waste much thought on imagining scenarios in which the Boston-accented firebrand to his right might meet a sudden death, because it was some minutes after he sat down when the first shell landed.

The shells were small, coming from the southwest, hitting the buildings and streets in uneven, unpredictable splats, never strong enough to create structural damage but enough to wreck a room or blow out a wall or obliterate a body, if it were lucky enough to hit one. But they were untargeted, volleyed one by one haphazardly into the air, landing virtually anywhere, so everyone in that section of the city was torn between two absurdities: running for shelter—the odds against a shell landing where you stood seemed, and in fact were, astronomical—or just ignoring the explosions, even as shrapnel flew over your head and windows cracked and fell out of their panes beside you.

On the Gran Via's back terrace, the shells were at first an erratic background drumbeat to the conversation, landing in the blocks surrounding the Florida. The terrace did, however, face south, a vulnerability that made Josie, for one, tighten and sweat with dread. But how to seek shelter, when Hemingway and Cowles simply sat there, swatting at each other verbally but otherwise not deigning to even notice the explosions?

"I know your type, Hemingway," Cowles declaimed, wagging a finger, "you're convinced you're the sun, right? And we're just planets and asteroids and space crap, right, revolving around you, and of course any sorry little planet or moon would be happy to get screwed by the sun, after revolving around it at a depressing distance for a while, right? After all, you are very bright and warm and important."

"Boy, who humped you over."

"The best, hotshot."

"I'm sure. But I didn't know it was a contest. Maybe that's your problem."

"My problem? I'm not the best-selling swellhead with a Sears catalogue of sexual conquests and a hairy-chested *Life* magazine photo spread every six months."

"Conquests? Virginia, you don't get me at all. I'm actually a very sad person. A day doesn't go by that I don't wish for one of those shells to land on my head. In fact, that's why I'm really here."

"Oh, I see, you think I can be appealed to by way of, what, a maternal instinct? I should feel sorry for your tragedy, your tragic greatness, and sleep with you for that reason."

"I never said I wanted you to sleep with me."

"You don't have to say it. I can read it on your chest. I can smell it on you."

"You don't know the first thing about me."

"You're right. Just the last thing, the last few things, which are all that's important."

"No, you don't. You had your mind set before you even sat down."

"Well . . ." Cowles nodded. "You're right. I did."

It had been going on like this for several drinks. Josie half listened, and focused on controlling her bladder.

"So? What you've been listening to about me is publicity and gossip and crap from writers who haven't sold as many books."

"And from women."

"Even worse."

"Oh, yeah? Women in general?"

"I'm beginning to think so. No, I meant women who've known me well, and whom I've probably disappointed."

"Ooo, a little self-knowledge."

"Whatever. They're hardly reliable, any of the above. You're a reporter, you should be wary of your sources and their motivations."

A shell hit the roof edge of the Florida next door, and tiny bits of brick and glass splashed across the terrace floor. Josie yelped from behind gritted teeth.

"What do you care what I think of you, Hemingway?"

"I can't say I care, but I'm interested. It's what we're talking about, isn't it? That's reason enough. Be a reporter, that's all I'm saying."

"OK, I'll go to the source, Mr. War-Zone Lover." Her voice softened a touch. Cowles was beginning to lose her malice,

Hemingway saw with relief, and to grow visibly nervous from the shelling. "You tell me one true thing that could disprove the picture of you I have in my head."

"One true thing."

"Just one."

"OK. I came here to write about the war, but as of yesterday I . . . A friend of mine was murdered, in Valencia, and no one wants anyone to know why or by whom. So I'm finding out. Come hell or high water."

"Really." Cowles wasn't buying it hook and sinker, but Hemingway could tell that by now she *wanted* to believe it. "You're going to . . . *investigate* it? A friend of yours was murdered? And you're going to pull a Hammett."

"It's true. Right, Josie?"

Josie nodded. "José Robles. The foreign minister told me himself."

Cowles turned to Hemingway, her blood slowly rising.

"Very nice. And how do you intend to do this, Hemingway?"

"I'm not sure yet. But I've talked with Gorev about it, who behaved as if I'd told him I saw his mother in bed with Hoover. I think he may be going insane. I've talked to POUM people who've known Robles forever and swore he could not be the Fascist spy the rumors are saying he is. Del Vayo, in fact, said one thing to John Dos Passos and another to Josie, in the span of forty-eight hours."

"And? What now?"

"I'm going to ask Pepe Quintinilla, who's sitting right over there."

The women arched and looked, and didn't need to be told who Quintinilla was.

"Oh, I've heard of him already," Cowles purred. "Ask him what?"

"Ask him what he knows."

"And he'll just tell you. The Republic's head of secret service."

"He'll tell me whatever he'll tell me. But then we'll see what he won't say."

"You might get yourself killed in this somehow, Hemingway," Cowles said. "If it's true."

"If it's true?"

Another shell hit, this time they could see it from the terrace—the tile roof below, a home, now consumed in clay shards and smoke, and then, increasingly visible, a small gaping crater of burned wood and ruins.

"Watch," Hemingway said. "Pepe?" he yelled.

Quintinilla looked over, smiled broadly, folded his paper, and strode over, his long limbs and croissant-shaped nose and exact manner exuding a Continental coolness.

"Señor Hemingway, I'm sorry, I've been absorbed in the news from Paris—did you hear that Roosevelt plans on signing a third Neutrality Act?"

"No, Pepe, but I'm not surprised. Look, this is Josie Herbst, and this is Virginia Cowles, both writing for American newspapers."

"I'm charmed, señoritas—"

And another shell hit, by the flat, deep sound of it landing on the asphalt right outside but perhaps a half-block away.

"Christ," Josie said.

Hemingway picked up his glass of brandy and sipped from it with one hand and gestured to Quintinilla to sit down with his other. Only Cowles, looking around, noticed that the thin crowd occupying the tables that afternoon was already substantially thinner. Everyone else was slyly, casually taking cover, back in their hotels' basements or in the wine cellar of the Gran Via, the ceiling beams of which were so old and dry anyway they threatened to crumble and collapse every Saturday night, when the restaurant was relatively full.

"Pepe, there is something of vital importance I need to speak with you about—"

"And me with you, Ernest! I've been reading your latest dispatches—*Le Journal* reprints them, out of the *New York Herald Tribune,* you see; you didn't know that?—and I must ask you, I must *eeeen-qwire,* Ernest, why is it you are reporting on the war as if it is a story of yours—I mean no disrespect. What I mean is if you do not report on the larger picture, the troops, the decisions, the politics, but just on the poor casualties, the way it is on the street, this is not the whole picture, *no?,* but a snapshot, a sketchy view, *si?,* beautiful and moving but, how do I say, like the painters, pointillist—" Quintinilla was jovial, and the debate he wanted to start was obviously intended for the game pleasure of both men.

"That's the point, Pepe, we already only hear about the decision makers and the politics and about abstract numbers of troops moving and fighting and casualty lists, that's what most reporting is, it's abstractions and regurgitated press conferences—"

"Yes, Ernest, but when I read the newspaper, I want the real meaning, the large picture, of what I'm reading about, not a human–interest story—"

"But it's all human interest! Politics all boil down to how people are hurt or killed or starved. *That's* the news. What Largo or Roosevelt are thinking of doing or saying they're thinking of doing, that's just bullshit—"

It went on for ten minutes or so, because the men enjoyed it and it was a good argument, and during that time another shell landed near the Gran Via, they could only hear it and feel it with their legs, and both men, with smiles, refused to even look around from their spot on the terrace to see if where the shell had landed was visible from there. Quintinilla let it disturb his rhetorical ramblings only to the extent of taking a moment to pronounce, *"Six!",* thereby inciting everyone to count the falling shells one by one as they struck. Josie, for one, didn't want to count but now had to, and each shell now seemed to represent an exponential increase in odds that she would die in the shelling if, in fact, she stayed put. But to duck out now would bring on shame and disrespect, both as a war journalist and as a Hemingway satellite. But she did have to pee.

Eventually, Hemingway turned the conversation around, away from critiquing his own reportage. They spoke in wine-sodden terms of the November assault and triumph, of the easily definable bravery and mettle of those Republicans, and how lucky those young men, killed or surviving, were to know so surely something real and proud about themselves. Most of such talk was Hemingway's, but he heard himself after awhile, got red-cheeked at his own sentimentality, and changed topics again.

"Pepe, as the Republic's Commissar of Investigation and Security—"

"No longer my official title, by the way—"

"What would that be?"

"Cannot tell you." Grinning. More wine and port came to the table.

"—from whatever seat you're holding at the moment in the Popular Front's efforts, I have to ask you about—"

A shell hit, very close, very hard, windows somewhere shattered, clouds of plaster dust swept through the restaurant, and as Cowles looked around she saw that virtually no one but the nervous waiters remained, unable to abandon a Hemingway table. Josie could not wait any longer and ran for the toilet.

"*Seven!*" Quintinilla crooned. ". . . —about?"

"About José Robles."

Quintinilla's cool, controlled, exacting stillness suddenly became, or seemed to become, an expert pose, a reservation of expression. But in fact he hadn't moved a hair. "Who?" he said.

He wasn't as drunk as Hemingway had wanted him to be, but the shelling was getting closer, and time may well have begun to run out. He refilled Quintinilla's glass with an aged ruby port Hemingway had assumed was out of a Spanish secret policeman's ordinary price range—that is, when Moscow isn't paying his bills. Impressed or not, Quintinilla happily drank it.

"Come now, Pepe, Robles, adjutant to the Comintern? He was arrested and disappeared, weeks ago, and he was killed. Del Vayo let it slip, to Josie's face. Señor Dos Passos is on his way to Valencia right now. Well, actually, I guess he's there already. Nosing around. Robles was murdered. You *must* know something about it."

"Ernest! Why would you assume that?"

"Because you're a straight shooter. You're a man in a field of bureaucratic mice. You will tell me the truth even if it hurts. We just need to know—there's not much chance we can do anything about it once we know, right? But the truth, it is good to speak it. This must not remain a secret. The old Spaniards said— right?—when the bull sits on the hot stone, it is time for silence."

"What exactly does that mean." Quintinilla reveled, the conversation's power balance tipping his way.

"It means never! The bull never sits on hot stones! Bulls never sit!"

"Not true."

"OK, but on hot stones?! Really, Pepe—"

"Have you found a body?"

"No. Wouldn't know where to begin to look."

"So why, again, do you assume the Popular Front has anything to do with Robles's death?"

"Del Vayo said so! If Franco kidnapped him out of his wife's bed in the middle of the night and disappeared the poor bastard, del Vayo wouldn't know a fucking thing about it!"

"Perhaps del Vayo, how you say, unintentionally implicated the government. Perhaps he meant to say, Robles was *probably* dead."

"But why would he say that, as opposed to saying Robles *probably* went on vacation to Ibiza?"

"Perhaps Josie's Spanish is not very good."

"Josie doesn't speak any Spanish. Del Vayo was speaking English. Where is Josie?"

The three looked around. Cowles had remained silent for an uncharacteristically long time, and had long since stopped drinking.

A shell whistled down, hit the back of the Florida next door, and the terrace of the Gran Via shook like a carnival ride.

"*Eight!*" Quintinilla sang out.

"Pepe, what have you heard? What do you know?" Another shell, quickly after the last, outside.

"*Nine!*"

"Pepe, why did they take Robles?"

"Señor, most respectfully, you are a journalist! You are both journalists! Could you imagine how quickly my head would be put on a pike if I were to be quoted in a newspaper? On *any* topic?"

"Off the record, I swear, Pepe. I'm not writing now, I'm talking about reality. You know I would never lie. And Virginia promises, too, don't you."

Cowles quickly nodded. "I couldn't use it anyway, not for Hearst."

Quintinilla's watery eyes narrowed and his chest labored for breath a little, he'd finally ingested enough alcohol to allow him to show his cards, which Hemingway knew he'd been dying to do.

"Ernest, Robles was a spy."

"No, he wasn't."

"Yes, Ernest, he was. That is why."

"Who gave the order?"

"Even if I knew, I couldn't tell you that, top-secret state information. Really, Hemingway. Even off the record. Should I in one gesture make myself an enemy of the state?"

A shell came and hit the corner of the Gran Via straight on.

All in a fraction of an instant the terrace jerked and shook, stucco and brick flew, windows exploded, Cowles dropped to her knees beneath the table, and a flying terra-cotta shingle winged into Hemingway's head, ricocheting off it and leaving a massive slashing scuff that instantly begin spitting blood. Hemingway grabbed a napkin off the table, slapped it to his skull, and looked back to Quintinilla as if he'd swatted a horsefly. The blood kept flowing.

"Señor," Quintinilla said, "we ought to go downstairs, find a nurse—"

"Pepe! I need to know what you know."

If not shaken by the shelling, Quintinilla now looked a little helpless, and let loose a surrendering sigh.

"Ernest, all I know is that someone said he was a spy, and they arrested him, and if they arrested him and executed him then somebody had it on good authority that he was working for the Fascists."

"But he wasn't. He couldn't be."

"You may not know everything."

Not the first time I've heard that, Hemingway thought, blood stinging his eyes. "But that spy shit, that's a smoke screen. An alibi. Only in Spain could the undocumented execution of a man as a Fascist spy be the alibi for something else."

"Undocumented? Are you sure? Well . . ." Quintinilla started speaking more slowly. "If you don't believe that story, Ernest, begin perhaps thinking about what you would believe."

What did he say? Hemingway saw immediately: Quintinilla repeated that spy business baloney but didn't buy it himself. Or didn't see much of a reason to assume it was true.

Cowles was caught up, her eyes wide. She didn't notice, but it was past sunset and getting dark.

"I'd believe someone lied about Robles, and killed Robles, to save their own skin."

"See? All you had to do was start writing the story!"

"Very funny."

"I mean that seriously." A shell. *"Eleven!"* Quintinilla was swaying; Hemingway could see that he didn't have much longer to stay on his feet.

"So who? How could Robles have threatened anyone?"

"Honest men are very threatening, Ernest." Hemingway was getting exasperated—all these vague answers. However true they might be.

"Where can I find the answers, Pepe?"

"Try Valencia."

With that, weary himself, Quintinilla put his glass down, bowed modestly to Cowles so he would not fall over, bid *buenos noches* to Hemingway, and loped back through the restaurant, staggering a little in the shadows.

Another shell hit outside.

"Twelve," Cowles croaked dryly.

"Hmpf." Hemingway checked the napkin on his head; the blood was just starting to cake. Cowles stood up from the table at last, gathering herself to go.

"Well, I'm still not going to fuck you." She was looking down, at her shoes.

"That's fine."

"But if it matters, I think you're not quite the horse's ass I thought you were. "

"Thanks, Virginia. I'll put that one on my résumé."

"And I do promise to buy the book that comes from all this."

"What a relief."

# 8

That book would never appear. Hemingway wrote a hundred or so pages in the fall, after it was all through, but then threw it away into the Key West trash and went back to the other book, with the *Americano*, the mountain cave, and the tight bombing-mission spine, which was a story someone might believe. The other story, the one that happened, he thought then, was for the birds.

After he was left alone in the Gran Via that early evening, and after the shelling soon petered out, Hemingway kept drinking with Sidney Franklin and Henry Gorrell of the United Press, and then with a few local Brits from the XV International Brigade, and then with whom else Hemingway could not say, as the hours ticked by and the bill got larger and Hemingway's memory enjoyed a deep, velvety blackout.

When he awoke, he was aware only that he was moving, in the backseat of a car. Dawn was breaking through the car windows, and he squinted. The car smelled of urine. Fuck, Hemingway thought, tell me I've been kidnapped, too. Those sons of bitches.

He sat up and saw that it was an old sedan cab, and the driver was alone and he was old and poor, wearing a tweed cap and smoking a cigar he thoughtfully held near the open window. Not kidnapped.

"But what?" Hemingway passed wind, tuba-like.

*"Que?"* The driver waved and smiled.

"What the fuck is going on?"

The driver still grinned. *"Español?"*

Hemingway's head pounded, which in turn made him remember his head wound. When he felt it, it felt like a small mountain of dried blood and scab on the crest of his forehead, in which large pieces of bar napkin were embedded, their edges and corners sticking out of the mess like shards of dried bread poking out of a pot of gumbo.

*"Que?"*

The driver had little English so Hemingway squeezed his eyes, tried to hurdle over his headache, and remember as much Spanish as he could, which wasn't a lot.

"Señor, where you are driving me?"

"Señor, to Valencia! Yes? That is what you wanted. We can turn in a circle if you want!"

"For what?"

The driver shrugged. "If you want to go in a circle!"

"No, why Valencia?"

"How in hell should I know? You said, to Valencia!" The driver's hand came up in a salute.

"I did?"

"Yes! Paid me one hundred American dollars! To Valencia!"

In English: "Jesus Christ! I did? For a cab ride to Valencia?"

"Yes! You were very happy."

In English: "I'm sure."

Could hardly take it back now, or turn around. Government cars were presumably impossible to find past midnight in Madrid, and Hemingway presumably had to offer a city cab a flashy wad of bills to even consider driving a very drunk American such a distance in the middle of the night. But then, one hundred dollars could feed a Madrileño family for six months. Hemingway settled back in his seat, trying to resign himself to his own inebriated folly, which he managed to do in the space of a few minutes. He tentatively scratched the edges of his head scab and reasoned that although he hadn't planned it—it was farther from the front than Madrid and he'd only decided to go to Valencia because he was stewed to the gills—it *was* where Robles was last seen alive. If Hemingway was going to make good at all on his own lofty, heroic self-declamations, the ones he'd been spreading around Madrid like IOUs, he'd better go, and . . . do some good. Find the truth.

The driver spotted Hemingway's thumbs massaging his temples, and passed back a flask of what turned out to be *patxaran*. This was new, although Hemingway deduced what he was gulping from the taste: the anise and sloe flavor of the homemade liqueur was so rich and complex it made his mind stop working. It didn't burn, but suddenly the morning sun coming over the hills of Cuenca was startlingly gorgeous, a heavenly panorama practically singing with hope and righteous power. Hemingway must've looked as if he'd had an epiphany, because the driver started chuckling. "You've seen the death of God," he said.

*"Que?"* It didn't sound chucklesome.

"Look. When we die, señor, afterward we are always on a porch relaxing and drinking and looking out at the meadows."

"If we are virtuous."

*"Si!* Well, imagine that if God died, that porch and the sun on the meadow and the brew he would drink and the relaxation he would have would be the greatest of all."

"Ah, *si.*"

The landscape outside the driver's window reflected his notion, wild fields and low mountains of red clay made roseate and peach and amber by the rising sun. Hemingway saw a burned church miles away, its blackened steeple standing out like a ghost against the sunshine. He'd noticed that, in this most medieval of Catholic countries, the churches served as prime targets.

"Who would burn a church?" Hemingway muttered, in Spanish.

"Republicans," the driver answered.

*"No."*

*"Si."*

*"No."*

*"Si.* Rome is with the Fascists. So priests are killed and churches are burned by the Republicans."

Hemingway knew it was so; he'd heard stray stories about summary executions in various parishes, usually of corrupt priests who also owned more land than anyone in their vicinity and paid peasants *reales* to work in their fields. But who knows how true the contexts and excuses were, and did they matter in any event?

Many people will die, Pilas had said. I will die, I'm sure of it.

"Are you angry about the killing of priests?"

"Señor, I stay out of it."

"You are Basque?" The *patxaran,* Hemingway knew, was a brew of Navarra.

*"Si,* señor."

"From where?"

"Guernica."

After fifteen hours of driving, the latter five for which Hemingway was conscious, watching the burnished fields pass him by, counting the war-wrecked villages he could see from the main road, and spotting at least two murdered bodies discarded into the roadside weeds, the cab arrived in Valencia.

Finding his way to the body took Hemingway another hour, as he first bullied his way through the government offices at the castlelike Palace of Benicarló with his sympathetic cabbie's rough translative help, and then to the local police station, where they were told that Robles's body was found by a goatherd boy about nineteen miles from Valencia city limits, left in the high grass on the lee side of a tall hill. It was now in a state of advanced decay but his mustache and clothes were still recognizable, almost four weeks after he'd been shot.

Dos Passos had left with a contingent of policemen about thirty minutes earlier. Then Hemingway and his overpaid Basque cohort, whom Hemingway found was named Ignacio, drove northwest from the city where the body was said to be and got lost, but arrived only twenty minutes or so after Dos Passos had, and after the cops were only beginning to take forensic evidence from the body.

Of course when the taxi pulled up in that barren fringeland everyone looked, and when Hemingway stepped out from the front seat Dos Passos rolled his eyes.

The morning was still bright, but the winds coming down were icy.

As Hemingway approached, he could see Robles, half obscured by long winter grass, rumpled in a sodden pile like wet clothes, his dry, blackened skin shining in the morning light. By this time the organs and flesh had grown desiccated in the cool spring, alternately being rained upon and then baked in the mountain sun. The eyes were gone, but the teeth were visible, the lips dried up and peeled back over them. There was little noticeable stench; most of the decay had finished. There was no question it was Robles: the mustache, the shape of the head, the black roof of hair reaching inches from the scalp, the English suit no Brigadesman or soldier or peasant could afford. The set of silver fillings in his upper molars, visible from a few feet away and confirmed by Dos Passos, cemented the deal.

"Dos." Hemingway sidling up, wrapping his coat tight around him in the cool air.

Dos Passos cast a sideward glance—he was upset, Robles was

a close friend, and he had decided already he had no patience for Hemingway's bullgoose nonsense. But Hemingway knew what the scene would be like before he'd made it to Valencia. "Sorry, chief," Hemingway said quietly.

Dos just nodded.

"What have they found." Hemingway took a step closer. The Valencia detectives—three of them, accompanied by a handful of uniformed militia—were prodding and probing Robles with long sticks they'd obviously found in the brush. Nobody was writing anything, nobody was measuring anything.

"What do you mean?" Dos.

"Are they investigating or are they just poking him like kids playing with roadkill?"

"I don't—"

"Have they found the entry wound?"

"Ernest, it's too late for that I think—"

"No, it's not. What about footprints? They've trampled the entire area."

Dos Passos scoffed. "Were you going to match the pattern in the dirt to every boot in Valencia?"

"See, Dos, that's as much as you know about crime scenes and shit like this. It's not a class they teach in Harvard, I'm guessing. In Chicago, they'd've known what to look for."

"That didn't take you long."

"Stop right there. I'm not getting on that bus, Dos, the let's-crap-on-Hemingway-every-time-he-acts-like-he-knows-something bus. There's information, here, goddammit, and these sheepheads don't know the first thing about what they're doing."

"Yeah, well, we're lucky they came at all. I spent three hours convincing some moron of a police chief to give me his men. He wasn't ready to concede that any one body found in the hills, no matter who it is, is worth looking at or even identifying. There are too many of them. The policemen here spend their time sleeping in brothels and playing cards in the cantinas. Until the war finishes up, they figure there's little that actually qualifies as police work."

"Fuckers. Look," Hemingway raised his voice, and the rather bored policemen turned, "anyone see a cartridge? *El cartucho?*"

The cops stared at him, then began to desultorily sift through the tall grass around the body without bending over.

"Aw, Christ."

"Ernest, this might just be a lost cause."

"Dos, I'm shocked to hear you say it. I'm supposed to be the one who says that. Look, this isn't a lost cause until we lose it. I didn't think you had come to Valencia because you thought it would be easy to find out who killed Pepe and why."

"I didn't think it would be easy, in fact I thought it'd be impossible, really, and it is, obviously. Finding out who assassinated one man in the middle of all this. I'm angry, but I don't know where else there is to go after this."

"You don't? You should've put in some time as a reporter, Dos. First thing you learn is there're *always* paths to follow, things left behind, gaps in the story, *never* is every tendril of a crime completely tied up."

"See, you're thinking of it as fun. I can tell. For me this isn't fun. I'm not doing it to entertain myself, or prove anything."

"It's not fun, Dos, but it is justice. Isn't it? Isn't that worth fighting for? This is like, c'mon, it's like a microcosm of the whole war, it's like November in Madrid—standing up to outrageous odds and defying the power that doesn't want us to press on—"

"But Ernest, that power you're bucking up against is the Popular Front; we're supposed to be here supporting it. Pepe worked for it, he believed in it. They're the *good guys.*"

The policemen were now standing in a group to the side, smoking and talking. They only looked over when the Americans' voices were raised, and they never looked over to the body.

"Fuck the Popular Front, one of them probably gave this order, Dos. Fascists didn't do this. This was inside work, this wasn't war, it was secret and criminal. You don't think the Republicans are capable? How many priests have been beheaded this year, Dos? How many churches burned?"

"The larger picture—"

"Don't give me the larger picture, you weren't talking about the larger picture in Madrid. You think Pepe should be forgotten as a martyr, for reasons unknown, to the cause, when we don't even know who killed him? The larger picture! Are you going to start thinking strategically, about the Republic and all that, when it comes to Pepe Robles getting secretly executed? C'mon, Dos, this isn't checkers, this is a goddamn mess and I'm beginning to think there are no good guys."

"That can't be true. Pepe was."

"OK, maybe that's what got him. That's what Quintinilla said last night—'Honest men are very threatening.'"

"Quintinilla! You would've had to get him very drunk to get a reliable word out of his mouth—"

"I did."

"What happened to your head?"

"Oh. Flying debris, shells last night at the Gran Via."

"And you stood there."

"Dos. C'mon."

"OK . . . Quintinilla . . . So who, who could Pepe have threatened?"

"That is all I'm saying, we have to find out. We know he wasn't a spy, that's just fucking propaganda."

Dos was wilting. Hemingway didn't know if his old friend could maintain the indignation the way he could—God knows, maintaining indignation in the face of authoritarian abuse came as easily to Hemingway as flyfishing or writing newspaper journalism. He could do it tirelessly, like a toddler holding his breath, until he dropped unconscious from the effort.

"Ernest, honestly, where do we go from here?"

"I don't know! But I'm sure as gull shit not going to just leave after coming all this way, and go back to writing NANA dispatches about the shelling I hear in the distance."

"You could write about this."

"I did already, they don't care. I think only about a third of the stuff I send them makes it into print anyway. Fuck them. There's got to be—"

The passel of Spanish policemen walked past the Americans, leaving the body where it lay, and nodded to the writers cordially as they made their way to their truck, having met the end of their allotted time worrying about a single corpse dumped in the runoff thickets of the Sierra de Gudárs One detective reached out and handed Hemingway a bullet casing as he passed. Then they were gone. Ignacio, napping in his cab, woke with a start and watched the truck drive away.

Hemingway looked at the casing: it looked like a Mauser shell, maybe a Gewehr 98. He hadn't seen one since Italy. If it was, then it was a German bullet, a Fascist bullet, that killed Robles. Hemingway slipped it into his pocket.

"Alright," he said, striding toward where Robles's ruins lay in a decomposing pile, "now, you look over here, at the skull, there's solid material still here around his eye sockets," bending over, pointing, though Dos Passos didn't look, "but the back of the skull is gone, so he was shot face on, probably kneeling, OK?, and fell forward. He was tied up, here's the rope, and dragged here—from where? Here." Hemingway got down on his hands and knees feet away from the body, and Dos Passos came over. "See the marks, the furrows in the mud, he was dragged from there, down the hill."

Hemingway hustled off through the scrub, and Dos Passos followed, up the hill.

They saw deep digs in the soil, where a man's feet might hit hard if he were pulled along and lost his balance, they saw grass dug up by boots pressing down for purchase, they found old cigarette papers and a clump of human hair still gripped into a clot, clinging to the gorse. They'd walked for forty-five minutes on the trail, the sun beginning to be hot, when they found a campsite, high but flat and laureled by heather. Logs had been dragged, and a fire had left burned wood in the cold clay.

"They spent the night here." Hemingway walked around the area bent over, focused on whatever his eyes and nose passed over.

Dos Passos stood with his hands in his pockets, feeling rather useless. "What are we looking for?"

"How should I know?"

The mountain vetch and flax growing around the perimetrical area was thick. But Hemingway found a discarded chicken bone, and an empty pint bottle of Gordon's gin. "So?" Dos Passos said.

"So, they were probably drunk. Or drunk, then hungover."

But then he found them, some thirty yards up path from the campsite, under a tangle of weeds: a simple pocket chain with two keys attached.

"What the." He walked them back to Dos Passos. "What are these?"

A rich boy, Dos Passos knew immediately—the flat handles of both keys bore a double-winged insignia, with a capital *B* at their center. "These are for a Bentley."

"Get the fuck out of here, a Bentley? Who out here could afford a Bentley? Why would anyone be out here, shooting men in the dark, if they could be driving around in a Bentley?"

"I cannot imagine."

"They must've dropped them. They were drunk."

"Somebody dropped them. But soldiers, or assassins, walking around with Bentley keys?"

"It had to be them. There's nothing around for miles that

suggests anyone's been through here since Napoleon except goats and shepherds. Look, these things are not weathered, they haven't been out here for long."

". . ."

"C'mon, Dos, use your fucking imagination."

"I'm trying. But I'm tired."

"Alright, let's go. You'll help me find a room in Valencia, right?"

"Sure."

Hemingway led his friend back down the hill toward Ignacio's cab, and the three headed back into the city, where the three men had a decent *comida* of roast chicken and fried potatoes. Dos Passos worried about leaving Robles's body where it was, but he was assured it could, after all these weeks, wait until tomorrow. Ignacio, feeling guilty now about taking one hundred American dollars for what was essentially one day's work, insisted, in Spanish and in bits of English, on paying for his third of the bill, and Hemingway let him. As the cabbie got up to leave and begin the long drive home, a young man, eager as a spaniel puppy but dressed in a mundane bureaucratic suit, approached the table with his happy eyebrows up, obviously looking for an introductory moment. Hemingway held a finger up to the young man, halting him, and spoke, respectfully and in Spanish, to Ignacio.

"When I'm back in Madrid, Ignacio, I might need your help again. I will pay less than this, however."

"Yes."

"Where can I find you?"

"The same place you found me yesterday."

"I have no idea where that was."

Ignacio remembered and smiled. "By the curb, in front of the Florida."

# 9

Mordaunt Worsleighson was all of twenty-two but had been nearly driven crazy already by his own brainpower, his own zealous energy, and his own idealism. He was rangy and broad-shouldered like a rugby player but trim and fire-eyed, with lank hair that fell across his forehead when he talked his usual blue streak in a way that made girls squeeze their thighs together. Though everyone assumed he was British, he was only of blue British blood, heir to the nonexistent estate of Worsleighson of Alamein, of Hindhead in the County of Surrey, sold off half a century earlier to pay off the debts of his grandfather Mordaunt's gargantuan plan to build a British streetcar system in every city in Sudan, which was scotched forever by the Mahdist revolt of 1884. The young Mordaunt Worsleighson, not a third because his father was middle-named Brookingdon and not Trawlingtoke like Mordaunt and his notoriously unlucky grandfather, was born and bred in Boston, but would settle for nothing less than British prep schools, and then Oxford. Worsleighson had by that spring finished his second Ph.D., and had read Lenin's *What Is to Be Done?* so often on trains and in garrets that he could virtually recite it aloud, complete with footnotes and Leninistic self-quotations. There was little in print, actually, that Worsleigh-son hadn't read, or seemed to have read, which included Hemingway's nine books, over and over again. Therein he absorbed the Hemingway worldview as completely as any reader had, without quite seeing it as, at best, an idealized struggle toward the truth, and toward an ethical rejection of the modern life, a rampart erected against a public onslaught of dime novels, cheap radio, dumb movies, and tabloid gossip. The cynicism itself, if it was detected by readers like Worsleighson, only accentuated the macho romance.

As of January 1937, Worsleighson had been an unofficial member of the Republican government, having arrived in Valencia with a pile of suitcases and a dazzling interview style that landed him the unpaid assignment of propaganda translator from Russian and Spanish into English for the Brigadesmen from England and the United States, and for English-speaking journalists like Hemingway. Nobody checked his translations, and so for that winter and spring the Popular Front's English releases and pamphlets all possessed a syntactical sophistication and hyperbole that could rarely be quoted comfortably in a news dispatch.

Worsleighson had heard Hemingway was in Valencia, heard it through the bureaucratic grapevine in the Palace of Benicarló. There he had a desk in a hallway so busy with secretaries and emissaries that his desk was routinely bumped, jostling his long-hand writing—Worsleighson abhorred typewriters—and introducing spilled-ink cock-ups that would force him to rewrite a simple piece several times over. He left his post immediately upon hearing that the author of *The Sun Also Rises* was in the city, and spent several hours combing the hotels and bars of the city before he found Hemingway in a busy mid-range restaurant lunching with John Dos Passos, whose work he also found to be almost intolerably brilliant, and bidding adios to a Basque man who looked like he'd just stepped out of an Iberian Hooverville.

Hemingway's raised finger went down, with more than a trace of irritation. Worsleighson bounded.

"Mr. Hemingway! It's true, I heard you'd come to Valencia, I shot out of my chair, may I introduce myself, I am Mordaunt Worsleighson—"

"I know that name—" Dos Passos.

"Yeah," Hemingway smiled, "that hump who wanted to turn Khartoum into Piccadilly Square, right?, until the Mahdi shut him down."

"My grandfather."

"Wasn't he also a racehorse entrepreneur?" Dos Passos offered. "Who got convicted of race fixing?"

"That," Worsleighson offered, trying to stay agreeable, "was my father."

"Oh."

"Worsleighson, we're eating." Hemingway wasn't in fact eating any longer, but drinking, delighted to discover that the restaurants of Valencia still functioned marvelously, and their wine cellars had not been notably disturbed, and that you could find a nice 1926 *cava,* like a Codorníu Teresa or three, without a sweat.

"Yes, sir, may I sit down?" And then he sat, leaving both writers at the table forthrightly agape. But Worsleighson's buoyant manner, he'd known since he was a child, almost always defused the ire brought about by his narcissism. He was an entertainer by nature, he couldn't help it.

"Worsleighson, is this official business? You're with the Front, aren't you?"

"Well, yes, but volunteering. How could you tell?"

"You couldn't be anything else."

"Oh. No, this isn't official business, God knows, no, but when I heard tell that you, Mr. Hemingway, were in the city, I had to abandon my idiotic translation duties as briskly as I could, which is to say an idiot could do them not that they are idiotic in and of themselves, serving the Republic as they do, I had to find you and put myself at your disposal, you see, I'm a veritable devotee, a Hemingwayian if you will, I've read all of your nine books and seven of the short stories not collected in them, and I believe I've read every one of your dispatches from Madrid—"

Dos Passos was three seconds away from tossing his napkin on the table and walking off.

"—and I'm convinced your agenda, if you'd call it that, never mind, your aesthetic is the moment's one true voice, the new call for purity and righteousness in the new century, and I am also delighted to tell you I was delighted to find out that you were a Republican and had decided to work for the Front."

"But I don't work for the Popular Front."

"Well, yes, not directly, but everyone knows NANA is a political tool used by your government, and—"

"Look, Worsleighson, NANA is not a government agency, and I do not work for the Front or any other political body."

Dos Passos had almost left, the sycophancy had been beginning to make his eyes water, but the spectacle of Hemingway get accused of being a propagandist made him relax in his seat.

"Yes, of course, Mr. Hemingway—can I call you Ernest? No, OK—this is just what I've heard over in *la palacio,* it's not important, my point is you are on our side, you are a Communist."

"No, you fucking twerp, I am not a Communist. Mr. Dos Passos, who's sitting right there, he's a Communist. But there are lots of those around, and I just wish you'd get to your point."

"I . . . You ought to get the scratch on your head bandaged properly, if I may say so."

"Scratch? This is a scratch to you?"

Worsleighson twitched. "What are you having, a Codorníu? Nice, but I know this cellar has several bottles of 1876 Cockburn's vintage port, and I'd be honored, nay, it would make my year, if I could order a bottle or two and share a drink with you gentlemen."

Hemingway looked at Dos Passos, who just smiled out the side of his face Worsleighson couldn't see, and shook his head.

"Worsleighson, you are the most shameless young turk I've ever met."

"All I did was get overenthusiastic, just now. It's a tendency I have."

"Go ahead, get the Cockburn's."

An hour passed, during which, in a flurry of port-to-port port drinking, Worsleighson vomited forth an unending, if oddly beguiling, stream of Stalinist fairy tales about the nobility of the worker, the utopian ideals of the Comintern, and even the necessity of the recent Moscow Trials, a topic neither Hemingway nor Dos Passos felt like exploring. Soon Hemingway felt compelled to intervene, to staunch the flow of bullshit with *something*, and so he told him about Robles, about where the two writers had just been that morning. Worsleighson did stop, and blinked five times. One thing Worsleighson couldn't do was hold his liquor especially well.

"Murdered?! And you're *sure* he wasn't a spy?" Which was when Dos Passos decided, having drank too much anyway, that he was done, and waited only for an opportune moment to leave.

"No, Worsleighson, he's not a goddamned spy, just take that for granted, will you?"

"Yes! Right! The adjutant to the Comintern—the Nationalists had to have done it! It's the war, right?"

Hemingway fished the shell casing out of his coat, which was slung over the back of his chair.

"The police found this near his body, in the grass."

Dos Passos leaned in. "I didn't see that. What is it, a Mauser?"

"I think so." Hemingway fondled it. "A Gewehr, maybe?" To Worsleighson: "A German gun."

"Aaahh, so it was Nazis!"

"Please, Mordaunt."

"You know what I mean—*Fascists*! Those bacteria! A spy mission from the Francoists, an assassination—"

"If that is true," Hemingway said, "then there are rats in the Republic selling information. No one outside of the Republic knew when Robles came to Valencia to see his family, right, Dos?"

"I don't know. Not many, I would guess."

"So, who's the Nationalist spy? Worsleighson, we could use you to find him, from the inside."

Worsleighson's eyes bugged out with excitement and intrigue-lust. "Ooo, an undercover traitor! In Valencia! Largo?"

"The prime minister?"

Dos Passos stood. "Ernest, I have to go, to see Margara. To tell her. Perhaps you should come along."

Hemingway was several degrees past half drunk by now, and shuddered with a double take at Dos Passos's suggestion, which was delivered as always with an almost insufferable air of rectitude. See Robles's widow *now*? Hemingway thought he'd rather step in front of a train than inform a Spanish woman of the discovery of her husband's month-old corpse.

"Wouldn't the police do that, Dos?"

"They weren't certain about the ID this morning, and seeing how they work I doubt they'll bother clearing the matter up for themselves, tomorrow or ever. So I'm assuming Margara hasn't been told anything. Even if she were, I feel I should go see her."

"Yes, you should. But I've never met the woman, and I'd be a stranger in her house on her worst day. Sorry, Dos, I'm staying here."

Dos Passos was visibly disgusted and left the restaurant, coat in hand, without another word.

Hemingway watched him go—dammit, that wearisome saint schtick of his. It hung in the air like a mother's disapproval.

"You disappoint him," Worsleighson slurred.

"Oh, shut up. The world disappoints him. And he prefers to moan about it instead of doing something."

"Like what?"

"Like what, Worsleighson? Like finding out who killed Robles, that's like what."

"But I thought we'd agreed it was Fascists—oh, but you're thinking we should track down the Republican spy that sold him out?"

"We?! Look, Worsleighson, I don't need a stooge—"

"*Excuse* me, Mr. Hemingway, but not only do I have two Ph.D.s and I work in the Republican government, but I've read and have more or less complete recall of every book published in English in the last seventy-five years about European history, there are two hundred and twelve of them you know, *and* I know six languages, including Spanish and Russian, so I dare say I cannot be accurately characterized as a *stooge*—"

"Alright, alright, cool your coal pit, Socrates, have some more port. I'm not talking about moles in the Republic. Look." He took out the Bentley keys, and laid them on the table.

"A set of car keys? Bentleys, yes."

"Found them about a half-mile uphill from where Robles's body still lies, not far from a fire site the killers apparently used overnight. Where'd they come from?"

"Yes, well . . ." Worsleighson, half-lidded and wobbly, was cut off by the approach, from the bar, of two women, both dressed in new Spanish clothes—cotton blouses that revealed a remarkable amount of cleavage for the day, and bright striped skirts, the kind flamenco dancers wear and slap when they dance. They were both in their thirties, both quite tipsy, neither of them Spanish, and both, Hemingway could read a half-mile away, divorced and on a touristy binge. Of course they turned out to be American.

"Hi! You boys mind if we join you? You seem to be enjoying yourselves! And we heard you're American! We're from Grosse Pointe! My, you two are a cute pair!" They spoke in a geyser of exclamations for a full minute, sitting down, scootching close, and gazing at Hemingway and Worsleighson as if the men were high-school boys sweaty from wrestling practice.

"Ladies, have some port." Hemingway poured it, never dissuading a woman from telling him he was desirable but at the same time planning to outdrink them and put their nonsense to rest in that manner. If they could keep up and still wanted to jump his bones, all the better. From the look of him, Worsleighson seemed muddled between delight and irritation.

"I'm Lenore, this is Peg! We're from Grosse Pointe!"

"You said that already."

"Wasn't sure you heard! Loud in here! We're on vacation, and there's no reason to be shy on vacation, is there? You are?"

"Mordaunt Worsleighson, at your service," and he affected a Brit accent that made the women coo.

"I'm Ernest Hemingway."

"The writer?" Peg raised her eyebrows innocently, while Lenore didn't react, as if Hemingway had announced he was the mayor of Ballantine, Montana.

"Yes."

"I've heard of you! What was that book, Peg, that you said Esther read, *Appointment* to something, *Sahara*?"

"That was John O'Hara."

"Oh, well, Esther said it was a very sexy book."

"Would we have heard of any of your books, Mr. Hemingway? And your forehead looks nasty."

Hemingway lost his savoir faire in a heartbeat. "So, what's your agenda, ladies? You're both divorced, obviously, and have decided to hit Europe with your ex-husbands' money and screw a few Spanish bellboys and drink too much bad wine and try to fill in your empty lives with luxury and indulgence—"

"That's it exactly!" And they roared with laughter. The men looked at each other. The sound of a shell landing echoed from some thirty miles away, a faint boom of distant thunder.

"Then what the heck are you doing in Spain?"

"What? Why not Spain?" Peg was pouring herself more port and spilling it, so Hemingway seized the bottle and poured for her.

"You're in the middle of a civil war, sweetheart," Hemingway belched. "You should be in Bermuda or some place that isn't littered with bodies."

"Or invaded by Fascists," Worsleighson growled.

"Oh, boys, you must take us for scaredy-cat Yankee housewives! The war hasn't stepped on our toes at all, right, Lenore?"

Lenore nodded, having grown a little sheepish.

"Thank goodness for that," Worsleighson said, thrumming with prejudice.

"So, you boys Brigadesmen? Work for the Popular Front? Or are you just journalists?"

The conversation had been antagonistic, in a sporty, booze-friendly way, from the beginning, but this tipped it. Worsleighson blurted, "I work for the government, indeed," but Hemingway's fuming *"What?!"* drew every pair of eyes in the joint like a bullet shot. *"Just* journalists? Lady, I don't know what you've got against journalists, but if it weren't for writers and newspapermen—"

"We love newspapermen, Mr. Hemingway," Lenore said soothingly, suddenly remembering that she was supposed to be having fun and that she had cleavage to display. "We've just met a lot of them already."

"Yes, no offense," Peg said into her glass. "We were wondering who else was in Spain, frankly."

"Well, it just so happens," Worsleighson began, "that Mr. Hemingway and I were just in the middle of investigating a *murder!"* Still caught in the fake accent, he said it in that irritating *r*-less way the British have of saying "murder," characterizing it as a fascinating parlor-game topic, like strange weather or a piece of morbid gossip.

*"Really?* In a war zone?" Peg colored her drunk enthusiasm

with a half-baked incredulity, and did very loudly. Heads turned, but Hemingway was far too deep into the port and far too focused on these irritating women to notice or care. He explained.

"Robles! Do I know that name?" Lenore's forehead crumpled. "What about the police?"

"Oh, Peg, honestly, during a civil war?"

"The police," Hemingway said, helplessly rising to the women's decibel level, "will do nothing—exactly, it's during a war. It's up to me."

"Us."

"Shut up, Mordaunt."

"What *will* you do, Mr. Hemingway?"

"That's what we were discussing. There are certain clues that I'm not sure I should share in a public place, and there are certain people I need to interview—"

"Like *who*?!"

Hemingway did not name names as the conversation grew in both length and volume, but he said enough, and in a clear holler, that people at nearby tables that Hemingway was no longer aware of, who may have been of nominal importance to him at first but were now completely nonexistent, either moved to the far end of the dining room, left the restaurant area altogether, or sat glaring fiercely. Whatever they did, Hemingway did not contemplate them.

But there were among them a few individuals who were listening carefully, whose ears were pricked up at the first bark of "Robles!", who were surreptitiously scribbling at their dark tables. The air in the restaurant—it was El Alarcon, on Calle de Murillo—was heavy with suspicion and tension; you could feel it in your ears or on your scalp only if you were relatively sober and paying attention, but that late afternoon no one was.

"So whose Bentley do these belong to? There can't be many Bentleys in Spain!"

"You're so full of beans, Peg, there could be hundreds."

"I doubt it—these people are poor—"

"Not the politicians and business owners and Russians and maybe even a few novelists, right, Mr. Hemingway?"

Hemingway harumphed, swallowing.

"Well, look, Lenore, these can't belong to a millionaire in, where, Granada, or Gibraltar, right? Why the hell would they end up here? I'd say that probability has it"—Peg tripped over a third *b* in "probability"—"that this Bentley, this car, is in Valencia or Madrid. Or maybe Barcelona, but that's stretching it, that's too far."

"And anarchists don't own Bentleys." Hemingway did a dance with his hand over his head, signaling to the waitstaff for another bottle of port, which for an instant they looked reluctant to fetch.

"C'mon, big-shot writer fella, Barcelona's a big city, with plenty of wealthy nonanarchists."

"But far," Lenore said.

"Maybe too far. Maybe."

"Who in the government, Mr. Wormstation, has a Bentley?" Lenore, very loudly.

"Call me Mordaunt, please," he replied. "I don't know, monitoring the parking of the cars is not part of my duties."

"Well, it's the first place we should look, isn't it?"

*"We?"* Worsleighson spat. "Here's what I know—those keys are to a Bentley 8 Litre, you can tell from the blue chrome coloring on the wings there, it was the largest and most expensive Bentley, produced in '30, '31, and there were only one hundred of them made. Exactly. I know, because I crashed one, into smithereens, a few years ago, and caught a whole lecture about how few of them there are."

"Poor boy." Lenore.

"Only one hundred?" Peg mused. "And it's an English car? What are the odds of there being more than a few in Spain right now?"

"Not terrific, you'd think," Lenore slurred.

"Largo has a Bentley," Worsleighson said quietly. Everyone paused.

"Why didn't you say that before?" Hemingway roared.

"Before? Before what? You just showed me the keys ten minutes ago!"

"Mordaunt, we've been sitting here for an hour."

Worsleighson held his head. "I'm not feeling terribly well."

"Is it an 8 Litre? Largo's car?"

"I don't know. I don't remember."

"I think," Hemingway kaboomed with a smile, as the third bottle of port arrived and he grabbed it by the neck, "we ought to lay siege—stealthily, catlike—to the cars at *la palacio de Benicarló*, which is where it'd be, right, Mordaunt? It's the official Republic boudoir as well, the cars should be there, and we'll see if the puzzle piece fits."

"Oh, yeah!" Lenore squealed.

"My dear ladies, this is dangerous work, you are not invited. Where are you staying?"

They were crestfallen but not really, the prospect of lurking in the shadows around the government building instantly brought forth visions of their expensive hotel rooms and their expensive hotel beds. "At the Fernando Rei."

"You know, everyone's been listening." Worsleighson hiccuped.

Hemingway stopped—what?—and then scanned the room as subtly as he could while stewed to the gills, and he began to sweat, as drunks do when they realize they'd forgotten something terribly important.

"Oh, shit," he said. The Michigan women also flopped their heads in circles, looking around, but despite that Hemingway thought he glimpsed a few figures who were pretending not to notice him amid the glaring faces and disgusted sidelong looks and muttered Spanish curses, and then he went back, stumbling, through his short-term memory to the last hour of talk, and his heart began to pound.

"Whatta goddamn gasbag," he said, and Worsleighson jerked his spine straight as if he'd woken up.

"Me?"

"No, me, you dullard." His hand snuck the key ring into his trouser pocket under the table.

"You think *they've* been listening?" Lenore hissed in a stage whisper.

Hemingway stood. "*Buenas noches*, ladies of Grosse Pointe," he said in a low voice for the first time all day, "please scamper home to your hotel, quickly and discreetly, and stay there, alright? It was a pleasure. Mordaunt, you've got the tab, am I right?"

There was applause in El Alarcon when they left.

Unopened bottle of sixty-year-old port in hand, Hemingway hit the sidewalk, Worsleighson wobbly at his side, and caught a cab. The sun was going down.

"So Worsleighson," in the broad, dark backseat, "what in the hell did you really want when you went looking for me today, anyway?"

". . . Just to know that . . . you were real."

"Real? Why, you thought maybe I was a fake?'

"I'd hoped you weren't."

They told the driver to drop them somewhere three blocks northwest of the Palace, and there the two very drunk men stood, as the ancient city grew dark around them without streetlights. "This way," Hemingway said, and they walked quickly, hunched over, trying to not let their footfalls echo in the empty streets but failing, of course, and heading two long blocks in the wrong direction before Hemingway reconsidered and turned back, by which time night had all but completely fallen. This city's a maze, Hemingway thought, not a single right angle anywhere. The dashing around made Worsleighson vomit, finally, an action that seemed to happen with no genuine impact or effort on his part—he just needed to stand slightly to the side, out of its way, and Hemingway waited it out standing in the shadows of an alley. The sound of it resounded down the corridors of curfew-silenced Valencia like a broken siren. Afterward the young Communist stood straighter, mildly refreshed.

"C'mon, fer Chrissake," Hemingway grunted just as he spotted a patrol car, rifles poking out of three windows, turning the corner. Hemingway yanked the wobbly youngster into the alley and pressed him with a broad hand up against the brick wall out of sight as the slow car passed, going east.

They crept around the corner and hustled with relative quiet toward the Palace, which, they could see as they approached from the west, was guarded under stationary searchlights by at least six rifle-carrying soldiers. They patrolled the front of the building behind a long, looping snake of barbed wire that curved up and over about three feet from the street's surface. Behind the guards a long line of large, dark, expensive cars sat, lined up neatly at the curb. The men huddled down behind a stone stairwell half a block away.

"Alright," Hemingway whispered. "First we need a diversion, which means you have to run at them, maybe yelling Franco horseshit, and while they beat the hell out of you I'll jump the barbed wire and crawl behind the cars, and I'll try the locks of the Bentleys, and—"

"What?" Worsleighson had been thinking of something else, of a novel he'd wanted to write about Rimbaud and tribal war between coffee-plantation Abyssinians.

"Goddammit, listen, Mordaunt—"

"I'm what? You're what?"

"I'll leap over the barbed wire, and crawl—"

Worsleighson stood up in one quick movement, stepped from behind the stairwell, and strolled—"strolled" is the word, though he did it rather shakily—toward the Palace, straight to the three guards stationed before the front steps, the spotlight bearing down on them and him. Hemingway clamped his hand over his own mouth, and watched the poor, silly, doomed lad affect nonchalance, even after the guards spotted him and raised their rifles and began yelling, *"Pare ahora! Pare ahora!"* He kept walking, throwing his hands up in a casual way, and Hemingway heard him toss out a laugh at the guards, who froze themselves, now there were five of them, their weapons cocked as the light glared on the scene nakedly, naked as a midnight firing squad.

Hemingway looked back where he came from—he'd have to bolt and run for his life.

Worsleighson made it to the guards; no shots were fired. He was gesticulating elaborately but not frantically, explaining himself. And the rifles went down. Hemingway saw him fish in his pockets, and fish some more.

The keys. He'd forgotten to take the keys.

Hemingway dashed out from the stairwell, his hand up, running over. *"Buenos noches!"* he hollered, both hands visible now, waving the keys, and when he made it to Worsleighson's side, Worsleighson said to the guards, *"Él es mi amigo, mi camarada! Él tiene las llaves!"* Hemingway handed the keys over to the nearest guard.

The guards did not raise the rifles again, and in fact two of the five who had collected in the moment of tension simply turned and walked away, disinterested.

"I explained to them," Worsleighson told Hemingway loudly, "that we'd found these keys and wanted to return them if they belonged to *Presidente* Largo or some other esteemed car of the Republic."

Hemingway nodded with a big smile as the one guard with the keys first went to the left up the line, tried the keys in the door of two Bentleys there, and then walked past them to the right-side batch of cars. There were sixteen in all, bumper to bumper, but only three Bentleys, and he tried the last. None fit, and none were 8 Litre models in any case.

The guard came back.

"*Se mantendrá las llaves,* we will keep the keys," he said in Spanish, "in case someone comes to ask."

"No," Worsleighson said, his befogged mind scurrying, "no, we didn't find them here, maybe the owner, uh—"

"Señors," Hemingway said, louder and clearer, but in Spanish that bordered on the idiotic, "we have already told the owner of *la* Hotel Florida that we have the keys and he will ask the American journalists and movie stars there, and that's probably where they belong because we found them in that region, so we need them back, it is getting late, *muy tarde.*"

"Sure?" The guard was clearly skeptical, but he also clearly didn't know why.

"*Si, gracias, mi camarada.*"

A shrug, and Hemingway took the keys, bid the guards *buenos noches*, and the two men calmly walked into the shadows.

They walked for twenty minutes in what they hoped was the right direction. But then the silence of the lightless streets gave way to the sound of an approaching truck.

Hemingway and Worsleighson stood in the center of an intersection and looked around. They saw no headlights, no truck; the night was too dark and moonless. But the rumble built and rose out of the distance, until in a panic the two men dashed out of the street for different building facades and an old army truck barreled out of nowhere, right between them.

And then braked. Three men jumped out of the truck; they carried rifles. Two of them each drew a bead on Hemingway and Worsleighson from the center of the street, and the third man shouted "*Vamos a disparar! No mueva!*" The Americans hadn't run because they were drunk; the days of nonstop drinking and the head wound and the ride from Madrid caught up with Hemingway on the sidewalk, and all he could think about was lying down, anywhere.

The gunmen grabbed the Americans by their coats, yanked

them stumbling into the street, the gun barrels under their chins, and kicked their legs until the two men knelt. Then, Hemingway first, Worsleighson second, the two gunmen each wound up with their rifle butts and slammed the kneeling men in the skull. When they fell over, howling, the men in the night swung the rifles like axes chopping wood and hit them again.

Hemingway could feel blood gouting in little spurts out of the reopened wound on his head.

The third gunman went down on one knee and hissed, *"Vaya casa!"*

Hemingway squeezed his eyes shut and made no movement.

Then the men retreated into the darkness. The sound of the truck started up and then faded down the night streets.

Hemingway groaned and launched up off the ground onto his hands and then his knees. He took his coat off, and then took his overshirt and ripped it in half, tying one half around his head, tightly around the spots he could feel were bleeding.

Go home.

"Worsleighson?" He felt for the younger man in the dark and found him, utterly unconscious. There was blood, but it wasn't running.

Hemingway stood and waited for his stomach to settle and for his balance to return. A crushing headache came with it, but then he picked up Worsleighson and slung him over his shoulder. He turned and walked. He squinted at the road signs, trying to read them although they were all doubled in his eyes and there was no light. He walked and held direction as best he could, leaning up against buildings to rest, feeling Worsleighson's heft go from bearably light to punishingly heavy.

And it occurred to him that he was simply heading back to El Alarcon—Dos Passos had never led him to a hotel. Now it was past midnight, and he was in a city he did not know. With a bloodied man slung over his shoulder.

The only sound he heard was the panting and claw ticks of a

pack of dogs Hemingway could not see, running together down a nearby street.

So this is how this century's going to be, he thought. City streets empty except when they're filled with war. Blood left behind in puddles. Left alone for dead in the middle of the night, trying to save a life or just survive, and getting lost instead. Dogs and rifles and bad men.

He walked slowly, for nearly an hour, though he couldn't have guessed at the time. It was too dark to see his watch.

He managed to read a street sign, La avenida Maria Cristina. There were a few cars, finally, and a single pedestrian. In the middle of the block there was a hotel, el Fernando Rei. Hemingway didn't remember it until he muttered the name of the hotel to himself, and then did: the lodgings of the Grosse Pointe ladies, both now presumably snug in their beds.

He hoisted himself and the Boston kid on his shoulder, both purple with blood, up the steps and into the hotel lobby, where the bellboys immediately ran to him and helped Worsleighson down and onto a chaise. The hotel doctor was summoned. Hemingway asked the desk clerk for two American women named Margaret and Lenore, and in little time both women, moist with cold cream, came out of the elevator in their night robes.

Hemingway was given a room, but he went with Lenore to her room instead, where she held ice to his head and let him fall asleep in her lap.

# 10

It took two days for Worsleighson to get out of bed, his concussion symptoms eventually subsided, his vomiting and headaches lessened. Both men stayed on at el Fernando Rei on Hemingway's dime. The hotel staff was conscientious and kind, and the Grosse Pointe ladies catered to both men like doting aunts without a trace of flirtation. Hemingway's head wound was properly stitched and bandaged. Valencia gradually seemed like a slightly sweeter place, all told.

Wandering the hotel corridors and inhabiting the restaurant's more swell corners, Hemingway struggled to figure out how he could ID the men with the swinging rifle butts. But he did not see them, nor their rifles, nor their truck. They could've come from anywhere, summoned by anyone. By an eavesdropper at El Alarcon? Or did they, whoever they are, know he was coming to Valencia?

So for two days he played the part of journalist: He asked for and was granted interviews with the Valencia police chief and the press secretary at Largo's office. Hemingway knew enough not to ask any dangerous questions, so he only sought to rule out the possibility of Fascist troops or spies having kidnapped Robles and dragged him into the hills. But both men proved either entirely evasive or virtually clueless on the matter. No one else in the Front, in any department, would consent to be interviewed; Hemingway nagged twelve different office secretaries for callbacks, but kept getting politely put off. The word was out, apparently. Or maybe Dos Passos rang all the same bells already and pissed the whole government off. Where'd Dos Passos get to, anyway?

Hemingway didn't have a drink the entire second day, until he met Eric Blair.

Late in the afternoon he'd decided to storm *el palacio* in person, unannounced, in a part of town that now gave him the shivers, and see how far that got him. It wasn't very far, but exiting from the long marble-columned, heavily guarded lobby after being stonily rebuffed he passed a tall, ugly, mustachioed man in a corduroy jacket walking in, a thick stack of files under his arm. He caught Hemingway's eye and an instant of concern came over his face as he went, so Hemingway turned and watched him. The man deposited the files with the clerk behind the desk, and turned to leave, and didn't seem very surprised to see Hemingway waiting for him.

"You're Ernest Hemingway." His hand was outstretched.

"Yes I am."

"I'm Eric Blair."

"OK."

"I write under the name George Orwell."

"Oh." They were still shaking. "I see. I've read *Burmese Days*. I thought it was swell."

They found a café that was dark, discreet, and empty. Hemingway's voice never raised above a mutter. They drank *cava*.

"So you're POUM. Why aren't you in Barcelona?"

"I was, then Huesca."

"This year?"

"Yes. It was very bad."

"Wait, you're not a journalist?"

"No, I'm a corporal. I'm fighting."

"I respect that."

"Why aren't you fighting?"

He had to ask, Hemingway thought. "I've got writing to do. Anyway, I've got bum eyes and, y'know, I'd thought I could do more good with my byline, rather than . . . just get shot . . . I did bring fund-raiser money with me when I came, and bought a dozen ambulances."

"I see."

"You think I'm wrong?"

"I'd never dictate to another man."

"You might think of doing it my way, you have an audience, right?"

"Not much of one. Anyway, if I were you I wouldn't dictate, et cetera."

"I'm not. You're right. . . . So why Valencia?"

"Party paperwork. Delivering petitions and mandates to the Front. The Comintern doesn't care, but POUM is trying to cooperate, trying to stay part of the coalition."

"Didn't know there was one anymore."

"Neither does the Front, apparently."

"No? I'll never keep it all straight." Hemingway rubbed his eyes and drank and wished the wine was colder.

"What happened to you, anyway, old chap."

"I got bludgeoned by mystery men in the night."

"And you don't know who or why."

"I know why—I guess. I've been looking into something . . . A murder."

"I say."

"And I've been a rhinoceros about it. Serves me right."

Blair appeared happy for the distraction, so Hemingway summarized the facts as a waiter brought them bowls of rabbit stew and huge wedges of warm *pan de horno*.

"So you're looking for a millionaire assassin? Bentleys, honestly!" Blair had broth on his mustache. He had one of the most experience-weathered faces Hemingway had ever seen. His eyes, deep in his skull, seemed permanently shocked by the world. But the man himself was cool, almost suave.

"I guess. Who knows. More likely it was stolen. The car, or maybe just the keys. I haven't a clue."

"If the Bentley keys were merely stolen, then who followed you and pounded you? The fact that you were targeted and assaulted seems to indicate that the murder is a . . . an institutional matter. Doesn't it?"

"I guess I'm assuming that. Men like Robles don't get killed in the middle of a civil war by common criminals, or by chance."

"Maybe. Did he gamble? Did he keep women?"

"No."

"You're sure it's political."

"As you say, I got beat up."

"Yes, of course."

"And if there's an underground in action here, they would've simply shot me in the head, too. They wouldn't care about bad press."

"I suppose. What if it is the Comintern? What if you find out that Robles was simply purged, like so many others?"

"Others? In Moscow I know, but not in Spain."

"Perhaps not noticeably, yet. But it's happening here."

"Well, if that's what it is, that's what it is. Blame Stalin and go home."

"I don't have to tell you how hazardous that is for you. If that's the end result."

"No, you don't."

"You're a nervy starker, Hemingway."

"Tell me this for certain, Eric, that the German bullet casing could not have come from a Nationalist gun."

"I think you can leave that notion aside. There have not been any Falangists or Germans or Moroccan infantrymen wandering around Valencia recently with forty-year-old German rifles."

"Spies."

"Sure, there're probably spies . . . Could be. But with that gun? The Nationalists are funded to the gills, they don't have to use obsolete weapons. We do."

"True enough."

"And anyway, there's no indication that Fascists are setting up covert assassinations in this war. No one else prominent in the Front has disappeared—without their arrest and supposed betrayal being publicly announced by Moscow, that is. And why Robles? Why kill a translator?"

"Yes."

Blair stretched. "Which means, my dear man, you are barking up an impossible tree."

"You think so."

"I do. But I'm sure you've been warned before by whomever you've confided in. I'm sure Dos Passos has advised you to mind your own business, yes?, and leave the Comintern and the Popular Front to their own nefarious ways and . . . inevitable implosion." Blair was on his third glass of wine and was clearly tipsy.

"You're drunk, Eric. You shouldn't drink."

"Yes, I'm not like you . . . don't hold it against me."

"Don't be silly."

They paid and left and walked, and the afternoon was lovely and warm, the first warm afternoon Hemingway had seen in Spain.

"So, Ernest, what have you been reading?"

"Uh . . . *We,* by that Russkie. Zamyatin. That was the last book I touched. On the boat. Joris Ivens told me it was essential, but I've got to say, it was so goddamn political."

" '*So* political'? How could a book be too political?"

"By being dull and preachy, that's how. Just being right doesn't make it worth reading. But who knows how right it is."

"I thought it was a fantasy. I'm going to make a point of reading it."

"It is a fantasy, but it's like Wells, it's making social points all over the place."

"But that's what fiction does, doesn't it, Ernest? Reveal the patterns of society, of injustice . . . pull back the curtains on political forces."

"No it fucking well does not. Maybe that's *your* fiction, Eric, maybe that's Dos's fiction, maybe that's what you make if you're fucking Hugo, and I've *never* been able to read him. Fiction is about the person, it's about the voice looking truthfully at the experience. That's all. If I can do that, I've done better than a hundred political novels."

"Good God. Forgive me for saying so, but that's just narcissism. It's as if there's no world outside the café table in front of you."

"Oh, fuck you, Blair! Is that the way my books read to you?"

"Uh, I've only read one . . . *Death in the Afternoon.*"

"God. Why that one?"

"I thought I'd learn about the institutionalized nature of bullfighting. I felt sorry for the bulls."

"Jesus Christ . . ."

"Well, I've just finished *The Magic Mountain.*"

"That's a book. A heavyweight."

"It was ambitious, but I was irritated. So aloof, so noncommittal."

"Eric, we better stop talking about this right now."

Blair grabbed a cab and escaped to his hotel room on the low-rent side of the city. Hemingway hoped he'd meet him again; the late lunch they had was fine. But boy, what a prickly pear about politics, he thought climbing the steps of el Fernando Rei. Just like Dos.

That evening Worsleighson arose from his bed, and the hotel doctor shrugged. The concierge had found a few books in English for Hemingway after calling the local shops, and so he sipped whiskey in bed reading Sinclair Lewis's *It Can't Happen Here* in its American edition, expecting to bristle at the politics but getting absorbed by the white-knuckled rage of it, before turning out the lights before ten.

# 11

It can happen here, Hemingway dozily thought, feeling the morning but not seeing it yet. It can happen anywhere. Germany, Italy, Spain, Russia, Greece . . . Okay, maybe it can't happen in Canada, the Canadians are too relaxed, too timid, too unambitious in their nationalism, what little of it you could find. Maybe it couldn't happen in Iceland, same deal. Or Finland, hard to imagine the Finns trusting anyone new with being dictator.

In the United States, there was plenty of frontier piety and isolationist selfishness and suspicion of authority. But there was also a sad desire to kowtow as well, to be patted on the head and tucked in by an all-powerful Daddy, and this was usually coupled with Christianity. There was too much kneeling in America, too much to be comfortable with, mass kneeling in public places. Hemingway never liked anyone telling him what's what, and that included an omniscient God, so from an early age he'd decided he wasn't a kneeler. He'd since yet to meet a kneeler he liked or could trust.

Worsleighson was up and Hemingway's door was unlocked. The morning light fell into the room like a waterfall. The lad bounded into the room, porcelain cup of hot coffee in his hand. "Ernest, you must get up, the coffee here is simply the best in the world, I'm a coffee aficionado not your typical Brit tea-bagger, and I'm telling you this is a miracle, notes of maple and cocoa! You've got to get up—"

"Shut up! Get out!"

"Alright! But c'mon, the day is fresh, we're going back to *el palacio!*"

". . ."

"Yes! I work there, remember? We're going to meet a Popular Front worker, an American. He's been to Moscow. His name is Liston Oak."

"And?" Hemingway was out of bed and buck naked, heading in a stiff bowlegged walk to the toilet. Worsleighson turned quickly toward the window.

"We can trust him."

Sure we can. Hemingway stood peeing. This brave and crazy Boston kid might be useful, but let's not just follow him into any old bear cave and start banging a tin drum.

At the same time, Hemingway was feeling a few jots less than perfectly cautious. They—*they*—thought they were calling every shot, and Hemingway knew, just knew in his cold little newspaperman's heart, that they only wished they could. Maybe it was the Lewis in his head—he never trusted any system to cover every slip, and this situation was unmanageable, nothing but berserk contents under extraordinary pressure. He doubted that it was the Comintern that killed Robles, at least officially. Wouldn't Hemingway have been whisked from his bed by now and never seen again? Would he have still been allowed to lounge around in full view in Valencia, under the Comintern's nose, if the machine had decided he was undesirable?

Maybe they were waiting to see what he'd do next. The city practically ached with secrets.

"OK, Mordaunt, let's go see your man. He better not be

another one of these alligator-eyed bureaucrats. If he is, I don't know if I can help myself from socking him."

"That'd be pretty."

After a taxi ride, Worsleighson jockeyed Hemingway right past the same sniffy palace clerks and grim-faced guards that had refused him the previous day. The palace was enormous, much larger than the marble-halled embassy in Madrid, with twin staircases that arced up three flights. Hemingway imagined the Winter Palace in Leningrad must look like this, but he'd never been.

They walked down a long hallway full of bustling government workers and lined with desks so you had to slalom. Eventually, after pointing to a hall desk and saying "That's mine," Worsleighson knocked at an office door. No one answered, so he just opened it.

There were three desks, all swamped with paper, and between a horn-rimmed woman and a bright-eyed Spanish teenager sat a plump American whose swollen eyes resembled a sea cow's after it'd been snagged with a treble hook.

"Liston, I was hoping to have a word?" Worsleighson said, with a smile. "This is Ernest Hemingway."

Oak jerked a little, but stood and stuck out his hand. "What an honor." His voice was surprisingly weak in his throat, relative to his girth. The teenager looked up from his work and stared. Worsleighson pulled two chairs in from the hall. "I'd heard you were in the country, reporting, right?"

"Yes. Mostly."

"How's that going for you."

"So-so. But I'm not a journalist right now."

"No? Not covering the Popular Front rally tomorrow? Then . . . what are you? What happened to your head? Worsleighson, you got hurt, too?"

"Can we have some privacy?"

Baffled, Oak sent his office mates to go get coffee. The door closed.

Worsleighson framed it. "We were wondering, Liston, if you could give us some guidance on a matter . . . unofficially."

"Unofficially." Oak was a nervous man, and he became visibly more so. His hands went to his knees under the desk. Hemingway tried to remember the last time he'd seen so many grown men close to panic and tears.

"Yes. We're just inquiring into the death of José Robles."

Oak went white. He got up and locked the door and sat back down. "That boy, that teenager translating the Russian here? You don't know? He's Coco Robles. He's his son."

"Jesus." Worsleighson sat back, feeling the tide rise. Hemingway sat up.

"That's Robles's boy? Working here with you? He can translate Russian?"

"Learned with his father, yes."

"What does he know?"

"About his father?" Oak was sweating now. "Everything. He saw him get . . . abducted. And when I heard that Robles was killed, I told him myself. I couldn't take the little fucker anymore, whining with questions every day."

"I'm going to have to talk to him."

"Feel free."

"How'd you find out? About Robles."

"The word got around. Unofficially."

"You can't tell me who told you."

"No, and it wouldn't do you any good anyway. He'd never admit it, or tell you who told him. You're playing detective, Mr. Hemingway? Maybe you should—"

"Should I?! What should I do?!" Hemingway sat forward. "I've just about had enough of you shit-eating Republicans telling me what I should do, Oak, and if I hear it one more time my head's liable to explode. You know something, I finally found a man in this goddamn country who actually knows something about what happened to Robles out there in the hills, you know,

Oak?!, something about how Robles, who was a good friend of mine, came to have a gun put to his head and was left for dead like a pellet-shot squirrel!" Hemingway rose out of his seat, but got quieter. "And I'll be *damned* if I'm leaving here without knowing what you know. They'll have to pry my fingers from *around your throat*. So help me God."

Oak's face was pulled tight, and his eyeballs were watery.

"I can't tell you who told me! But it doesn't matter, everyone knew!"

Worsleighson's hands were gripping his chair arms. But Hemingway remained half risen out of his chair.

"Oak, you look like a scared man, my guess is you're very worried about your position in the Front, you're worried that the word's gonna come down from on high and you'll be pulled out of your bed one night"—he stood, leaning over the desk— "and brought to Moscow and forced to confess that, what, you had goddamn homo sex with Trotsky! Or something! Some such bullshit! You're scared, Oak, and I'm guessing my visit here today, especially when I RAISE MY VOICE, is not doing you any favors, and I'm guessing, too, that if I or Worsleighson here were to put in a bad word in the right ear, just a little hint of something about you, then that's it for you, you're shat out of this assembly line as waste product. Am I right? I've seen trembling fools like you, all over Spain, you're as easy to spot as diseased trees. So I'm going to ask you one more fucking time. Who told you?"

Oak exhaled and swabbed his head with a handkerchief. "Del Vayo." Quietly.

"Oh, for the love of God. We know he knew, he told Josephine Herbst."

"Sorry."

Hemingway turned to Worsleighson. "Dos already spoke to him."

"And you probably couldn't threaten him very easily." Oak.

Hemingway sat down with a large sigh. For a moment everyone waited for him. "East Jesus. Sorry, Oak . . . I've been more than a little frazzled and . . . squashed by this thing."

Oak did not look mollified. "It's okay, Hemingway . . . Wish I could help." Which did not look true on his face.

"Do you think del Vayo ordered it?"

"Do *I* think? Hemingway, I don't think. And I'm certainly not going to think about that. I don't care, frankly."

"Of course."

"But no, I don't think del Vayo did any such thing. Why would he? Why would anyone? We're all just trying to hold our pants up in this war, Hemingway."

"I know. But someone did. Who. Whoever actually did it, carried out the order, used a Gewehr."

"Excuse me?"

"A Gewehr, I think I'm saying it right. A Mauser. A German rifle from the Great War."

"Someone's father's war gun, you mean?"

"Yes. Who would have those? Not the Fascists."

"Not likely. And not Republicans, we wouldn't even know where to get rounds for it. We've got artillery coming in from all over, and we have a hard time finding shells for British or French guns. But no German."

"So it'd be a single gun, a private gun."

Oak shrugged.

"Liston, off the record," Worsleighson said. "If I were some variety of Valencia bastard who wanted to disappear or erase an officer, or a bureaucrat, maybe like you! ha!, in the Front, but wanted to keep it a secret, who would I get to perform such a thing? Unofficially."

"Someone who would use nonregimental ordnance." Hemingway.

"I don't know, gentlemen. Please."

"Think. Hard."

Oak squirmed. He wanted to say nothing, but he wanted this meeting to end as soon as possible. He couldn't have both.

"Well, Coco says he heard them, and they didn't speak Spanish. They spoke something else, he thinks it was *quinqui*."

"What's that?!"

"A dialect. Gypsy or something, I don't know. I barely know any Spanish."

Worsleighson raised a finger. "It's northern, it does have Romany roots."

Hemingway with the look. "So, Oak, *quinqui*, what does that tell you?"

"It could mean . . . *las Termitas*."

"What the fuck is that?"

"The Termites. An underground gang, criminals. They're *quinquilleros*. Which is some kind of ethnic minority, gypsies, and *las Termitas* are supposedly militant nationalists for their kind, wanting to be recognized by the Republic. But when we hear about them it's as criminals."

"That's a wild shot, isn't it, Oak?"

"You asked me."

"I didn't ask you for bullshit."

"I'm not bullshitting you. You want *quinquilleros* in this city, you end up with *las Termitas*. They'll do anything for money. I can't think of anyone else in Valencia about whom you could say that. Not now, anyway, not in the war."

"I think that might be a naïve thought."

"Not if you're sitting at this desk. Anyway, they're *quinquilleros*."

"Where do you find them, these *termitas*?"

"I have no idea. Ask around. You'll probably get yourself killed."

"They're assassins . . ."

"They are whatever you pay them to be."

# 12

The day was just beginning. Valencia was warm and would stay that way. Hemingway and Worsleighson, who had just hatched a sour egg of apprehension in his innocent gut, were nearly at the front doors of *el palacio* when Coco Robles appeared behind them at a gallop. "Señor Hemingway, wait. I'm Coco; Señor Oak told me you were asking about my father." His English was impeccable.

Hemingway stopped and turned. "Yes, son, I'm trying to find out who killed him."

"You are? Why?"

"Uh . . . It's complicated. Oak says you think they were *quinquilleros*."

"That's what I think. But they hit me with a pipe quickly, knocked me out. You should talk to my sister, Carmena."

"She's how old?"

"Twelve."

"Where do you live?"

The two men left the boy behind and walked north. It took them forty-five minutes to reach calle Pintor Zarinerva and the old three-story house of flats where Robles had installed his family almost two years earlier.

"OK, Mr. Instant Recall, what do you know about *quinquilleros?*"

"Uh, well, *quinqui* is an ancient form of Castilian, probably mixed with Bohemian Romany, called *quinqui* because they were reputed to be ironmongers, toolmakers, *quincalleria,* but were actually more often petty crooks. They first came to Spain, or appeared in Spain, in the 1500s, possibly but not certainly from Bohemia, and possibly descended from Constantinople Muslims who turned nomad to escape persecution, in Italy and Normandy and elsewhere. Uh, during *la Reconquista* and the Inquisition they were burned and killed like Jews and Muslims, but not in large numbers because they were very hard to find. They're reputed to be tribal. Almereyda of Bilbao wrote in 1698 that they practiced ritual cannibalism every winter solstice, but only ate the toes, and they regularly copulated with snakes."

"You don't organize this stuff in your head at all, do you, you just accumulate it."

"I suppose. I never thought it'd be a sore point."

"It's OK, don't get tetchy. Nothing more recent?"

"Not in the history books, no."

"Geronimo," Hemingway said taking the steps to the Robles home and ringing the bell and dreading a Spanish war-widow scene. But Margara, a statuesque woman of thirty-five, opened the door with no indication of surprise or emotion on her face. She looked perfectly grim, but strong as a thick tree in a storm.

"Señora, do you speak English? My name is Ernest Hemingway."

"*Si,* Señor Hemingway, I recognize you from that issue of *Vanity Fair*—the paper dolls of you, as a caveman and a matador? Adorable. My husband had all your books. I've since given them to the library." She turned away, leaving the door open. The men stepped in. Carmena sat at the table in the kitchen drawing wolves with charcoal.

"Oh . . . Yes, well, I just wanted to ask you some things—"

*"Por que?"*

"I'm . . . inquiring into Pepe's . . . demise."

"His what? Why, señor? Who are you to do that?"

"I'm nobody. I'm just a questioner. No one else is being the questioner. So I am."

"Is 'questioner' a word?"

"It is now."

"You act as if Pepe was a close friend. But I've never met you."

"I knew him in Italy. And I visited him at Johns Hopkins a few times."

"The time he came home at dawn with a fat lip, reeking of scotch."

"That was probably it."

She had been keeping her back to the men, putting things in the kitchen away, wiping down dishes, but now she turned.

"Señor . . . I'd offer you a drink, I know you like to drink, but I've nothing. We can barely afford food."

"I'm sorry. I can help."

"Shut your mouth. You should know better."

"Mr. Dos Passos came to see you?"

"Yes. I didn't take his money, either."

"I just—"

"Ask your questions."

Hemingway took a deep breath and went to sit down at the table across from Carmena. The child looked at him with her eyes only, not her face.

Worsleighson stood silently where he was, his hands holding his hat.

"I don't know what to ask, I'll be honest with you. Just what do you remember. From that night."

"What I remember." Margara Robles folded her arms across

her chest. Hemingway got the sense of how thin she was. Of how maybe she fed her children and not herself. "They were dressed in black. With hoods. There were four of them. They spoke some cretinous dialect. They hit me with pipes and threatened to rape me. They beat Pepe until he was unconscious, and took him away. That's all I remember."

"I want to try to find them."

"That's all I remember." Margara lit a cigarette and watched it burn.

Carmena looked up, with her face this time.

"One wore shoes that had cement on them," she said.

"Cement?" Hemingway refocused on the girl, whose expression was guarded.

"Cement, in the creases. They were a cement worker's shoes."

"Did the men hurt you?"

"No. They didn't even look at me. Another one, not the cement worker, he had long hair in his ears. He was the captain, the one giving orders. His voice was deep and scratchy, like he smoked a lot. He smelled of cats. His coat was wool. He didn't move too quickly. I think he had a bad back."

Hemingway and Worsleighson looked at each other, eyebrows airborne.

"Carmena, do you always remember everything?"

"Yes. I remember more."

"And your English. But you grew up in Baltimore, didn't you?"

"That's right."

"Sorry. Go ahead."

"Another man was shorter than the rest, but he was wider, fat. He smelled like blood. Like chicken blood, a little bit like raw eggs. Maybe he works in a slaughterhouse. Or owns a farm? Maybe he just stole a chicken and didn't wash. None of them washed, they were all dirty. The one with the chicken-blood smell, he wears glasses. Because he didn't have any on, and twice he bumped into the table and the chair, like he couldn't see them well enough."

"Was he maybe drunk?"

"No, his steps were sure. He just couldn't see in front of him. The one with cement shoes smelled badly of wine. The others a little, but only from their breath, not their skin, not their clothes."

The girl slurped from a water glass on the table. Hemingway hoped Worsleighson would remember it all.

"Are you sure?"

"A drunk man smells a certain way, yes? Not like wine, but like he needs a bath. Sweaty."

"OK."

"The fourth man was larger, stronger, than the others. He has lice, I think, because he smelled of camphor, and I smelled it more whenever he bent over toward me. He was the only one who was married. He had a ring."

"The others could've taken theirs off."

"They didn't have dents on their fingers. The large married man had shoes that were falling apart. They were tied on with rope. They were big and black, maybe Army boots with pieces missing? I don't know. His coat was thin; he had two sweaters on under it. I could hear change, *centimos,* in his pocket. Just a few. And his breathing was heavy, like he had asthma. Maybe the camphor in his hair made it worse."

"How do you know what asthma sounds like?"

"Coco has asthma."

"*Centimos*—could they have been keys?"

"No, *centimos.*"

Margara kept looking down, as if alone.

Hemingway sat back. "Carmena, you are the smartest little girl in the world, you know." The girl just cracked a crooked, sure-I-am smile. "Is that all you remember?"

"No. The cement worker made no sounds with his throat. I thought he couldn't, that he couldn't speak. His hair was gray. But he wasn't old. His hands weren't wrinkled."

"You couldn't see his eyes?"

"No. But he seemed . . . slow. Oh, and the captain guy sneezed a good deal."

"Did you see any rifles, Carmena?"

"No. No rifles. They had only the pipes. The fatter one tried to roll a cigarette, over there, while they were beating my father. But it fell apart, and he got angry and smashed a pitcher. They spoke in whatever language it was, but I heard the captain call the fat one *bexhet*."

"Bex, shet."

"Yes. I don't know if it was his name or if it was a curse. It's not Spanish, I don't think."

"No," Margara said. "It's not Spanish."

*"Quinqui,"* Worsleighson offered.

"Are you through, miracle girl?" Hemingway was smiling, and so the girl did, too.

"Yes! Except the large man had a stain on his hand. This big. It was dark gray, kinda silvery. But a stain. There was grime, dirt, on top of it; it's been there a while."

"Holy smokes, Carmena. Remind me to not introduce you to my wives."

Which was when Margara had had enough, stubbing out her cigarette just as Carmena asked, "How many do you have?"

"That's enough. *Vamos.* Leave us in peace."

"We'll let you know what we find out, Margara." Getting up, making his way slowly to the door.

"Don't bother."

"But señora—I will need to honor José. I'm sorry Señor Dos Passos didn't let me know about whatever service you had, so I could attend."

"He probably couldn't find you," Worsleighson said.

"There was no service, no burial," Margara said. "José disappeared."

Hemingway stopped in mid-stride. "What?"

Margara shrugged. "Señor Dos Passos went back to the foothills two days ago, but someone had taken the body. It's gone. We did not get to bury him. We haven't even a death certificate. It's as if he'd never existed."

"Good fucking God," he growled. Carmena was listening.

"Where's Dos Passos now?"

"He left. To Paris."

Hemingway became scared, for the first time in Spain. He'd been assuming up to this moment that Robles was exterminated for some nefarious reasons by some covert purpose, and because the war was so all-encompassing, and because the Comintern's involvement struck the fear of God into every Republican's soul and preoccupied nearly everyone, it seems, with paranoid worries about being suddenly judged an adversary of the revolution instead of its faithful soldier. He'd assumed Robles was just a lost figure in the smoke, a forgotten casualty, a loss everyone seemed too distracted to pursue. Even the beating near *el palacio* could've come simply because Hemingway was an intrusive figure with a big mouth and no direct connection to Moscow, a bulldog that needed to be slapped down.

But if someone went through the bother of disposing of Robles's corpse, in a landscape littered with dead, mere days after Hemingway had disrespected Valencia police at the scene, then two things were at least semiclear: Someone was still concerned about their culpability, and that same party was and had been closely watching Hemingway.

"Margara, that probably means whoever's responsible has been surveilling . . . I've been under surveillance."

"Of course. You're the important one."

"I'm serious. They probably know I'm here."

"So? What's the big deal? They obviously know where I live."

"Jeez, it's like you're related to Dos Passos. I mean, be careful."

"They've already beaten me with pipes. What could you tell me that would make them want to beat me again? I'm just the widow."

"I don't know, maybe you're right, but they might be worried, scared, they might just decide to clean the slate. You never know."

She was not alarmed. "Don't worry about us. Just get out."

# 13

We have to go back to Oak."

"Why?" They walked back south, looking for a cab as they did. The old apartment houses around them looked like they'd stood already for a hundred years, lined with lovely egg-and-dart terra-cotta.

"*Las Termitas*. We can identify them, right? Hey, don't you work doing something?" Hemingway was full of juice—after his initial chill faded, he took the fact of the body's disappearance as a raising of the stakes. A challenge. Let them follow me, he thought. The fuckers.

"Please. I volunteer."

"Yes, but what we're doing isn't the reason you came to Spain. You're a Communist. What if we found out the Comintern tortured and killed Robles? Will you tell me it had to happen, for the sake of the revolution?"

"Please stop talking."

A cab driven by a fourteen-year-old boy barely tall enough to reach the brake pedal brought them to the Benicarlo. Worsleighson escorted Hemingway in, but went to his desk instead of

Oak's office, feigning concern about his work, and then slipped around the corner by a bank of tall windows and waited.

"Liston? Hi. I have one more question." The secretary looked up. Coco was not at his desk.

Oak glared and shook in his seat. Hemingway had been right, Oak lived in permanent fear of being purged ever since he'd returned from Moscow, where he saw too closely the first phase of machinations within Yezhov's NKVD, the show trials, the midnight executions.

"Hemingway, I'm not saying anything more. Get the hell out of my office." Hemingway stepped in instead, and in one dash the secretary stood in her bosomy sweater and whisked past Hemingway out to the hallway.

"I've just been to Robles's house and spoken with his twelve-year-old daughter, and I'm not through with you yet, Oak, and I'm not in the mood to be turned out because, from where I stand, you're the one with your head on the block, not me."

Oak looked about to burst. Hemingway edged closer and put his hands on the desktop. "I tell you, I'm feeling full of crazy, best-selling-writer bullgoose self-importance right now, Oak, goddamn! nothing like it!, and holy shit, it just occurred to me I haven't had a drink yet today—you're a lucky son of a bitch! I might've really raised hell! But no, I'm as sober as an organist, and you will tell me at least one more thing, or I will fall on you like Constantine's sword and cleave you in two, you worried little titmouse."

Oak wasn't little, but he seemed to grow smaller. He shook his head no.

Hemingway took one loping step around the desk and landed his knee in Oak's lap and grabbed him by his collar, pushing up. "I just need the name of whatever little rat bastard you know in the underground of this godforsaken city that will tell me where I can find *las Termitas*. That's all. The one that gives you information. Whoever it is is probably some kind of weaselly little felon anyway, a stoolie, right?, and I can't imagine you'll take a beating for that kind of guy, a little shit like that, not a man like you."

"I don't know who—"

Hemingway arched his elbow back and hammered his knuckles down once into the bridge of the man's nose, the sound resembled an oak bat hitting a cantaloupe. Oak howled, and Hemingway stood and quickly uppercut him to close his mouth. Oak went back over his chair, his feet sailing in an arc past Hemingway's ear. Before he'd even landed, Hemingway started around the desk in three steps to lock the door, then circled to where Oak was trying to get off his knees.

Still on all fours, Oak pulled a desk drawer open and the whole drawer came out and crashed to the floor. Hemingway stepped over, and Oak had his fat hand on a revolver, and it came up.

He didn't have the chance to choke words out. The gun wasn't pointed at Hemingway for more than a shaky second before the writer grabbed it by the muzzle, frame, and cylinder and ripped it away from the man on the floor. Hemingway stepped around the desk completely and Oak tried to pull himself up on his overturned chair.

"You can't shoot me," he blurted.

"You're goddamn right about that," Hemingway said, grabbing the fatter man by his coat collar, turning him over with a yank, and smacking him across the face at full swing with the steel gun. Oak grunted and blood quickly welled from a gash on his cheek. The man made almost no noise.

"Why don't you yell? That would be bad, wouldn't it?"

Knocks came at the door anyway. *"¿Que está pasando allí?!"*

Hemingway hit him again flat across the face with the pistol. Oak sat back down on the floor, his eyelids fluttering.

"What else are you planning on whipping out," Hemingway said, firing open all of the desk drawers. "What's this, a stiletto? My God, is this standard issue for Comintern flunkies these days?" He threw the knife into a corner. "You must be such a terrified puppy, Oak, what else—no"—finding a finger-darkened edition of *The Sun Also Rises,* leafing through it quickly—"Oak, you like my book? It's the best thing I ever did! Damn straight this is your favorite book, right? Or was until now! But you bend the pages like this to mark your place, the book will fall apart! What, you had to pause on every page, look at this!" Tossing the book. "What's this? Look you muttonhead, behind this drawer, a little dictograph is taped to the inside wall," bending over and tearing it out, holding it up, the size of a small Brownie camera. "Who's listening, Oak? You *are* in big trouble! But look." Hemingway pulled the wires out, dropping the box to the floor.

Oak watched him.

"Did you know that was there?"

"I didn't know where it was," is all Oak said.

"Yeah, well, now they can't hear you—" The knocking came again, and Hemingway could see through the white glass on the door that there were a number of people outside the door. He heard Worsleighson talking to someone urgently in Spanish. "No one's listening now, Oak," Hemingway said at a lower pitch, but still holding the gun like it was a football he was getting ready to pass, "so just tell me who's your man, give me a name and place, that's all. C'mon, I'm already feeling a little bad about busting you up so much."

"I can't."

"You won't." Hemingway cocked the gun but didn't aim it. "I'm out of ideas, Oak. Why not? This man. This lowlife."

"He . . . he's got friends in the Front."

"Friends? So what?"

"Uncle."

"Uncle?!"

"He's Juan Negrin's nephew." Oak whispered now.

"The minister of finance? And his nephew is what?"

"An opium junkie and *chapero.*"

"A gigolo!" Hemingway laughed loudly, standing straight.

"OK! Name and place."

"Vico. Eduardo Vico. He has no address. Look in La Rosa y el Canon. It's a dive on the east side of the city."

"Where."

"Paseo de la Cuidadela. Somewhere down there."

Hemingway nodded, looked to the door. "OK. Now I have to get out of here. C'mere, explain to your compatriots that we had a friendly misunderstanding."

"Fuck you, Hemingway. I'm not going anywhere." He sat on the floor like a sulking boy, blood dripping down his shirt. Hemingway jammed the pistol into his trousers.

"Alright. I'm keeping the gun."

He strode over to the door and flung it open. "Relax, señores—" But there were two guards standing close and with guns, poised at hip level, and a mob of Front workers, and Worsleighson trying to push through the crowd in the narrow hallway toward Hemingway, who quickly grabbed the barrel of one rifle, held it down with a locked arm over and against the barrel of the other, took Oak's pistol out of his waistline, and pointed it at the nose of the guard to his left.

"Just settling a gambling debt with Señor Oak! Nothing to worry about! Don't play cards with Señor Oak, whatever you do!" The guards couldn't back up for the crowd and the walls, there was no swinging room, and began stumbling once everyone saw the pistol and tried to disperse, in a muffled panic. Hemingway tried to move into the mess, but made it half a step.

Worsleighson finally cut his way to Hemingway, grabbed his arm and pushed it down, lowering the gun. *"Amigos,"* he hollered above the noise in perfect Spanish, "do not worry, I will take this crazy gambling American out of the Palace and make sure he never comes back! No need to call the police! *Es bien! Es bien! Nada más ver!"* Worsleighson made the gun disappear in the folds of Hemingway's jacket, and escorted him by the arm, with a bracingly authoritarian manner, down the hallway toward the lobby area, waving in "stop" and "don't worry" gestures to every curious onlooker, all the way out the front door.

They kept walking, briskly.

"Well, that was quite a hugger-mugger," Worsleighson finally said, letting go. He was already beat, but Hemingway's adrenaline was spiking.

"Let's walk east, we need to find a bar."

"What bar?"

"Any bar, I need a rum and I need it now. Then we'll find that other bar."

"Liston told you to go somewhere."

"You betcha."

"You think going there is a safe thing to do, especially now?"

"Mordaunt, that man would've told me where his children were hidden. I'm convinced."

"If I were you, I'd lay low for a week."

"I have been laying low, too fucking low!"

"You were just telling Margara Robles that you suspect you're under surveillance everywhere—"

"Yeah, so? They're watching me, I'll give them something to watch. Come at me, motherfuckers. You know, if they're watching me, they're watching you, too. You might not have as much cache with the Front as you did a week ago."

"I didn't have much then, either."

"Ah, now we're doing something, *now* we're on to something! *Now* this is a goddamn war zone!"

"Ernest, my dear fellow, all you did was beat up a paranoid bureaucrat."

"Well, yeah, alright, so? Don't piss on my parade! Did you have three men point guns at you in the last ten minutes? Look, Worsleighson, if this isn't up your alley anymore, then scram, I don't need a naysayer on my hip!"

"I didn't say that—"

"Fine! On one hand you're telling me it's too dangerous, on the other it's no big deal, you're getting to be like a wife! Are you going to help me with this thing, or not?"

Worsleighson stopped, sighed, and said, "Yes."

"OK! C'mon. I'm thirsty as hell."

"I wonder if Liston is going to live out the night."

"Don't be melodramatic."

"I'm not."

"You think it'd be all my fault if he didn't? Did you hear that I ripped a dictograph out from inside his desk?"

"No, I didn't get that—"

"Who in the building was listening to him, you think?"

"I'm not inside enough to have the faintest idea."

"Every office probably has one of those things in it, half of the government is probably spying on the other half!"

"You're assuming the tap was there before we ever went to see him."

"Yes, I am. Because he was nervous from the get-go."

"Yes. But maybe it was installed for us. Maybe they figured we'd go to Liston. I know him, and he is the only American officially working for the Comintern in Spain."

They passed an empty cantina, and Hemingway doubled back, and set up rums with lime on the bar.

"Installed for us? Worsleighson, you're a worrisome punk. It's not all about us. Haven't you been watching what's going on around you?" Drinking. "We're a sideshow. We're wild cards, and Robles's murder is a tiny hand, a quick play of five-card where a pair wins, in a long and expensive table game. We're not the high rollers, we're the mice catching the peanuts that fall to the floor. You think I'm pushing the metaphor? You're right—but look. Are they watching? Sure. Will they touch me? I doubt it. Am I willing to let them try, in order to do what I think is the right thing to do? Yes, goddamn it. Yes."

"I don't know how long I can tag along, at this pace. My head is starting to hurt again."

"That's understandable, Worsleighson, you've been a stand-up mate so far. But there's risk here, and you're young. Do you write, son?"

"No, I don't have the gift."

"Horsecrap. You've got the memory of a sequoia, and the nerve of a thief. That's all you need. That's better than Booth Tarkington had."

"Faint praise."

"Don't be picayune. You should try. But for now, you know what I have to do."

"What?" A second round came, and Worsleighson began calming down and warming up.

"I need to find a junkie gigolo in a bar named . . . what the fuck was it! The Rose and Cannon. *Rosa* and *Canon*. He knows about *las Termitas*. We're close, Worsleighson, we're close. You with me? At least through today?"

"Yes."

"OK, I need you to write down, here, use a flyer, I'll get a pencil from the barkeep, write down everything you remember from what that Robles kid said."

"I can do that. Why?"

"In case you decide to go home. Two drinks right now and I'm already forgetting everything."

# 14

La Rosa y el Canon used to be a stevedore's *taberna,* open at eight in the morning for the night shift crowd coming off the docks, empty for lunch and siesta, and then ready again at four for the next off-duty wave. But by 1935 a good portion of the export traffic had been redirected north to Barcelona, and the war dried much of it up after that. The bar that Hemingway and Worsleighson found, after an hour's walk and one more detour for cocktails, was a shadowy, shuttered joint with dirt-thick windows and, despite being apparently occupied in the middle of the afternoon, a locked front door.

Hemingway's impatient knock—never, *ever,* had he encountered a public house that had the nerve to lock its door in the middle of the day, the very idea was an *outrage*—was answered after a few minutes by a phlegmy bark on the other side. *"Quien es?"*

*God, why can't these people speak English,* he thought. *Or French.* *"Una bebida!* I'm thirsty, that's who I am!"

The door opened a crack, with two chains crossing the divide, at chest level and eye. A withered, swollen old man stuck his face up to the opening. Hemingway couldn't quite believe the size of his nose, which was probably swollen with drink but looked like an elephant seal's.

"*Chupa mi pinga!*"

Hemingway heard the "dick." "Look, any *ingles* in there? I want a drink. I was sent!"

The old man hocked up something, chewed on it. "Sent? Who?"

"Juan Negrín."

"*Quien? Republicanos!*"

"Juan Negrín. Minister of finance."

The man started laughing, then coughing. "*Gilipollez!*"

"I need Eduardo Vico."

The coughing faded as the man walked away from the door. For a full minute they heard nothing inside. Hemingway looked at the door—hanging slightly open, you could see its hinges, which were rusted and falling out of the rotting doorjamb. He reached up and dug his fingernails into the wood, lifting one hinge plate from its mortise.

"Ernest, I don't know—" Worsleighson said.

The hinge came free of the wood completely, and the bottom one looked weak as well, so Hemingway simply took a step back and kicked the door square in the middle with the sole of his boot. The door flopped inward with a clamor, still hanging by its hinge in the air like a sheet on a line, its bottom edge now tilting out toward the street. Beyond it was dark. Hemingway stepped around the door and went in.

The Rose and Cannon was as dire and shabby a gin mill as Hemingway had ever seen—the deadfalls in St. Louis, frequented only by immigrant brewery workers and ranger-hunted steamboat sharps, looked like Versailles by comparison. The smell in the air was urine, and the floor was thick with cigarette butts and rat turds. No one manned the bar, which had only three visible bottles of unknown contents behind it in any case. The handful of chairs and stools were mismatched, probably stolen from other watering holes over the years or retrieved from the trash. There were two round tables, and an unconscious man slept across one on his stomach, his head hanging off the edge.

The old man with the distended nose was gone. There were three other men in the room, and one wore a dress.

He was, in fact, decked out like a prostitute, with high heels and tight skirt and red-haired wig. This man glanced over in an obvious fashion. The other men—one seated and smoking, the other standing at the bar beside the transvestite, both slim and ashen—were already glaring toward the door, and neither moved a hair when Hemingway and Worsleighson walked in, and when Hemingway strode over to the dust-covered bar and hit it with his open hand. "Bartender!"

But then they all slowly looked away.

Hemingway shouted across the room. "Hey! Any of you fellows speak English, *Ingles*? I'm looking for Eduardo Vico."

They all turned and glowered. Hemingway knew he had to try to tread delicately when dealing with Soviet-style politics, but this was merely a hovel of crooks and jonesers, there was nothing new to fear here.

The man in the wig and tight skirt walked over, trying for insouciance but unsteady on his heels.

*"Americano?"* he said to Hemingway, standing an inch too close. Hemingway backed up. "You looking for a friend?"

"What? Wait a minute, that's exactly what I'm *not* looking for!"

"You look . . . lonely."

"Alright, cut the shit. Is this just a hangout for fairies?" To Worsleighson, who, Hemingway saw, did not seem nonplussed. Hemingway did a double take.

But then the man at the table stood and walked across the room, and Hemingway could see simply by his gait that there was something not quite . . . heterosexual about him. Then the transvestite put his hand on Hemingway's shoulder to pat him seductively, and Hemingway recoiled like a fired shotgun, bumping into Worsleighson.

"Easy, *muchacho,*" the man in drag said, vaguely amused, but too vaguely. Hemingway saw that he was high, on something other than just booze. He looked to Worsleighson.

"I, uh, don't know, Mordaunt—" He spoke under his breath.

Worsleighson leaned on the bar. "Ernest, surely you can't be shocked."

"I . . . can't say I've known much . . . many fruits . . . You're OK?"

"Ernest, I'm a product of English boarding schools. There's nothing they could show us I haven't seen."

Hemingway chuckled, bucked up, and turned back to the bewigged addict at the bar. "Sorry," he said. "I'm not used to such . . . poised men." The man dozily furrowed his brow.

*"Elegante,"* Worsleighson said.

The man smiled. "Why do you need Eduardo?"

"Just for information," Hemingway said, trying for friendly but not too friendly. "I know his uncle. I don't know this part of town."

"Uncle? The minister? How well?"

"We're very close."

"You are a lie. What, you want a good restaurant or something?"

"No. Why am I a liar?"

"Because Eduardo's uncle sent him to a sanitarium in Switzerland two weeks ago."

Hemingway's shoulders folded—dead end after dead end.

"Maybe Liston didn't know," Worsleighson said.

"Eduardo, he liked his *chiva* very much."

"Yes, I know."

Hemingway exhaled like a draft coming out of a cave. Was it time to go home? To who, Pauline? Was it time to go find Martha, and try to get that racehorse up and running again? Or was it time to go—where? Fascists were nearly everywhere; Africa wasn't even safe. Cuba, maybe. Or Australia, never been. Wherever he went, his failure would follow him, he'd still have that book waiting to be written, the one that's supposed to vanish the lingering fart smell *To Have and Have Not* is likely to leave behind it. That new book. What is it? If it can't be about this civil war, then what?

The transvestite patted Hemingway on the back consolingly. "Luis," he said to the other men down the bar, "*Algunos* brandy." The smoking man stepped behind the bar and poured three small tumblers full of what promised to be the cheapest, crappiest brandy in Europe.

"What could Eduardo tell you, that we cannot?"

"I'm looking for *las Termitas.*"

"Oh. *Mi dios, los quinquilleros,* why on Earth . . . Well, we know about *las Termitas.*"

"You do?"

"*Si.* They have . . . come here. You want to find them?"

"Yes."

"Why?"

"They may've killed a friend of mine."

The three homosexuals looked at each other.

"Are you ready to kill them?" The man shifted his wig, a little unnerved. "All of them? Because they are *loco,* scum. You must mean a man's business, to go to them."

Hemingway took a breath. "I do."

Worsleighson wasn't so sure—he didn't warm to the idea of charging into a gangland headquarters and taking on a small criminal army. "Excuse me, but if you know them, yes?, maybe can give us a name?"

Hemingway nodded. "Good idea. One of the men we're looking for, he has . . . glasses."

The transvestite shrugged. The other two men drew closer, listening.

"One of them," Worsleighson said, "has a silver stain on his hand, probably from silvering mirrors or from photograph development . . ." No response. "No? Another one, a big man, has asthma? Difficulty breathing? A wheeze." Nothing.

"One of them smelled of camphor," Hemingway said. The three men of la Rosa y el Canon were losing interest. The transvestite's right eyelid sagged.

"What about *bexhet*," Worsleighson said. "A name? A *quinqui* word?"

*"No se."*

"One is mute, he cannot speak."

The man in the red wig looked up. "Baena." The man behind him nodded. "Baena."

Hemingway finally downed the brandy.

"Who's Baena?"

"He's *las Termitas*. Isn't that what you wanted?"

"I mean, what can you tell us about him."

"Nothing, except his name. He is ugly and cruel. He cannot speak because his throat was cut once by another *Termita*."

"Why?"

"Because, it is said, he borrowed a horse. Without asking."

# 15

The day had grown gray, and Hemingway was already busted from all of the walking and all of the confrontations. Maybe hire a car full-time, he thought—why'd he let Ignacio go back to Madrid? The two men couldn't even find a cab on the east side until they were blocks away from el Fernando Rei, but Hemingway climbed in anyway, the balls of his feet tingling and sore. The transvestite at la Rosa y el Canon said that *las Termitas* frequented the back rooms of the bars off la Plaza Del Ayuntamiento, gambling what money they could steal on dog-fights and dominoes. But all Hemingway could think about was putting his bare feet up, their yeasty fumes filling his room. And finishing the Lewis he'd started. And drinking beer—he needed something kinder to his stomach, but as there was no decent beer brewed anywhere in Spain, he'd have to make the staff search around for French farmhouse ale, or a Belgian abbey brew, or something like that, something gentle but with some Gallic weight to it.

Perhaps, he thought, I'll find some paper and a pencil and put something down. *It was midday yet the door to the tavern was locked. The three homosexuals inside seemed to be waiting, not drinking or talking but waiting. Perhaps, Robert thought, they were waiting for their bodies to slow down, or speed up, or respond somehow to the opium or kif they'd ingested. This life was all about waiting, for the next blast or for the last to wear down, or for someone to arrive with more . . .*

To hell with it, he thought. What do I know about dope? And this word, *"homosexuals,"* there's got to be a better, simpler word that isn't just a stupid insult. *The three men seemed to be waiting. There were no women . . .* Aw, fer Chrissake. The thing about writing stories was, you had to feel that it's worth your while and the reader's while and the tree they cut down to make the paper it's on *before* you write it. There has to be that hope, at least; it's not laying bricks, something you can do whether or not you own or even like the house you're working on. The bricks add up regardless. Words add up, too, but not meaningfully unless you think they should. They won't line up like bricks do, creating a strength of wall due to their essential shape and integrity. Words each have a hundred shapes and natures, and you have to see, almost like God, what's going to come of it before you even begin. What grows between the words. If there's a gift to this, that's it—the knack for seeing the algebra of a story before it's written.

At least he thought so—at least he'd written enough by then to think he might know something about how it goes. If only it was something you could push, because you need to have something happen, like a mule or a factory line or your own body when you're hunting in the mountains and decide not to go home empty-handed.

He got a sheaf of paper and wrote in his room, with a nice corked ale from Flanders which wasn't as cold as it should've been but which warmed him and the room well enough. He wasn't sure if he knew what he was doing, but it flowed and that was fine, that was a joy. That was his late afternoon and evening. Worsleighson did not hang about—the boy might well be through with this business by now, and was only looking for a way to say it. Only room service came, with another large bottle of ale it had found in a distant shop, and Hemingway tipped them grandly.

In the morning, Hemingway woke from a dream in which Scott Fitzgerald stalked around the Oak Park parlor from Hemingway's boyhood, weeping drunk and breaking furniture, as Hemingway's mother scurried after him trying to prevent each vase explosion or thrown chair. Hemingway himself was small, a boy, watching from the door that led to the entrance hall, and he was upset and angry and wishing his mother would just tackle the bum and knock him out with a poker.

"Stop where you are, Mr. Boozegob," she was screaming, "before you kill the cat!" Fitzgerald squinted at her and put his foot through the fire screen.

Awake, Hemingway washed and dressed.

"We have to go to the Popular Front meeting, Ernest." Downstairs for breakfast, Worsleighson was bathed and trimmed out as best as he could in trousers he'd been wearing for five days, and a second-hand tweed jacket the hotel staff found for him, after his other had been permanently stained with blood.

"We?"

"I have to. And you should. There's a war on, you know."

When did this whelp reacquire his sense of class superiority? Wasn't he just an sycophant a few days earlier?

"Mordaunt, you're a pain in my ass."

"And for that, Ernest, I will be the envy of all the fellows at home."

They ate and they departed for the ballroom of the Husa Reina Victoria Hotel, where the Popular Front was staging a rally under the guise of being a group meeting to vote for and honor a changing of guard in the party's executive board, from one Spaniard who had probably grown to like the Russian presence in Spain a little less than he once had, to another Spaniard who claimed to like it all the more. The ballroom itself was vast with twenty-foot yellow ceilings and white marble floor. The crowd the men found there at ten in the morning was immense and thick as an evening train platform's, and the noise was crushing. The crowd included Russians, Frenchmen, black Americans, Brazilian army officers in full uniform, English diplomats, and even what Hemingway took for a few Norwegians, red-haired tub-sized men who seemed to be speaking backward, and everyone was talking, oblivious to the black-suited speaker at the microphone at the front of the room who hollered like a Dartmouth football fan about the *republica!* and all of the *camaradas!*, and whose voice boomed and echoed through the speakers until it was barely distinguishable from feedback static.

Hemingway decided not to look for the complimentary wine he'd suspected was being offered on a table somewhere, and instead to scout the room, why not, collecting material for a NANA dispatch, the last of which he'd sent, who knows, was it a week ago? "There's no story here," he said to Worsleighson just as the young Englishman got himself backslapped by some slick gadabout lads in their twenties and vanished into the throng.

Hemingway spent a few minutes watching a Russian in a military uniform hissingly berate a mustachioed Spanish bureaucrat in a corner until the Spaniard appeared to be close to crying, a scene that seemed to sum up the revolution in these days, the more Hemingway saw and heard. But then the inevitable interruption: a thick, over-boisterous bellow of "Huckleberry!" It was a boozy nickname only one man had ever called Hemingway in his life, and that was years ago, in Paris.

Hemingway turned as if someone had fired a rifle at the ceiling: Coming out of the crowd, his hand extended, was Leo D'Armoux.

D'Armoux had no real career and probably many names. When Hemingway knew him, in the '20s, D'Armoux was a gambler and a pimp, with the gamiest Cherbourg accent Hemingway had ever heard, and the instincts and energy of a sewer rat.

He gambled because it was fun and undemanding of his time, which was otherwise taken up with whoring, liquor, and smoking opium on le Porte d'Ivry. He pimped because several whores asked him for protection, which he barely provided. If what little money he needed didn't come in these ways, he'd steal. He called Hemingway "Huckleberry" because Hemingway was American and so was Mark Twain, and Hemingway only tolerated the nickname because he remembered it was a derisive term his grandfather used, in an amused voice, to describe local Illinois goldbrickers he knew.

Hemingway got familiar with D'Armoux from gambling; too often Hemingway, barely twenty-five, would squander what little cash he and his young wife had playing *vingt en un* in the backrooms on the Rive Gauche. He'd be ashamed to go back to Hadley, so he'd let D'Armoux, who often won, take him out drinking, and these handful of occasions almost always ended with a fight or an impulsive assault with a wine bottle or an on-the-spur plan to heave a brick through a shop window and rob the place clean.

Hemingway would always be happy to get home to his garret in one piece. The last time he saw D'Armoux was in 1926. After a card game that left D'Armoux more or less even and Hemingway only slightly depleted, the drunk Frenchman insisted that they visit a lady friend of his, an ex-fiancée, he claimed, who owed him money that would give them license for some drinking in what was left of the evening. Guessing he'd at least see a new apartment and meet a new character and maybe even catch a story out of it, Hemingway followed him to Aulnay-Sous-Bois, where on rue de Belfort the two ascended a walk-up, and D'Armoux thundered on a red door. A sunken-eyed blonde who looked to be fifteen years old opened the door.

In short order, D'Armoux began bellowing at the girl, whose name was Viviane, about the money, which she claimed that she'd paid off a year earlier, and which D'Armoux, who had a prodigious memory, was pretending to have forgotten so he could collect it all over again. Hemingway stood by the door as they raged at each other. D'Armoux hit her to the floor and began breaking things in the tiny apartment, looking for money. He found a bottle of Pernod and happily began slugging from it, and then decided, as the girl mousily tried to clean up the detritus even as it rained on the floor around her, that instead of the money Hemingway and he should simply rape her, there and then. *"Vous et moi, Huckleberry!"* He threw the girl on her bed and she screamed. Hemingway was already sick in the stomach for having stood by as long as he did; he wasn't sure when D'Armoux had crossed the line from being a pig to being a menace. But once D'Armoux flipped his suspenders off, Hemingway knew the line was far gone. He shot to D'Armoux's side, telling him, "No, no, no, we're going," and when D'Armoux shrugged him off with a backhand slap, Hemingway brought his boot sharply down on the side of the man's left knee, holding his bicep up, dislocating D'Armoux's kneecap with a corklike pop.

D'Armoux howled and fell down toward his left side, and apparently folded the leg and the dislodged kneecap the wrong way, howling louder. Viviane ran out into the hallway and returned with two large men—larger than D'Armoux who stood somewhere above six-foot-two—and they picked up the whimpering cretin and roughly carried him out, to God knows where.

Viviane thanked Hemingway and offered to let him lie between her legs *sans frais,* but by this point he was delirious with anxiety and fatigue and lingering adrenaline. Hemingway said he'd take a rain check, *"une autre fois peut-être,"* and walked home.

Now eleven years later D'Armoux came at him, with a pronounced limp and a cane, and Hemingway shook his hand.

"My goodness, Huckleberry," his accented English flowing thickly, like syrup, "it's been many years, I never would've guessed I'd find you in Valencia!"

"Leo, it's a nice coincidence. How are you?"

"I'm a gimp forever, thanks to you. See my knee? All because of your weak stomach."

"That's right, I'm just a softie."

"I bet you cry at Shirley Temple."

"Of course I do. Serves you right, you bastard. No question about that."

"Did you ever see Viviane again? I bet she offered you a free one that night."

"She did. But no, I never saw her again."

"I did. I married her."

"Really."

"And then got an *annulation,* after she had a black baby."

"Never a dull moment, Leo."

"That is my English motto. I like to have mottos."

"OK. But what're you doing here, Leo?"

"Me? I'm an attaché to the Front, I am *asistente adjunto* they call it, to Juan Posada's office in Madrid."

"But you're a criminal, Leo. How'd that happen?"

"*Triomphe!* Eh? I'm older now, like you, more responsible. I have responsibilities! No more petty business. Now, I work only for the powerful, and for the revolution! There comes a time when a man must think of something bigger than himself."

"So you're a Communist now."

"Sure! Why not? The Communists pay me, so I am one of them. But you know, between you and me, I do not *attaché* anything. They ask me to do things, secretly. I have skills, they use them. Many secret things need to be done in this war."

"Don't I know it."

"But of course I cannot speak of my work."

"It is secret."

"*Oui.* But we can about your work. I see you have been publishing. Quite a reputation! Even in Paris. That book, *Hommes sans femmes?* Very popular. Even on the radio they talked about it. Tell me, can you make money doing that?"

"Writing? Yes. Some."

"I ought to try it."

"Good idea. Go ahead. It's easy."

"Yes? You just write what happened, correct? Nice and simple."

"That's it. Nothing else to it."

"I have some stories! And you are in Valencia, why, to find stories? You could write about me!"

I could at that, Hemingway thought. You'd be the year's most loathed fictional scalawag. You'd come gunning for me.

"I'm here as a journalist. Filing stories for American newspapers."

"Ah. That pays well, too, I'm guessing. There must be wine here, no? Let's find it!"

"Alright." Hemingway didn't feel that the reasons to say no were terribly compelling. They cut through the crowd until they spotted someone with a wine glass. D'Armoux inquired, and the small man pointed over his shoulder toward the far back corner of the room.

There was the table, not very lavish and largely ignored, and the men snatched up goblets of Chablis. One quaff and Hemingway's kidneys began to ache.

D'Armoux began to tell a story, one that he dreamily said he was contemplating writing down and selling, about a game of Russian roulette he played in Algiers in 1931, at a table in a café cellar with two Algerian Arabs and a German fighter pilot–turned–Nazi delegate, all of them blind drunk and each betting 8,000 Algerian new francs. The Nazi was the first to go, in a fast bloody tumble to the floor; when the game had been drawn down to two and D'Armoux had the revolver, he simply turned it and clicked through two empty chambers before finding the bullet and shooting his last opponent, who was running to the stairs, in the back, and then scooping up all of the money and what was in their pockets besides.

"A happy ending," Hemingway cracked.

"*Oui!* What more could a magazine want out of a true story?"

The story was not revelatory to Hemingway. He knew D'Armoux was a sociopathic monster who'd probably taken a few lives before then, and was apparently in Spain being paid as a goon or assassin or both. But the story and the Chablis cleared Hemingway's head: How could it be a coincidence that they'd find each other, in Valencia, right now? D'Armoux wasn't the kind of man you stumble into; you had to seek him out, in the worst of places. Before coming to Spain, he'd probably never been in a crowded public building in his life. And besides, reprobates like D'Armoux were exactly the sort recruited and assigned by the Comintern to secretly purge uncooperative officials, or threaten perceived enemies of the cause, or bear down on crusaders who, say, were loudly bellyaching about an unsolved disappearance, and who had just bulldozed into a government office and slugged a bureaucrat behind his own desk. And emerged from the office to point a gun at a palace guard.

It's as if I had begged to have D'Armoux appear, he thought. Of course he's in Valencia for me. Did that third man in the army truck outside the Benicarlo, the one that hissed *go home,* have a limp? He didn't think so.

But wait: Posada? What's that weasel got to do with any of this? He hadn't even thought of Madrid per se in days. How long has it been? Wasn't he supposed to be trying to get Martha back?

Posada? Hemingway squinted to himself. Sure, being the police chief in Madrid meant, under the new Republic, being in charge of secret operations and "unofficial" public management actions that even Madrid's mayor or half the bureaucracy in Valencia wouldn't be told about. But Posada was just a climber, a shrugger and brownnoser, without an agenda or even an honest revolutionary impulse anywhere on him. He held that office and owned that penthouse because a friend, or a friend of a friend, recommended him to the Comintern agents as an obedient, crafty servant, a pliable political animal. Hemingway vaguely remembered that he'd heard Posada before the war had been a mortgage broker and, on the side, a bookie. Now, he was one of those Spanish bureaucrats who hoped for a permanent seat of power after the war but who also stood a good chance at not surviving the Russian manipulation of the Republic. There was no shortage of them. So, was it significant that D'Armoux works out of Posada's office, or is the Frenchman simply a general journeyman thug for the Front? *Asistente adjunto?* Is he even telling the truth?

He realized that all this time he had been assuming he would be led to the doorstep of Julio Alvarez del Vayo, the foreign minister and propaganda chief, and he realized he'd assumed this because del Vayo had lied to both Josie and Dos, and because del Vayo was in a powerful enough position to snap his fingers and get a man disappeared in the wilderness. But maybe he'd been wrong—maybe the first-cause domino-drop that started this whole megillah was strictly military or operational, and del Vayo, who was really an inflated public-relations manager for the Front, massaging its image as it's presented to the world, was not involved. Posada's job, on the other hand, was to have a hand in all kinds of black nastiness.

Maybe del Vayo lied just to get those pain-in-the-ass American reporters out of his office. Or maybe he'd been warned. Either way, the compass point quivered toward Posada, and living evidence of it stood in front of Hemingway in the form of a large, limping French cutthroat.

Hemingway checked with a shift of his body for the weight of Liston Oak's gun in his inside pocket. He sipped his wine, and consciously separated his feet on the floor slightly, balancing his center of gravity.

"Leo? How'd you know I'd be here?"

D'Armoux's jaw dropped.

"I didn't! How could I? Did I not look surprised?" He had looked surprised.

"It was Worsleighson, wasn't it? He had to come, so you assumed he'd drag me. Or have you been watching me all this time, back and forth from the Benicarló?"

"Huckleberry! You are delusional! Why would I be assigned to follow you around? You're just a journalist, correct?"

That *just*.

"C'mon, Leo, don't bullcrap me. . . ."

The Republican pontificator speaking into the microphone said the word *"Carlistas!"* and both men turned and listened— apparently, Hemingway deduced, picking through the Spanish, Franco had consolidated the conflicted parties of his movement, the Falangists and the Carlists, and announced himself now, that day, April 19, the political as well as military leader of the conservative rebellion. A chilly milestone in the war's progression, mentioned now to ignite the room with common purpose.

"May toothed worms devour Franco's eardrums," D'Armoux growled.

"My God, Leo . . . you're displaying political commitment."

"Commitment? Well, it's hard not to have it, how you say, get under your skin, working in a war. Seeing the innocent die in such numbers."

"Well, I'm glad we're on the same side."

"Yes." D'Armoux was looking away. "But, so, you think you are being . . . betrayed? By us?"

"I don't know the word, Leo. Watched. Threatened. Don't play me for a chump. It's the way the Comintern works, and every schoolkid in this godforsaken country knows it."

"Yes . . ." D'Armoux appeared embarrassed. If Hemingway hadn't known better, he would've sworn he was seeing moral conflict and humiliation overtake the man. He let the awkward pause linger.

"Leo? . . . If you told me you were the one following me, I'd actually be a little relieved. Because I know you." He was lying—he'd rather have to confront a perfect stranger, rather than a man that he knew has the conscience of a hammerhead.

"Really. Well . . . don't let on to anyone then, Huckleberry. We could both be in danger."

"Of course . . . But I'd be in danger from you, only."

"From me *first*. If I'm eliminated, someone else will step in."

"But what am I doing, Leo, that's so dangerous?"

"You know very well, Ernest. But you're only a danger to yourself. Go back to Madrid and take up with those *putas* again. Buy some more cognac from the dead shop on Calle de Ayala. Parse out the crackers in your closet. Fuck your young American mistress."

With that, D'Armoux, his naturally feral grin spoiled into a grim frown, walked away and out of the hotel.

# 16

The conversation with D'Armoux seemed to have taken up an hour of portentous pauses and subterranean meanings, but actually lasted all of twelve minutes. Hemingway stood alone in the room now, slowly realizing what D'Armoux had really said, that Hemingway has been under the watchglass of Comintern spies since . . . when? Since Dos Passos came to Spain. At least.

Fine, he thought. Let them watch. He was startled, a bit, to realize he didn't feel the need to think more deeply about his predicament. Let them threaten. Let them hit him with rifle butts. Let them assassinate him and lose his corpse on a rubbish heap. He'd be fucking goddamned if he'd run scared now. I like this, he thought, this obstinate irresponsibility. Because it was irresponsible: He had kids back in the States. But in that room, emptying his glass down his throat, he was suddenly, irredeemably, briefly happy.

He wished he had a pad and a pencil and a small desk in a corner to write, his head was giddily full of sentences, his adrenaline started to quietly percolate like it did when a story was brimming up. The pressure was building; he knew if he had a chance to sit down something good would come out, steadily, like steam out of a gauge cock. But he didn't move. He knew the pressure would rise and quickly begin to fall, and even if he were able to find a silent corner, by then it would be too late. You can't panic, he knew, you can just hope it'll come again. Try to remember what bubbles up. Enjoy the charge. Which wove nicely with the sense of danger he felt standing in the crowd, on the edge, some kind of edge. The room was thick with portent, in a way he could write out later. It smelled like carbon.

He had to find this Baena shitheel, he reasoned, before nightfall. He scanned the room for Worsleighson.

The tall Boston boy was not visible in the crowd, and Hemingway eventually tapped on the shoulder of a wide-shouldered man in a leather jacket, who turned and smiled and stuck out his open hand.

"Excuse me, I was looking for Mordaunt Worsleighson, I thought maybe you knew him, saw him come in—"

"So you're Hemingway." Smiling wider. The young man radiated trustworthiness, like warmth off an oil lamp. And he was American.

"Yes. I was looking for Mordaunt."

"He left." Hemingway leaned in to hear, unbelieving. "Yes," the American explained, with a Boston flatness, "after he came in and we were talking a man came over and cornered him, kind of, whispered to him, and then Mordaunt told me he had to go. He looked white. He said that if Ernest Hemingway should ask, I should tell him that he, Worsleighson, had to leave. Go home. To America."

"Shit."

"I'm not going to ask."

"Was the man who cornered him French?"

"I didn't hear him, I couldn't tell."

"Did he limp?"

"Yes, he did." *Son of a bitch*. That was it for Worsleighson, scared off the continent in two minutes flat.

"Sorry," the young American continued.

"Thanks."

"I trust Mordaunt will get home safely. He's blessed, like a fool or a drunkard."

Hemingway knew D'Armoux's freezing-out had more to do with scaring or intimidating him than it did with actually addressing Worsleighson as an "enemy of the state," or whatever. But D'Armoux must've done it before coming over to Hemingway, moments before. He must've had it all planned out.

How much did *they* know? Hemingway tallied the last week's worth of conversations and data—did they watch him go to Obdulio Pilas? Possible. They must know that he had gone to see Margara Robles, but he hoped they didn't find out that Carmena had a photographic memory. He hoped she was clever enough to not to give herself away. But could they've known what happened in La Rosa y el Canon? Could they know he knew the name Baena? Impossible, he decided. Unless they invaded the tavern afterward. . . .

Hemingway took a step away from the American, thinking too hard for small talk, and then turned back. "What's your name, my friend?"

"Walker. Daniel Walker." Shook again.

"You fighting with the Brigades?"

"Yup. I'm a munitions man, just got back from the hills." A young Spanish girl with short, badly cut hair came up from behind him and held his arm with two hands. They smiled at each other. Whatever they had just come from, it seemed to Hemingway, was grave and deadly enough to make them shine with the promise of survival.

"I salute you."

"Thank you, Mr. Hemingway. I look forward to reading one of your books. When I get home."

The girl smiled broadly at Hemingway—clearly she was happy, and just as clearly he had saved her life—and then disappeared

into the mix. The speaker on the stage had wrapped up his propaganda rant, and an eight-piece brass band began to play. Hemingway had to shout.

"Listen, Walker, did you know José Robles?"

Walker's brow furrowed. "No. Not in person. I heard he was
killed."

"That's right. I was wondering if you'd heard anything, in
the field, or . . . among the Brigadesmen . . ."

"No. I only know a woman in Madrid who knew him.
Well."

"In Madrid?"

"Yes. Portugese. She's an obstetrician. Her name is Floripedes
something. Crispo? There aren't many woman OBs in Madrid
right now. She trained some medics with me while I was there.
She might be able to tell you something."

"Why do you think?"

"She was Robles's mistress."

# 17

Baena. Hemingway hailed a cab at the curb in front of la Husa Reina Victoria and asked the driver, a middle-aged man with a deep tan, to take him to the places where the *quinquilleros* drink and gamble in the back rooms on the avenues tentacling off la Plaza Del Ayuntamiento. The cabbie, who had admitted to knowing English at first, refused to understand anything Hemingway said after that, and shrugged and shook his head. Hemingway got out and hailed a second cab, whose driver, older, understood it all plainly and said, *"Coma mierda,"* over his unlit cigar.

The third cab driver was younger, and was game. More than that, he said he knew a little Spanish Rom, not *quinqui* per se, and knew the Plaza dives, with a wiggle of his flat hand: a little. *"Se que hay rata pelea!"* he chortled, wrenching gears.

"You know there's . . . what? Rats?"

*"Si! La lucha!"*

"Fighting?"

*"Si!"*

"Oh, boy."

They drove in a four-door Chrysler Series 66 from 1931 that

looked as if it'd been already driven off a cliff. The trip took over a half hour; so many roads were closed by barricades, often for no apparent reason, that the young cabbie very nearly had to drive in a circle around the neighborhood and come at it from the north. The cluster of streets north of la Plaza Del Ayuntamiento had to be the direst, saddest, most woebegone avenues Hemingway had seen in Spain, saved from being ruined by shells but squalid and poor and crumbling. The war had not touched them, but a few centuries or more of poverty and vice had done worse. No glass was uncracked, no stucco was unchipped, no door had been painted since the days of Ferdinand VII. The town hall building in the huge square, an ancient, terra-cotta-adorned templelike beauty, was closed permanently by the Republic. Most of the storefronts lining the area were empty or boarded up, although several *tabernas* without signs seemed busy, their customers spilling out into the street, where children swarmed in packs and begged passing cars for food or money. Serious Spanish sun poured onto the Plaza, but most of the windows were shuttered.

The cabbie pulled up to a curb and pointed to a battered double door that used to be painted red, where two large men in dirty tweed smoked on the steps.

*"Dígales que ud. conoce a la Princesa Wallada,"* the cabbie told him, and Hemingway threw both hands up. "Tell them!" the cabbie repeated, trying his best, pointing back and forth. "You know, *Princesa* Wallada!"

"Who the fuck is that? Is that a password?"

The cabbie threw up his hands. *"Era una princesa Mora . . ."*

"A Moor?"

*"Sí!"*

Hemingway gave the cabbie a wad of Republican banknotes and with hand gestures got him to understand that the taxi should drive around and pass down the avenue every now and then, to pick him up. Who knows what he'd find, how long he'd be. He might search all day and not find the men he was looking for. Where was Worsleighson when you needed him? Or at least that list he'd made in the bar on the way to La Rosa y el Canon, of Carmena's cataract of remembered details?

He stepped out. What was this he was being steered toward, a rat fight? How can you make rats fight? What these goddamn peasants wouldn't do for fun. He put on his best blood sport face and strode over to the beefy men outside the double door. He'd forgotten, for some time already, that he still had a bandage on his head, and his eyes were still darkened and bloodshot by the various head injuries he'd already accrued.

"*Princesa* Wallada," he said with an affected impatience. The men looked at the American wearing the face of a car-wreck victim, looked at each other, chuckled between them, and then walked away down the sidewalk.

Hmpf. He opened one of the faintly red doors and walked in—it was in fact a bar, and it was crowded. He smelled opium mixed with the tobacco smoke that by itself made it a challenge to see the far wall to any degree. There were mostly men but a smattering of whores, too; the unshaven men were all wearing dark wool jackets and flat tweed caps, the uniform of the low-class urban European. It was loud in the bar but only as an aggregate of the men's private mutterings and growls—no voice could be separated from the roar. He wouldn't know what *quinqui* sounds like in any event. Beneath the smell of smoke Hemingway smelled shit, farm animal dung, probably on a dozen different shoes. In the middle of the day the place was so dark Hemingway couldn't guess at its decor, or lack thereof.

But at least it was a functioning public house, thank God— Hemingway beelined for the bar, found a stretch of bar rail, and demanded a double gin with some kind of fruit, *frutas*. The bartender, moving quickly once he saw Hemingway's hand go into his pocket, produced a pint glass half full of Beefeater, and a whole lime he quickly sliced into quarters. "*Bravo*," Hemingway boomed, and paid the man. The lime was squeezed in, and Hemingway bolted half of the glass.

He looked around: nobody was paying him any mind. There could certainly not be any spies for the Comintern here, though D'Armoux could walk through the door any minute. This was exactly the kind of place that scofflaw would love.

Quick, then: There was no way to know if the clock was ticking.

Hemingway turned and stood away from the bar, his eyes down, drink in hand, nonchalantly roaming, gazing quizzically into his drink like a far-gone souse whenever another man glanced his way, otherwise just half-liddedly examining the crowd, and the walls (now visible, and not much to look at besides desilvered mirrors with liquor logos), edged toward the back of the bar where there was a hallway and a doorless lavatory with a trough, and a closed door with another man, one with a face full of knife scars, waiting outside.

Hemingway walked up, drink in his left fist, his right hand free to reach for the money in his pocket or for the gun in his jacket. "*Princesa* Wallada," he growled with a grin. The bouncer nodded, eyes half-closed as if he were exhausted with a jabbering five-year-old, and rubbed his thumb and index finger together once. Hemingway retrieved his folded wad of notes, and looked for some place to put his drink, so he could peel one off. Instead, the scar-faced guard simply reached over and plucked out two bills, and then, just because he could, a third. Hemingway realized he may've just paid upwards of 3,000 pesetas for the privilege of seeing two rats fight.

The room beyond the door was large and fashioned into a wood-plank arena, with chicken wire serving as barrier walls, and as a ceiling—presumably, the rats could climb. There were benches, and men betting and other men taking tallies on pads, and one behind a low table making odds, taking bets and paying out. There was a dog-track-style racing clock on the table, and it was running.

In the pit behind the wire was a bull terrier, and it was fighting with large brown rats. Or rather, the rats sought shelter and escape, scampering in harried circles while the dog, apparently highly trained for this particular activity, was catching and killing as many as it could, as quickly as it could. It would grab a rat in its jaws, chomp down and whip its head simultaneously, and then toss it aside, already in motion for the next rodent running by, which it would seize before the previous rat had even landed on the boards. The bets were on the number of rats cut down in the prime of life during the allotted time. The rat blood continually sprayed in circular spritzes through the wire. The dog was covered with bites, too, and was streaked with blood from all directions. But it did not pause: its motions were not defensive or even predatory, really; they were choreographed, a trained athletic set of maneuvers, not unlike a matador's. Hemingway could see the sport in it immediately—it wasn't just placing two dumb animals in a pit and seeing which kills which. The strategic grace of it, the heightened ability required, was instantly obvious.

So was the disgusting, almost neanderthal flavor of the scenario. You've got a dog, he idly thought, you train him for this? Not that rat hunting isn't good work for a dog, but what he was watching wouldn't translate to the real world. It wouldn't be surprising to find out that ratter dogs like this were utterly useless at catching rats unless the luckless rodents were first stuck in a pit with no exit and no place to hide. Hemingway had read about the dog-baiting and bearbaiting in England in Henry VIII's day, and that's how this dank horror show made him feel: stuck in a medieval world of catastrophic hygiene, everyday street sewage, rotten teeth, spoiled meat, and rats so ubiquitous that a dozen different and serious games were invented to employ them.

He sat down and watched the men instead—a sorry, desperate, toothless gang that, though there was some overlap, made the hunched, hairy mob outside in the bar look like Oak Park socialites. He tried to remember Carmena's litany of facts about the four hooded murderers, but could only recall the silver stain on one man's hand, and something about camphor, in the hair? Oh, and the slit throat. Christ. He sipped his gin. Scanning the dog-baiting fans on the benches, he noted physical details—a dead eye, a forehead scar, a profusion of black hair and beard that suggested its owner had just returned from a decade in a cave—but nothing rang a bell.

This wasn't the Spain he was looking for, that's for certain. Would he ever get to see an actual battle?

He sat there for twenty minutes. The bull terrier had to be pulled eventually, due to exhaustion and loss of blood, but had managed to snap the necks of some forty rats in his second five-minute bout, and this apparently made his owner a velvet winner. The next dog, also a terrier, was larger but slower, and though it seemed inviolate to the angry rats' teeth, it was not a hot ticket. Eventually, Hemingway's large glass was empty. There was no reason to think the particular *Termitas* he was looking for would be betting on dog-baiting at the moment; there were other places along the plaza to look, other shitholes to sift through. He'd been caught up with the competition long enough.

Hemingway got up and left the arena, through the smoky drinking hall and out to the street, which was littered with a few drunks and urchins. He didn't see the cab, and didn't know at all where to go next. Damn, he thought, I should've learned Spanish.

The afternoon threw cold winds down the avenues north to south. He could just see himself wandering the alleys of the lowest neighborhood in Valencia, into the evening. What the hell have I gotten myself into?

He turned and strode back inside, past the crowd and past the bouncer at the back door. Once inside the arena space, where a

German shepherd was being chased in maddened circles by a pack of squeaking rats, the dog's owner sitting with his face in his hands, Hemingway went to the man at the betting table. The man was doing nothing with his paper, just laughing at the spectacle beyond the wire. Hemingway sat down on the bench beside him. He asked him if he knew English—he did—and asked him about a man he heard of who might know a man about a particular dog. Hemingway fumbled out a line of fuzzy bullshit that was undecipherable even to him, and the man's name was Baena.

The bookie, whose enthusiastic mustache possessed at least a half-dozen pigments from white to auburn to pitch black, eyed Hemingway for a moment, took him to be a real man, not a tourist or a slummer or a cop, and shook his head.

"Ach. Too bad." They watched the shepherd run. "Oh, you know, he had a friend, another man, a trainer, I think . . . What the fuck. Oh: Bexhet."

The bookie at the table nodded. "He's outside there, drinking."

"He's fat, chubby, right?"

"*Si*, and wears *anteojos*. Spectacles."

Hemingway thanked him and headed for the door. He didn't have a moment to congratulate himself on fishing that name out of the abyss, in a long shot, without any help, because he was that moment wading into the dark waters, and he had to think on his feet. The time for talking and puzzling and promising onself was over.

Through the door and into the dark bar, and his eyes needed a moment to adjust. He scanned the bar, then the tables, for fat men, and there were not many. Food wasn't plentiful enough. But he saw one, two, neither with glasses, and then spotted Bexhet, sitting with a low tumbler of red against the wall at a table, laughing with a cohort and slouching, obviously stewed to the tips of his toes.

Half of the voices in Hemingway's head agreed that they couldn't believe he'd actually found, in a large war-torn country, one of the four men who killed José Robles. The other half were scrambling for ideas about what to do with the evil pig now that he had him.

Hemingway didn't wait—he took one step to the table's side, reached across it, and grabbed Bexhet by his woolen lapels with the speed of a lizard's tongue. The fat man was so startled his eyes and mouth gaped involuntarily, while his friend next to him grabbed Hemingway's arms and begin shouting in *quinqui,* a nasal gibberish that sounded to Hemingway like Hindi yowled through a whirring desk fan. The other men around the table, sitting and standing, began yelling in a panic, hands grabbed Hemingway's collar and shoulders, trying to pull him off, but his left knee went up on the table and his hands pulled Bexhet to his wobbly feet and yanked him across the table, glasses spilling everywhere, both men shoved backward now by the force of Hemingway's body, knocking several other men over and creating an explosion of yelling in the bar, and all in three or so seconds.

*"Get the fuck off!"* Hemingway bellowed twice, and the bar patrons, who were hollering in their tongue, let him go. Hemingway pulled Bexhet again to his feet, which weren't much good to him, and the fat man was crying, asking in *quinqui* God knows what, but obviously asking *"who are you, what do you want."*

Hemingway didn't even reach for Spanish, he just hissed, *"José Robles."*

The fat man's watery eyes bulged in dread. Hemingway shifted his weight and started dragging the man to the door; Bexhet could only stumble drunkenly, sobbing. No one in the bar knew what the fight was about, or why the fat man was crying. But the waves parted for the pair of them; apparently, among the *quinquilleros,* one man's bad tavern fortune is his and his alone.

The outside door flew open, and every head on the block turned as a large American with a bandaged head came through the door like a truck, catapulting a fat Spaniard who was begging for mercy in *quinqui*, falling to his knees and being dragged up from them again. Hemingway had him by the coat and by the back of the neck, and he was squeezing hard.

He led him into the first alley they came to, hustling northwest up the street, and threw him into the brick wall. Bexhet's head hit hard—Just like that poor bull's weeks ago, Hemingway thought—and the man crumpled under his coat, choking and sobbing.

Hemingway pulled his head up by its hair, arced his closed fist back, and landed it into the man's right eye. Skin cracked in two places and blood flowed into the man's eye socket, which kept the eye irritated and closed even as it swelled.

Hemingway's Spanish was bad, but he hoped the fat gypsy's was at least a little better. It had to be, right?

"Del Vayo? O Posada? A Russian? ¿Quién? ¡Cuéntame!"

Bexhet just shook his head, to the names and the demand, to everything.

Look at this quaking mess, Hemingway thought. He doesn't know a thing.

"Baena, *donde es,*" Hemingway spit.

Bexhet looked up, openly terrified. What shook him was either the realization that this crazy head-trauma American guy with the large hands actually knew details about the Robles affair, or it was the realization that this American might kill him because, as he tried to communicate with a frenzied head shake and shrug, he had no idea where Baena, the throat-slit cement worker, was. Or it was both.

"Don't give me that." Hemingway hit him again, connecting mostly with the skull above his ear. Hemingway's knuckles shuddered from the pain; it was like punching a bowling ball.

Bexhet was gasping, and his eyelids fluttered. *Oh, no,* Hemingway thought, *if he passes out that'll be the end. It's getting dark. How long do I have before D'Armoux shows up, or before the* quinquilleros *decide to exterminate me?*

"*No más,* I know not," Bexhet sobbed. Both men managed a child's Spanish.

"Baena."

"I know not! *Por favor!*"

"The other. Big. Bad breath." He meant something like "hard breathing," asthma. Bexhet shook his head, clueless. Hemingway couldn't remember any detail about the one Carmena called the contingent's "captain." Just the mute one and the big one. He gestured, miming a hulking giant, pointing to his hand. "Big. Hand with silver."

Bexhet's eyes understood but he said nothing, until Hemingway pressed the man's head against the bricks and raised his fist again.

"*Goemilxea!*"

"What?!" Hemingway made him repeat the name twice. Then he lifted the fat man to his feet once more. "*Vamos,*" he said. "*A Goemilxea.*"

Pushing him and threatening him the whole way, Hemingway followed Bexhet through several miles of Valencia byway.

The evening Hemingway had worried about the whole afternoon finally arrived, but much to his surprise the streetlights in this part of the city worked. He still had the pistol in his coat, and he wished he'd had another drink at the bar, just one more to fend off the dehydration and the headache, which he anticipated more than he actually felt because the full-blasting adrenaline load in his system had obscured all other things. Maybe this one, the one with the godawful name, could tell him where the captain is, or whose Bentley it was, of who did the hiring. Because it was apparent all over again that these peasant alley rats would have no personal reason to kill a particular government official, unless that official was at a card table with aces in his shirt cuffs.

Bexhet stopped at a street corner and pointed across the intersection at a tenement, mumbling something in *quinqui*. He apparently hoped that the mad American would just say thanks and go knock on the weathered door alone. Hemingway heaved him across the road and threw him on the steps.

Just then the door opened, and a very large, John L. Sullivan–sized man in yet another wool jacket stepped out of the door, his face down, but then it shot up, and he saw Bexhet lying on the steps and then he saw Hemingway, whose eyes were stetched open with tension. He bolted back inside and Hemingway ran after him, stepping over Bexhet and dashing down the building's narrow and unlit center hallway after the hurtling man, who exploded out the back door into an alley cluttered with garbage bins and scrap wood and yipping dogs.

Hemingway followed full bore, bouncing off the walls of the alley, catching sight of the running man only as he'd made it back to the street. Up the street, in and out of the streetlamps' cones of amber light, Hemingway could faintly see the man checking in a panic for a doorway or an alley to escape into. The streets were mostly empty; no one in a civil war would care to get involved with two men running like predator and prey across the cobblestones in the dark. They ran like this for ten minutes, and Hemingway did not tire, he felt invigorated and risk-drunk and strong as a mountain lion.

From a distance of some twenty yards he saw the big man hook left into an alley, which Hemingway saw a minute later was not an alley but broader, a municipal corner with a hitching post that must've been a century old, and an old steel sewer door, its two dovetailing leafs opening out of the ground to the night sky like a mouth.

Had Hemingway thought for a moment about the likely con-
sequences of going underground at night, into what he knew—
because he'd read about it—was one of Europe's oldest intact
urban sewer networks, reputed to have been installed by the
Romans, he might not have simply leaped into the gaping man-
hole, grabbed the iron ladder, and scuttled down it at full speed.
But he did, and he landed at the bottom and saw nothing
because there was no light. Only the sound of running liquid,
the feel of pressurized fumes moving down the vast tunnel,
and the heartbreaking stench of human excrement, dominated
by the smell of fresh shit but also pervaded by the scent of much
older, fossilized waste, so old and atomized that it smelled rather
robust and pleasant, like good soil for potatoes.

But Hemingway's adrenaline, pumping like a drug, kept the
distractions numbed. He didn't move, because he couldn't see,
and listened intently. That hulking *quinquillero* must be nearby,
because he is also blind in the darkness, and wouldn't dare either
to take a wrong step into a river of sewage. Carefully, silently,
Hemingway took a searching step away from the ladder, the only
point of reference for either man. The ground was solid. He listened for breathing and heartbeat, but heard nothing. He crawled
his hand along the stone tunnel wall, inch by inch, he might be
getting near to that lumbering bloodletting motherfucker, or he
might be inching farther away. Another step, no more than a
foot, and Hemingway's outstretched hand touched something,
metal, on the wall, an iron hand lantern. He leaned over to it and
gently tipped it: He could hear oil. Now the challenge was taking it off its presumably rusty hook and getting out a match and
lighting it without making a sound. But why? Keep the noises
faint and mysterious, so the *quinquillero* cannot bumrush you, but
otherwise he can't make a break anywhere.

Hemingway lifted the lantern off, fished a match out of his
pocket with a surprising minimum of noise, and struck the match.

He looked around: Just a few feet away, on the other side of the ladder, stood Goemilxea. He was breathing like an over-weight racehorse after a meet; Hemingway began to hear the wheezing. He didn't move. Hemingway slowly lit the lantern, and the area glowed. They were just a few feet from a hellish, deep, inky stream of excrement and runoff; the tunnel went black in both directions. The two men stood in a wet stone al-cove, maybe fifteen square feet surrounding the ladder. It re-minded Hemingway of *Phantom of the Opera,* and how there seemed to be room in the Parisian sewers for massive organs and such. These walls were old and beautifully crafted from carved blocks, but there was nothing here except tunnels for crap.

Hemingway looked at the man, who was gradually finding it harder to breathe. He did have a silvery stain on his left hand; it looked to Hemingway like argyria, from the silver salts you use to make mirrors.

"Who are you?" Goemilxea asked, in clear if raspy English.

"You fucking *quinquillero,* where'd you learn English."

". . . I listen . . . to the BBC."

"I'm a friend of José Robles." He skipped a beat, wanting to feel the moment weigh in the air. "I've been looking for you and your friends, and I have found you."

"Robles? . . . What for? . . . It's a war, man. Who cares?"

"I care, and I'm tired of that excuse. You're right about one thing, though: It's war and no one will wonder where you went or who killed you."

"I have a wife."

"Good for you. So did Robles . . . You're a silverer."

Glances at his hand. *"Si."*

"Shoulda stuck to your day job."

"You can't just kill me. Why cannot I just kill you?"

"You can hardly stand up, fuckup. And I have a gun."

"A friend of José Robles . . ." He seemed to be scoffing, amid the wheezes.

"That's not funny, you gyppo. You did the blood work, you got paid, now you have to pay back."

"I was never paid."

"I know. You lost the keys."

The large man looked stricken—this was the story of his life, it looked like. In a single stroke he was a beaten man. "You found them?"

"Yes. Whose Bentley. And where."

"They said the car was in Madrid. But I do not know who it was of. Some big-wigger . . . important man. Someone who was gaining from the Russians."

"A Spaniard?"

Goemilxea thought. "I don't know. I was not told."

That doesn't narrow it down too much, Hemingway thought, but it sets up possibilities. Del Vayo, Quintinilla, some other NKVD executive. Someone in Largo's office, over Oak? Gorev? But why?

"I need to know who it was." The *quinquillero* just shrugged, leaning against the wall. "You have to be able to tell me more than that. Somebody will pay for Robles."

"Cannot."

"Who was your captain . . . Ugh. The guy who took the orders and gave them out."

"*Americano,* why don't you go to fuck your own self."

Hemingway resolved right then to kill the man. He'd been tiring, and the longer the conversation went on the easier it became to simply have sympathy for this peasant crook as he struggled for air helplessly with sounds that chilled the blood, and it was also becoming easier to simply chalk the whole escapade, from Dos coming to his hotel room to dragging Bexhet across the bar table, up to war and fate and cynicism and moral exhaustion. Hemingway saw the signs of letting up, of loosening his grip on the justice he'd been seeking, and resisted. Even if my blood is not up, he promised, this rat bastard will not see daylight. I will shoot him down and dump him into the shit river, and that will be fucking that. Even if I don't want to by that point. It's only fair. It's only right. It has to happen, even if it'll make me feel like a monster. Like a D'Armoux.

"*Quinquillero,*" he said, steering clear of using the man's name, "tell me, why did you use a German gun?"

"*Que?* How do you know that? Bexhet wasn't even on that hill!"

"We found the bullet casings."

"You can tell the difference?!" His wheezing turned into thundering, painful coughs.

"Yes."

". . . Accident, the rifle jammed . . . We found another on a corpse up in the hills."

"Lucky you. What would you have done, just beat him with the rifle butt?"

Goemilxea hacked, and fell to his knees. Hemingway took Oak's pistol out of his coat and cocked it and stepped over, aiming down at the back of the man's head.

The man coughed and sucked in air as if through clogged netting. Hemingway did not waver. The trigger will get pulled, the gun will fire, this man is done. Shot to the head, just like Pepe.

But Hemingway waited for the cough to pause, and the breathing crisis to subside, because, he supposed, he was just too weak to do it otherwise. Standing there, Hemingway smelled the camphor, which sent images of his grandmother's attic into his forebrain, and the cedar dowry chest of lace and cotton tablecloths that also contained newspapers from the American Civil War, which he thought as a kid were the most beautiful printed things he'd ever seen. The light would pour in dusty beams from the single four-paned window. At least one of the papers, he remembered, the *Alton Observer,* was actively abolitionist, and used fiery, righteous preacher language. One issue reported on the battle of Chickamauga.

The coughing did not stop. Hemingway waited some more, but soon Goemilxea was choking, convulsing, huddled on the floor. The gun did not lower for several minutes. Hemingway tried to empty his thoughts as he waited. He finally realized that the sewer was very cold, like an icebox. Soon enough the *quinquillero* on the stone floor was still.

# 18

Hemingway climbed to the street, found a nearby tavern, staggered into it without a thought as to what kind of bar it was or who drank there, bought a bottle of brandy, and went outside. He stood on the empty street corner, under a golden spray of lamplight, and drank. It should've been the best and most satisfying tipple he'd had in weeks, but of course it wasn't; it bothered his stomach and conjured an instant headache. But he needed it all the same, like a night of dreaming after a tragedy. He didn't figure there was a chance in hell that his roaming cabbie would be able to find him now, even if he were trying. So Hemingway began to walk back south, to where he estimated he'd been dropped off.

Was Robles avenged? Or, rather, was justice served? Or, rather more precisely, was the right thing finally done? He didn't think so. The man just murdered by his own lungs was only a stooge, a mercenary. There was no release when that man stopped moving. And Hemingway didn't for a moment think it was vital to find Bexhet again, or the other two gangsters, the "captain" and Baena, the mute cement worker. If it hadn't been those cretins, it would've been some others. They were just soldiers.

It was like the war: You don't hate the Moroccan conscriptees because their government sold them to Franco and Mussolini. The bombs don't matter, it's who fires them into the void. Hemingway knew he'd have to go back to Madrid, finally, and find that Bentley. The keys still sat, sharp-edged, in his pocket. When he found the car and cornered the almighty prick that set this ordeal up like a rack of pins, then he would find out exactly what evil Pepe was killed in the name of. Then the war would make sense. If it didn't, then at least his corner of it would be clean and safe.

After a while he found himself back at the side road near la Plaza where the first tavern was, and it was still open. He steered clear and waited for his cab on the other side of the street. It started to rain, cold and thick. He didn't want to start walking again at night in this old city without a single right angle on its map. He hoped his cab was still circling. He sat on a doorstep under an awning and dozed for half an hour, during which time someone took off with his brandy. He was awoken by the smiling cabbie.

"*Gracias*. Name? *Nombre*," Hemingway said, groggily getting into the cab.

"Ah, Antonio."

"*Gracias,* Antonio." He handed him a wad of bills. "*Vamos a* . . . Madrid." Antonio made a surprised face, counted the money, asked for more with his fingertips, and then slammed the Chrysler into drive.

Hemingway looked at his watch—it was broken, the face was busted in. A gift from Pauline. He took it off and left it on the floor of the car. It must've been nine or so. They'd be in Madrid by breakfast if the cabbie drove like the dickens. Hemingway tried to remember if he'd eaten anything that day after leaving the hotel, and realized he hadn't.

He slept for an hour or more, dreaming of rats in cages as the night passed them outside, when the cabbie said one English word that woke him up and sat him up straight: "Followed."

Hemingway then slouched, seeing the light of headlights blare through the back window into the cab, mottled by the rain. He turned and could only squint. Close.

"How long, Antonio—*cuánto tiempo?*"

"*Tres, quatro minutos, supongo.*"

"Antonio, could be danger, *quizás . . . peligroso.*"

"*Peligroso!*" The young cabbie did not seem upset. "*Fascisti?*"

"No, *Rusos . . .* Probably not Russians, but thugs. *Asesinos.*"

The cabbie chortled to himself; he didn't need to know more. The rain was getting torrential, and the road ahead of him was more or less straight, but only packed dirt, northwest of Requena to the south of the mountains. Any moment, Hemingway thought, the mud will be an issue. It was a rough ride as it was, but the road to at least Utiel had seen some shelling and troops in the last year, and potholes were everywhere, filling with water. The cabbie pressed on the gas, trying, what?, to outrun the other car on a straightaway, or somehow outdrive it with nowhere else to go but forward?

Hemingway was getting gravely anxious again—this was the dark soul of a war zone, when anyone at all could end up in a shadowed ditch and no one would know about it for days, or longer. That was why foreign journalists stayed in their hotels. Certainly being famous and wealthy wouldn't matter. He checked Oak's gun and opened it: four bullets.

"Antonio, anything, what is it, *beber?*"

Antonio dug around in the front seat, passed back a flask. It tasted like kerosene.

The cabbie accelerated. Hemingway could hear the turbo whine build, and the headlights behind them began to recede. Every time the car hit and splashed through a deep shell pit in the road, Hemingway would be hurtled up to the ceiling and fall back down like a knot of popcorn, and the bolts and welds holding the vehicle together would cry out suddenly with the stress.

They hurtled, and within moments the car following them

was hurtling, too, getting hair-raisingly close to the back bumper, the light filling the cab, and Hemingway glanced over Antonio's shoulder at the speedometer, which read zero. Broken.

Hemingway estimated they were hitting seventy miles per hour, but it could've been a fifty that felt like seventy in an old car on a rotten road in the rain. Didn't matter: the Chrysler sounded as if it would've shattered like a ceramic if it hit anything bigger than a maple stump.

They raced for the better part of fifteen minutes this way, eating up miles, the two rickety vehicles roaring and throwing mud, the downpour reducing visibility to a ridiculous quantum.

Hemingway didn't hear the gunshot, but he heard the back window shatter and saw ahead the hole and spidering cracks appear in the windshield. He slumped down out of view. Just let me grow old, he thought. I know sometimes I waste my days, and think about cutting it short, it's hard to help sometimes, but God Almighty not this way, this is asinine, in this desolate, idiotic country, with these huge corrupt governments just chewing people up like horse meat for dog food. Old age wouldn't be bad. Even if I stopped writing. Even if I got fat.

He realized he was praying. Antonio was hunched down, focused on the road. The car roared and shuddered around them.

Hemingway took the pistol out with the idea of shooting back through the hole in the window, like Jimmy Cagney in a movie, but realized he'd hit nothing, probably, and he'd waste the bullets. He could get more in Madrid, but who knew whether he'd need them before they got to the city, it was a long journey and a long night.

A second shot, and the back window fell apart like thin ice. Now the sound of the second car and the rain outside joined the cacophony, and icy spray from the car found its way inside.

Hemingway could only see a sliver above the front seat, ahead to the road. The pits in the road so far were mild and Antonio hardly tried to evade them, but then there loomed a dark hole ahead of them three feet wide that didn't seem to have a bottom, just blackness, and there was barely a second and a half to react. Antonio sped right at it. Gripping the seats with locked arms, "No no no—" Hemingway began to say, feeling his empty stomach rise up his throat, but then Antonio turned a little at the last minute, riding the edge of the soggy ditch on his skinny wheels and laughing.

The car behind them, going perhaps fifty or more, tried in a panic to mimic Antonio's driving, but one wheel dipped into the ditch and the axle snapped with a piercing clank. The left front wheel flew off and the front grill went down into the ditch with a wet smash, and the back of the car—which Hemingway could make out now through the back window was a Ford V-8—arced upward into the air, somersaulting, and turned completely over, smacking down on the far side of the ditch on its roof, wheels spinning.

Antonio had already braked, skidding, and looked back, Hemingway tossed to the floor.

"Holy Toledo," Hemingway grunted.

"*Dispare mi coche!*" Antonio hissed, still excited but fiery now, grabbing an old pistol out from under his seat and running from the car.

"Wait a minute!" Hemingway kicked the door open and hustled behind Antonio toward the ruined Ford, its wheels slowing. "*¡Espere!*"

Antonio didn't seem to hear. Already saturated with rain, he jumped into a crouch behind the upside-down Ford and pulled out a body from the driver seat, dragging him over to where the Ford's headlights still lit up the road.

Hemingway saw that the man, a slim balding man of perhaps thirty, was already dead, his throat ripped open by windshield glass or frame. Antonio knew it, too, and ran already to the other side to pull another man out. Hemingway stepped over in the rain and saw that this man was D'Armoux. There was no mistaking the bulk, the ropy arms, the boxer's profile. Antonio fished the cane out from the car, and a handgun.

"*Lo conoces?*" Antonio said, his chest heaving. "You know?"

"Yes," Hemingway said.

D'Armoux just moaned, but his eyes were open. Hemingway hoped he wouldn't start talking.

"*Por que?*" Antonio asked, "*Quiere asesinar a usted?*"

Hemingway didn't understand exactly, but he understood well enough. "It was his job. *Su trabajo.*"

Antonio shook his head—*crazy foreigners*—directed his pistol muzzle dead at D'Armoux's nose, and shot him. His face burst into a mess, but in the darkness and rain, as Hemingway averted his eyes, it looked like just more mud.

# 19

The Chrysler arrived at the Hotel Florida in Madrid at 10:30 AM, but Hemingway didn't look at the time. He'd woken up after a four-hour snooze, paid the disarmingly calm Antonio twice what he'd earned, and thought only of barreling up to 108, plundering the pantry, opening a good bottle of cognac, and lying down again. He'd watched two men die in the space of just a few hours, and his back hurt from being curled up too long on the cab's backseat. He'd just begun to realize how close he was himself to being responsible for D'Armoux's death. He pulled no trigger, but that man ended there in the rain because of him. It was that fucker's choice, and he was a mercenary, bloodthirsty prick, but so. Hemingway'd seen men die, but had never had an active role in a death before, a marble-hearted snuffing out, killing a wounded, unarmed man and then leaving the corpse behind. The inside of his heart was a slightly different country now, cloudier, brutalized by midnights and less beguiled by mornings. Did the shitheel deserve it? Yes. Did that matter? Not yet. Maybe not ever.

As it happened the hotel lobby would not, as he should've guessed, let him breeze by. First, Virginia Cowles accosted him, surrounded with her own luggage, her makeup precision-perfect.

"Ernest! Where in the name of Christ have you been? Sidney's been pacing like a lost dog. He thought you'd gotten killed. What's with your head?"

"In Valencia. Business."

"I'll bet. With Dos?"

"Virginia, I'm very tired."

"Well, hotshot, I'm going home, got a book deal with Harper's, had enough of this asylum, you can tell me the story when you get back to the States, which I'd love for you to do, it's been a bit dull around here without you. Did you find Robles's killer? That's what you've been doing, yes?"

"Christ, Virginia. Yes and no." He stood with his shoulders slouching.

"Alright, Sherlock, go and get your friggin' drink."

"OK . . . Hey, Virginia, can I ask, have you seen an obstetrician since you've been here?"

"God, no, do I look like an idiot?"

Hemingway promised to keep in touch went to the main desk for his key, and the elderly clerk passed on a stack of cables. NANA, Pauline, Max Perkins, Pauline again, the Consulate, NANA again, *Esquire,* and Martha. It read: "Having fine time in London stop. Met E. M. Forster at party, very ugly stop. Would like to return to Madrid if you're done being asshole stop. Love Martha." It was dated April 17, three days earlier. Shit, he realized, she's probably been thinking I've just spent the time rolling around with the upstairs whores, not even bothering to respond.

He asked the clerk to send a cable back, but then had to take a minute to compose it when all he wanted was to rest and drink. He handed the notepad to the clerk—"Just got back from Valencia, battling forces of evil stop. Was just going to come looking for you stop. Please come back stop. Ernest."—and then read the last cable.

From Dos.

Dated April 16, from Paris. "Robles vanished. Heard Gorev in Moscow, on trial. Ask J."

What the. Nothing like being discreet—how many Comintern eyeballs examined this note before now? Hemingway had to massage his forehead, trying to unpack the message, and got nowhere. That Dos, dribbling oblique clues from faraway, after leaving the country in a disillusioned funk. What did he know that he didn't spill before?

J.? Good Lord. Who's that supposed to be? Hemingway wished he knew more about the machinations of the government, it would certainly make piecing together the littered shards of suspicion and doubt a little easier. At the same time, he was glad he didn't know, not so much for any reason that pertained to Robles, but simply for his own peace of mind, his own vision of the world (not so fast was he willing to give up the hopes of the Communist left, even if the Soviets have so smashingly succeeded in poisoning the well), even if the previous day had given him a sharp taste of what being an amoral apparatchik might be like. Whatever—why wasn't he writing, instead of this happy horseshit, why hadn't he just stayed home in the quiet of Key West and just worked, made sentences?

It was because there were other voices that didn't tell stories and didn't make it onto the page, voices that grew deafening in solitude. And it was because he couldn't write about being a best-selling novelist living in tropical luxury. He was trapped between the need for order and time and the need for chaos. Of course neither made him happy.

Bloody fuckers, he thought, Dos and Robles and del Vayo and Worsleighson and Blair and every last one of the sensitive, watery-eyed pinko idealists who push these huge rocks over the hump and down the mountain without a single reasonable thought as to how it'll land or who it'll crush. Of course he held tight the ideas that the powerful should be taken down at the knees, and the poor should be fed and supported and not oppressed. That Fascism is a blight as surely as anything ever devised by nature or man, as surely as the Black Death or a siege of Vandals, was not open for debate. But does it have to be this way? Does it have to be such a ruinous, inhuman debacle?

Which way is that, exactly, with the fields of Europe littered with corpses as monarchs vie for territory? Why, yes, in fact, it does have to be this way, it is this way, grow up and cast a cold eye and go smell the mustard gas.

He was dog tired. He crumpled Dos's cable into his pocket and headed for his room, which he got to with being waylaid only by Sidney Franklin, who'd been sitting around the Florida for days reading newspapers and wondering where his boss had got himself to. Hemingway assured him he would explain, but later, please go and read another newspaper, he had to rest. Franklin's selfless obedience, Hemingway knew, was more a matter of wanting to be regularly paid than actual puppyish devotion, but it was touching nonetheless.

Hemingway's room was actually warm—the heat, at some point, had begun to work. In his pantry he dug out a dried Italian sausage, a box of English crackers, a jar of roasted peppers in olive oil, and a bottle of Chablis from Chassagne-Montrachet, and ate and drank on his nightstand as the midday light tumbled into the room. Soon he felt like a new man, especially by way of the wine, and resolved to not again be without some form of serious potable for at least a few days. It was his goddamn right.

He found he didn't need to nap, and he found he maybe had something to write. There was that American he'd met at the Popular Front meeting—Walker? He seemed to have promise, an American with everything to lose, fighting the war for justice's sake, high in the hills where he didn't belong, where the scattered Republican forces and village brigades were holed up, harboring ancestral grudges and bitter about the lives they'd lost and the lives they'd taken, and never quite sure to what degree they were part of an army and to what degree they were simply fighting like tribal bands, on their own.

Hemingway wrote in longhand for an hour, discarded the first five pages because the story was better begun in the middle, without exposition, and named the American and the Spaniards, supposed there had to be a cave, and figured that if the Yank was a munitions man, there had to be a bridge nearby. . . .

By noon he'd begun a book, and felt as if the world had turned itself a little right side up, finally. He opened another bottle of wine, a red Lirac, whatever that was, and set out into the corridors, first striding up the stairs to the third floor, rounding up a few of the under-worked whores for a drink, and asking them if any knew an obstetrician in the city, and after they howlingly joked about his need for one, they admitted that they did not. They knew only midwives. Then, swearing he'd return later with his money out and his pants down, he headed downstairs, poured the aged desk clerk three fingers of wine in a dirty glass he had, and asked him if the phones worked—which they did for the moment—and if he might be so kind as to call a few doctors and clinics in the city and ask if they know of an obstetrician with the first name Floripedes. Hemingway sat and drank in the lobby, reading a week-old *London Times,* had a chat with Sefton Delmer, whose dispatches, the man claimed, were being stonewalled by the *Daily Express,* and then the clerk said yes, they've located Dr. Floripedes Crespo, in a clinic over on Calle del Arenal, and would he like a cab?

He would, he said, he'd like Ignacio, the Basque in an old sedan, and the spindly limbed clerk put down the phone and stepped out the front door, whistling and pointing. In no time Ignacio was pulled up and stepped out, to open Hemingway's door.

"Señor! Good to see you," he said in Spanish, "how was Valencia?"

"Trouble, Ignacio, just trouble. I want to pay you for one day or two, maybe more—is that good?"

"Yes, sir!"

"Are you sure you know no English?"

"Not to speak, no!"

"Here, have some wine, it is French." Ignacio produced a coffee cup. Sitting in the cab, the men sipped and appreciated it. The day around them was sunny and warm, like Spain in April should be.

On Calle del Arenal, Hemingway disembarked and asked Ignacio to wait. Inside, there were only two rooms, a reception area and an examination room. Only two women waited, and the nurse at the desk simply sat and eyed him suspiciously over a magazine.

"Dr. Crespo *acqui*? Do you speak English?"

The nurse, who was maybe nineteen, looked aghast, as if Hemingway had sternly asked her if she mates with goats. She shook her head in disgust and went back to reading.

Enough of this, he thought, and walked right through the examination room's door to the alarmed keening of the nurse behind him, and confronted, in close quarters because the room was small, a hugely pregnant woman lying exposed on the table with her legs spread and hanging in stirrups, and a not-so-surprisingly elegant Dr. Crespo standing between them, her right hand deep in examination. In a second all three women were roaring at Hemingway to *salir, idiota!* and the door slammed shut.

He spent twenty minutes waiting in the chairs with the two women, one of whom fell asleep, and one of which was apparently waiting for the patient inside. He was tempted every minute or so to duck outside to Ignacio's cab and nip at the wine he'd left there. He didn't.

Floripedes Crespo came out finally, bidding the pregnant

woman *adios,* and turned to Hemingway with an intolerant frown. But he introduced himself, and established that she spoke English, and uttered the name José Robles, and then her resolve softened like butter on a windowsill.

"You are not a . . . government agent."

"I promise you, I'm not. I'm just an American. A journalist."

"No, you're not," with a small smile, "you're a novelist, I know who you are. Your books are in the windows here and in Barcelona. Or at least they were. Pepe mentioned you, whenever we were in a bookstore."

"Well, I'm not an agent for anybody, anyway. Nobody but myself."

"Alright. Who's been beating on you? You look like a boxer."

"Just everybody."

"Will you have lunch?"

"I thought you'd never ask."

She took him a few doors down to a café, which had only a goat sausage casserole and corn on the menu, but Hemingway, having eaten, ordered a bottle of local red.

"But you've already been drinking. I can tell. It's not even noon."

"Yes, well, I know, but, uh, it's OK, not your problem, anyway, enough about me, tell me, how tough is it to keep your practice up during the war?" The damn woman had his tongue in knots. She was beautiful and smart and also possessed Robles's air of unwavering rectitude. She was intimidating, goddammit. Jesus, didn't these people do anything *wrong*? Well, yes, they did— they had infidelities. That, at least.

"I do fine, women are still getting pregnant. There's plenty of call for a general practitioner, too."

"Of course. Are you married?"

"No. Why do you ask."

"Uh, just filling in the picture. I understand you were Pepe's mistress."

She gave him a long, boiling look.

"I don't like to be referred to in this way."

"I'm sorry. You tell me how it should be said."

"I was Pepe's friend. That's all. A comrade. I did not wait for him to divorce his wife and leave his children and save me from spinsterhood. I did not look to marry him. I didn't put demands on him. Neither was I a game he played. Want to know how to say it? We were orphans in a storm, and we held each other up."

"I see. Thank you." The wine came, and Hemingway felt self-conscious, forecasting her disapproval, but he downed a full glass in a flash.

"You drink too much."

"Too much for you, perhaps. Please, I have a wife."

"So I understand."

"So, you and Pepe."

"Well, it's over now, isn't it. What are you looking for, Señor Hemingway?"

"Ernest, please. I'm looking for his murderer."

Dr. Crespo looked down into her lap and drew a large breath. She was a tough woman, like all of the women he'd met in Spain, but Hemingway sensed he was soon going to find out how tough.

"I see. Have you found him?"

"I saw his body. In the Sierra de Gudárs. But it's disappeared. Disposed of. How much do you want to hear?"

"I don't want to hear any of it. But I suppose you'll tell me. I still don't know what you want of me. How did you find out about Pepe and I?"

"An American Brigadesman mentioned you, in Valencia."

"Oh. Daniel."

"That's him."

"So . . . I don't understand."

"Please relax. I'll give you a thumbnail. Pepe's wife told me that the body went missing, my friend John Dos Passos returned to retrieve it and it was gone. No death certificate, nothing. Now, I've been on some kind of dumb-fuck crusade, I don't mind saying so, and I've seen two men die in the last twenty-four hours, one with a bullet to the head. I have every reason to assume that the man who caught that bullet, a French hatchet man and cutpurse I knew from years back, and who worked here in Madrid for the Front, disposed of the . . . body. But he's gone now. Someone else, probably, will be following me soon enough, after the word gets out that I'm back in Madrid."

"Gets out to whom?"

"That's just it. I'm talking about the Popular Front. The Frenchman was an *asistente adjunto,* he told me, to the government."

"You spoke with him?"

"Yes . . . my God, it was only yesterday. At a rally."

"Huh. Have you slept?"

"Yes. The Fascists, as far as I can tell, have nothing to do with any of this. This is just the Soviet-style bullshit coming to roost in Spain. I hope you're not one of those lingering idealists who are happy with the way the Comintern have been shaping this revolution."

"I'm not happy, no. I'm a doctor."

"Yes. So, in Valencia, I found the goons that arrested Pepe."

"You did?"

"Two of them, anyway, and one of them was there for certain in the foothills where Pepe was shot. He's dead now, too."

"You killed him."

"No. I was going to, I was standing right there and ready. But he just died."

She took some wine and drank it.

"So, now you're looking for what?"

"Well, those idiots in Valencia, they were just hired thugs, they're not even Communists. They're just petty crooks, gypsies. They didn't even know, I'll bet, who Pepe was or why he was being taken out. I'm looking for who hired them. Know what I mean? Those guys were the soldiers, like the Italians in the CTV, they're not Mussolini. I've got nothing against the Italians, even if they're in the army just for pay, like those Valencia piglets. But Mussolini I'd put down. I want the Mussolini. I want the scumbag who gave the orders. And I know he's in Madrid. The dead man told me so."

She nodded slowly and ate.

"I don't know how I can help," she said resignedly, as if she'd already come to wish the conversation hadn't begun. He was not sure she believed a word of it. She was stern and cagey; he'd met the type of woman before, as unreadable as lizards in the sun.

"I don't know either, I just figured since you represented . . . let's say a secret part of Pepe's life, I figured there might be something you remember, something Pepe mentioned that he might not have broadcast everywhere else . . . that might give me a direction to go in." Let's not tell her about the Bentley, he thought. It's probably simply parked somewhere, waiting for the moronic *quinquilleros* to come and claim it. How am I going to find it? Even if I somehow did, and manage to pin it to some Front string-puller, what's to be done about it then? What questions will go unanswered?

Did the car's owner have the slightest clue why the car hadn't been picked up yet? Did he care? Maybe there is no car, and the gyppos in Valencia were set up, just like Pepe. That'd be just fucking great.

"Ernest? Do you really think I'm going to take you to bed, just like that?" She wasn't smiling.

"What?"

"You've come to see me, a woman you know had a clandestine relationship with a married man, a man you know is now dead. You don't have a plan, or even a straight question to ask me. So you have obviously decided that I'm probably a pushover."

"What? Listen, doc, I don't lack for women to fill my bed

here or in America, and if I did there're no shortage of whores upstairs in the Hotel Florida. I didn't have to be nosing around a city under siege looking for a strange woman with a history of married men, just to get laid."

"Have you gone to the whores?"

"That's kinda personal."

"Excuse me?"

"OK. Yes, I have, a few times. I've been here for over a month, away from my wife."

"Well, a month, oh, dear, that is a long time."

"Fine."

"Your second wife."

"Yes, in fact, we're all allowed a few, aren't we?"

"Oh, sure. Why not? My sense of it is this, simply, Ernest, that you use women, as subjects, as vaginas, as mother surrogates, as decoration. I don't think you can even help yourself. You see a woman with some kind of perceived vulnerability, you lunge. I'd like to know, if you'd found out that Pepe had, oh I don't know, a male lover in Madrid, would you have scampered over to him so attentively, with such vague questions."

"Jesus. I don't know. Honestly? Maybe not, because I don't know how to talk to . . . them. Homosexuals. I haven't had a lot of practice. Women, though, I know. I'm sorry if my questions are too vague for you, but they're all I've got, and if you don't want to entertain them any longer, if I'm bugging you, I'll hit the bricks and leave you to your uteruses."

"Uteri."

"Really."

"You're not bugging me." She poured another glass of wine, and cracked her spine with a loose wiggle that made Heming-way suck in air. "I'm just trying to be honest. You see, I've read your book, the stories, *Hombres sin Mujeres*? Even the title. You feel threatened by women like me. You must hate your mother. Do you hate your mother?"

He summed her up: The doctor was beginning to warm, drinking more freely, and she clearly enjoyed lording it over a strong man, perhaps not an entertainment she got to indulge in too frequently. So, let her lord. Hemingway lowered his eyes just a little, like a shamed schoolboy, and he decided he'd be honest, too, and open the fire hose.

"Yes, actually. I do hate my mother. Lots of writers act as if they do, and then weep at the funeral. I won't, when she goes. I'll dance a chaconne at the graveside, with my pants around my knees. Except I won't bother going; I'll throw a party instead, wherever I am. That everlasting bitch cut away at my father like a termite eats at timber, and she tried to do the same thing to me, tried to get me to tow that Congregational bullshit, wouldn't for a single minute let me be myself. Even after I came back from the war with a wound and a medal I was still a teenage heathen and a libertine in her eyes, because I liked jazz and novels and girls. I was twenty-one, and she kicked me out into the street—and I was still on crutches. My brother and sisters weren't on her target, just me, and I'll never forgive that almighty, malevolent harridan for the claw marks she left on my life, like *big fucking bear-claw* wounds. Because I know what you're thinking and you're right, I do not entirely trust women and yet I need them; I'm wary of their efforts to control me and yet I seek them out; I hate my mother and I long for the woman she never was for me. Sure, I'm a man who sees things from a fiercely masculine perspective because I cannot, and will not ever try, to see things from hers. So, Mrs. Freud, so what? You think I don't know these things? You think it matters? It doesn't matter. The world still needs men, doctor, men who aren't womanly or weak or pliable or always looking for 'understanding' or 'sensitivity,' but men who do the world's rough work, who seek out the truth, who live their lives like they have only one risky bet to make with their very beings and they dare to make it. I love women, Dr. Crespo, but I'm a man, I love women because I'm not one of them and they're not anything like me, and secretly I know you're thankful I do. Go ahead and be prickly about it but you are thankful that there are men in the world and not just a lot of women. You'd be thankful for that if I were to enter your home, or lie between your legs and whisper in your ear in the dark, my hands holding yours. I think you're grateful right now, because no woman would talk to you this way. No woman would pit their will against yours to your face, and still fall to their knees in awe of your womanhood. But a man might. A real man."

# 20

The love they made in Floripedes Crespo's expansive apartment on a narrow side street memorably named Calle de Nostradamos, after he'd waited for her final afternoon appointment to open and close, so to speak, and after she'd brought him home under an array of pretexts (photos of Robles, discussion of Austen, a faucet leak), and after they'd finished off a tin of smoked oysters she'd been saving and a fresh bottle of wine, was brutish and long; she echoed up a deep loneliness, and he responded in kind. She was the most orgasmic woman he'd ever known—she spent some time in foreplay simply grinding her crotch against his naked thigh, and came three times that way alone. Fingering was another half dozen, cunnilingus another score, and after he sank into her and they rutted for three-quarters-of-an-hour without even a break for water, the number of orgasms, she said immediately afterward, had passed forty. Hemingway had only one, unsurprisingly. But that was fine, coming was never his favorite part of sex anyway; it was the travel, the distance from here to there. Ultimate satisfaction per se, lasting as it did a mere moment, held little allure, and so of course he envied the good doctor's inexhaustible ability to come again and again, to explode and lose herself indefinitely, which looked a lot like the perfect life, no matter how you shake it. If that were me, he thought, I'd never get anything done.

He had wanted to fuck her, no question, the moment she got indignant about being called a "mistress," but he also knew he had to get into her home, where Pepe would've known her. He knew she was hiding something—too much foofaraw about Hemingway's agenda being "vague," almost flat-out saying that there was in fact something to be unvague about. Whatever it was.

As soon as she was snoozing, Hemingway crawled out of her bed, naked, and began searching the flat. It wasn't large—two bedrooms, a living room and kitchen, in a building that was probably a century old—and Hemingway had to tiptoe around, silently looking through kitchen drawers and rifling through her desk in one bedroom, and trying as he might to dig into her hall closets without making any noise.

It didn't work after only a few minutes, Hemingway on his knees with his bare rump in the air, Crespo appeared in her bedroom doorway, naked and standing like an Amazon with her hands on her hips.

"What the hell are you looking for, you nosy American?" Her voice was chilly, and iced by a hangover headache.

He shot to his feet. "Uh, sorry Floripedes, but . . . Alright, I'll be straight with you"—the two of them stood almost toe to toe—"I'm pretty sure you've got something here of Pepe's, a file or cache or something, and I don't know if it's what I need, but I know you're hiding it, and so whatever reason you think you have to hide it, I want to see it."

"The what? What? I didn't understand a word of that. Are you delusional? Am I supposed to know what you mean?"

"You know."

"I do? Get dressed and get out, you crazy ape, before I call the police."

"If you can find one! Your phone works? I know the chief of

police, sweetheart, drank his champagne, and I can tell you he doesn't give a shit. Now I'm going to tell you what I'm going to do, I'm going to search your apartment, and if I make a mess, I'm fucking sorry, but I've come too far by now. Do you hear me, Floripedes? I've come too far. Now go make coffee."

"Eat shit, Yankee," she said, striding back into the bedroom and coming right back out with a desk lamp, hurling it at Hemingway—he ducked, and the lamp smashed against the front door.

*"Jesus!"*

"Get out!"

"I wasn't going to bust up your furniture or anything—" And Floripedes found golf clubs and grabbed one. Hemingway had to rush her, anchor her raised arm against the wall, and grab her throat with his right hand, squeezing enough to make her cheeks red and her mouth gasp open.

"Floripedes," is all Hemingway said, shook the club free, and shoved her into the bedroom. She flopped on the bed heaving with bitter sobs.

He returned to the closet, fearing that he'd crossed the line and hurt this woman for what might end up being next to nothing. Still naked as a bushman, he hit all of the closets: shoes, clothes, suitcases, shoes, shoeboxes of birthday and Christmas cards, gramophone records, cardboard boxes of Christmas ornaments, shoes. Crespo fumed around in the other rooms, and when he came into the bedroom, beelining for the closet, she threw herself on him again, her large breasts moving wildly on their own, he threw her off and opened the door. The closet didn't have much room for shoes or anything else because the floor of it was stacked two feet high, to the back wall, with cases of white medical packages, all of them identical Eli Lilly boxes. He picked one up.

*"Mierda,"* Crespo muttered on the bed.

*"Morfina.* Morphine? Floripedes, morphine? Where'd you get

all this? What's this for?" It took him a few moments. "You're not a doper . . . There must be three hundred boxes in here. Christ, you sell this stuff?"

Crespo was on her back, braced up on her elbows. Her breasts hung low on her ribs, her belly slowly heaved a little, and she spread her legs even wider than they were, her vagina and its black hair still visibly moist. He could still smell her. She sighed in resignation.

"Yes. I sell it. To *adictos*. You think my patients, these pregnant women in a city of no men, you think they can pay me?"

"I could have you locked up—"

"Please, Hemingway, who'd care—"

"Doctor, I'm telling you, I can have them come for you by nightfall, a licensed doctor selling narcotics in the new Republic! You doubt me?"

"You care so much about Spanish junkies, wealthy American writer?"

"Not terribly. But I could make it happen. Unless you give me what you're hiding."

She got off the bed and threw on a silk robe and headed toward her front door, grabbing keys. Hemingway followed, yanking on his boxers.

"I can't imagine Pepe knew about this, selling dope," he said as they walked the hallway.

"No, of course not. But some of the money has gone to medical supplies and arms for the Brigades, all the same."

"The Russians catch wind, you're a dead woman."

"I know."

She unlocked another apartment door, turned on the light. Inside it was uninhabited, dusty, sheets over the chairs, boxes stacked high.

"This is my real apartment, where Pepe and I used to meet. I closed it up."

"When did you see him last?"

"In January."

"He was in Madrid in February."

"Perhaps. He didn't see me."

From the hall closet she dragged a lidded box of files.

"That's it. It's government documents. Nothing controversial as far as I could tell, but Pepe wanted them put aside and forgotten. For posterity maybe. He did not want me to admit to anyone that I had any government papers, no matter what they said. Not even a memo on the weather."

"But why? Are they classified?"

"Classified? Don't think so—I read some of them, and they bored me to death. No purge trial lists or anything."

Back in the first flat, Crespo made coffee. Hemingway lifted the box onto the table and began to skim through the papers. He asked for a drink, any drink at all, and got a glass of musty icebox wine.

He could only catch occasional Spanish words, no more than he could in conversation, but it seemed that she was right: The papers, hundreds of them, were copies of routine communiqués, meeting memos, requests for transfer, admonitions from the Comintern in matters of legislature, requests for information, and reports on Comrade Stalin's moods, meals, and support. Hemingway could see by the reference initials that many of the papers were in fact the Spanish translations Robles had made himself from Russian originals, some of which were also shuffled into the mix, unreadable. Others were from the Largo offices, to Moscow. Gorev's name came up a good deal, but not in ways that suggested trouble.

It was getting dark.

Hemingway saw nothing, not a single incendiary secret or criminal plan worth keeping secret. Not even a single execution order, or tactical strategy for military defense. Did Gorev deliberately keep Robles strictly to the innocuous bureaucracy of running government? Or was much of his operation undocumented, or kept secret from Moscow? Hemingway didn't know and didn't want to find out. He felt like Dante, not at all interested in the presumably monstrous machinations that went into running the seven circles of Hell, and very glad he was no resident but a tourist, just passing through.

Only one aspect of the box of papers hit Hemingway in the eye, and it was the third time that week: Juan Posada. Handfuls of memos and itineraries were addressed from Posada's *oficina de seguridad* on Calle de las Huertas. Apparently Robles commuted between the offices, and translated for both. Hemingway wouldn't have thought twice about it except for D'Armoux's boasting admission to being employed by Posada, which all by itself, given the nature of D'Armoux's skills, put Posada in a different category than Hemingway had previously thought to put him, far from the mere "police chief" and political counter-jumper he used to be, and closer to an authentic power broker and, quite probably, a man with blood on his hands. But since when would that unlikely tapeworm be commissioning illegal assassinations, and for what reason? Did D'Armoux have express orders from Posada to kill Hemingway on the road from Valencia? Or was the Frenchman crossing his own *t*'s, an overenthusiastic maniac doing Stalin's business as he saw it?

And now, to find out that Robles also worked for Posada—and therefore may've had reason to confront something he shouldn't have, read something he shouldn't have, overhear a conference dangerously beyond his pay grade. Hemingway didn't know what Robles's security level had been, but given his earnest, unpolluted Communist idealism, it'd make sense to assume it wasn't terribly high. Robles wouldn't have been able to assimilate the homicidal shadow actions and self-serving manipulations of the Comintern with his sense of revolutionary hope, just as Dos couldn't seem to. The landscape was filled with Marx-quoting dreamers, homegrown and imported, so smitten with the Communist dream they managed to overlook a startling amount of savagery and convince themselves that the little they did allow themselves to see was all for the good of the revolution. As far as Hemingway knew, Robles died believing in the veracity of the Moscow Trials, no mean feat of cognitive dissonance.

But Robles must've come up against something he couldn't swallow. It's that simple. Something he had to be killed for, far away from Madrid, in the night, by strangers who barely spoke Spanish. Disposed of like a shotgunned coyote, or a Berlin schoolteacher.

It was Posada.

He had to see the shitheel. But if Posada was in fact the one— the head honcho who said alright, let's pay the peons to take José Robles out to the foothills and shoot his goddamn brains out, and if those punks don't take the Republic's new currency then give them a car, any car, the Bentley—if Posada was this man, then he also had had Hemingway followed, beaten, and shot at. He would already know that evening that Hemingway made it back to Madrid unscathed, and that D'Armoux, his *asistente adjunto,* was at least missing on the roads of Cuenca. He would not be delighted if Hemingway simply showed up smiling on Calle de las Huertas and asked for a meeting. No, he wouldn't like that at all. Another Leftist intellectual to fuck things up for me, he'd think. Another to take down, somehow—but how? He's Ernest fucking Hemingway! The man would be scared of being exposed, of Hemingway knowing what Robles knew. He would have the look of a cornered fox.

That would wait until tomorrow, Hemingway knew. Floripedes Crespo made some kind of dinner out of leftovers, chicken, and he asked if he could stay in her bed for the night, and she said *ciertamente.*

# 21

The next day did not go as Hemingway had planned, or half planned, because he met a man named George Mink.

He didn't merely meet him. In the morning, bidding Dr. Crespo *adios* and resolving to do what he could to never see her again, Hemingway cabbed it back to the Hotel Florida for a change of clothes. Walking into 108, Hemingway noticed immediately a vague sense of disruption. The bed was made, and the curtains were half open as he'd left them but . . . a little *too* half open? He shot immediately to his larder, opened the doors—items had been taken, packages of dried foodstuff, no wine. He started scoping the room, thinking someone had probably planted a dictograph somewhere. Was it too late for that, though?

It was. The bathroom door flew open and three black-coated, black fedoraed men filed out—"What the fuck! Get out," he blurted—but they came right at him, two of them holding the food they'd grabbed from the closet, and grabbed his arms and he saw that one, bald under his hat and with gray eyes, had a gun in his hand and the hammer was back.

"*Vamos,*" this man said, and Hemingway shrugged inside, letting them take him. No fighting. I'll flirt with death, he reasoned, like the slut bitch she is, but I won't marry her. It's about time, actually, that the Front came out of the shadows and talked to my face.

Back downstairs, outside the Florida, inside a huge black Rolls.

But he wasn't headed toward the station office on Calle de las Huertas; they headed northeast, back to the neighborhood he'd enjoyed, so many weeks earlier, from inside an oil drum pummeled by a dying bull. But before the streets became familiar Hemingway was blindfolded, with a shove and a yank, careless of his fading head bandage. He sat between two of the long coats in the backseat, his hands folded in his lap.

Walking in, the blindfold came off, and he was led up the stairs.

"Mr. Hemingway, delighted to meet you," said the wide man in an empty third-floor flat, in a building the unblindfolded Hemingway assumed would be condemned if anyone bothered to inspect it. Falling plaster, broken windows. Not a hopeful sign. "I'm George Mink."

He was tall, and had thin hair and eyes set so deeply you couldn't make out their color. Hemingway had heard of Mink— both Josie Herbst and Herbert Southworth of *The Washington Post* had known him in Socialist circles in New York, and had run into him, and interviewed him, in Spain. Josie said he was an oily liar, and Henry said he was an outright sociopath; both suggested that he should be avoided like a leper. Southworth repeated a rumor, that in the United States Mink was a freelance yegg and liquidator for the War Department, with a history in the Philippines, and in Spain he was a gun for the Front. His name isn't really Mink, Josie had added, and he's not really American.

He was a menace, that was clear to the eye, Hemingway thought. He was still, like a snake on a branch.

"I hope you've heard of me," he continued. Hemingway couldn't think of anything to say that was both defiant and less than suicidal, so he said nothing. The man's accent was too flat to read, deliberately drained of particularity.

The room was empty of furniture except a few wooden dinner chairs and an old desk in the corner. Beside one chair sat a large, gray, weathered Ford car battery, with unattached alligator cables curled on the floor.

Hemingway made a deduction that he hoped wasn't wrong: that they intended only to scare him, and had no orders to execute.

"Yeah, Mink, I've heard of you, I've heard you tinker with this Soviet torture bullshit. I can tell right here in this room, this is what you live for. This is your vocation. It's nice when a man can do what he loves. Well, boy, I'm very frightened, like a little schoolgirl."

Mink hitched his chin up and two of his goons grabbed Hemingway by the arms. Because he'd been cooperative and passive so far, they didn't grab very hard, and Hemingway immediately yanked free, cocked his fist up turning and punched one man at his side straight in the ear with a swinging force that began at Hemingway's waist and that threw him off balance. The man's neck jacked at an angle and he fell to the left, hitting the right side of his skull against a chair seat going down, and did not get up.

The other two men leapt on Hemingway. Mink stood still. Hemingway ignored the man at his back and crouched down in a linebacker's crouch and rushed the man at his right, shouldering him in the gut, lifting him off the floor and crashing him into the wall over the old oak desk. Then, still holding the thug around the waist, Hemingway stepped back, dragging him forward, and then fell on him with all his weight, so the man's head would hit the desk going down. It did, like a coconut pitched at the side of a barn.

The third man behind Hemingway had by this time, two seconds or so into it, produced a police billy and in full swing hit Hemingway in the back of the head once, twice. Hemingway dropped to his knees.

"You're a tumult, Mr. Hemingway," Mink said with a smirk in his voice, as the club wielder and the second man, his steps unsteady, dragged Hemingway to the chair by the battery. The first man lay unconscious, bleeding from his ears.

Hemingway was handcuffed to the chair. The man with the billy went down on one knee and undid Hemingway's belt. "Not even a cocktail first?" Hemingway said groggily, but said it just as he shot his knee up into the man's chin, knocking him back, the chair almost tipping over the other way. This time Mink, to his side and behind him a bit, hit him right on his old bandage with something wooden, tearing it off, and Hemingway's eyesight got fuzzy.

"Cuff his ankles." The man was able to do it before Hemingway's faculties inched back into play. He could feel blood running down his face.

Then Hemingway's pants and boxers were pulled down, and his knees spread. Mink had the alligator clips. He attached one to the back of Hemingway's left ankle, and the other to the soft skin of his scrotum, which Mink grabbed and tugged up like it was the corner of a rug.

"Ow, fucker," Hemingway muttered, his ears ringing, his head pounding. Mink locked a clip onto a battery terminal.

"OK, Hemingway, I'll tell you what," Mink said, standing up with the last clip to the wires in his hand, "I've spent a good deal of time in Moscow, I've met Joseph Stalin, I've been trained by the most merciless motherfuckers on this planet. You wouldn't believe what I've seen those bastards do—things *I* couldn't do if my mother's life depended on it. Me, though, I don't have a taste for human blood, but I don't care about it, either. If it runs, it's like rainwater on a window to me. I can get any tough son of a bitch to tell me anything I want him to. I can make anyone, men who could eat glass and kill horses with their bare hands, I can make them confess to complete nonsense. But I'm not here to get information out of you—we know everything. And I'm not here to make you confess to something, because there's nothing the Popular Front needs from you right now. We have plenty of Trotskyite weasels to hang up in public, and at the moment it's been decided that we're just keeping a lot of stuff under the radar, if you know what I mean. For the good of the people. You and I, we never met, and never saw this room. What I am here to do is to ask you, the nicest way I know how, to go back to Key West. Leave the country. Pretty please. This is me asking nicely, not telling, but asking. On bended knee."

And he snapped the open clip onto the other battery terminal.

"*ACH!*" Hemingway spat, and winced and thrashed, almost knocking over the chair. "*Fuck,* that hurts!" This he said rather matter of factly, calming. His eyes were tearing but he was able to catch his breath. It didn't hurt, in fact, nearly as much as he thought it would.

What the. Then it didn't hurt at all.

Mink sputtered. "Come now, a fucking writer?" He roughly ungripped the clips from Hemingway, quickly scratching Hemingway's scrotum—which hurt more than the electrical charge—and stood and touched them together. There was a faint buzz and a tiny spark. Then nothing.

"Fucking God!" he cried. "You imbeciles! Is this battery dead?!" The other men shrugged. "C'mere!" Mink roared. The lackey with the bump on the back of his head came over and Mink, holding both clips in one hand, grabbed him by his hair and attached one clip to his left ear, then the other to the right. "Owww!" the man whined, and then nothing. Mink slapped him, kicking the battery.

"Always bring a backup," Hemingway said, his eyes clear now.

"Oh, shut the fuck up you goddamn stinkard." *So, he's British,* Hemingway thought.

"You could go out and steal one."

"Ah, very good; Emiliano, go get the battery out of the Rolls."

"Uh, Christ. I was kidding, Mink. . . . You could call it a day."

"Oh, no, wouldn't think of it." Hemingway's pants were still down, his genitals swelling with the adrenaline and the residue of electrical charge.

"You can't kill me."

"I'm not going to kill you. I'm just going to hurt you."

"Why? Hurt goes away. It heals."

"Not in the mind it doesn't. When I'm through you'll hide under your mother's bed whenever anyone even says the word 'Madrid.'"

"You don't know my mother."

When the man with the billy came back upstairs, the conversation was entirely in screaming Spanish, but Hemingway gleaned that it began with something about the battery being bolted to the chassis and they'd need a wrench, *una llave,* and Mink yelling why don't they have *una llave,* and Emiliano the flunky yelling back why in living hell would they carry a set of *llaves* around with them on government business, and suggesting they could go knock on doors to borrow *una llave,* and Mink, half laughing like a mental patient, howling about how fucking stupid Emiliano was, we can't go around the city borrowing tools so we can remove a battery from our car in order to torture a famous American journalist we have handcuffed to a chair in an abandoned building. Mink took the billy from the other man, threatened to hit him once, with a jerk, and then turned and walloped Hemingway over the head, knocking him out good.

Hemingway dreamed. Hadley, the Alps, picnics, mountain café keepers with huge white mustaches, feeding Bumby bits of goat cheese. God that baby was cute, the Hemingway in the dream thought, remembering the scenario even as he stood in it, smelling the breeze off the Swiss hills.

When he awoke in the abandoned building, he was alone. The battery was still there, but the cables were gone. There were dried drops of blood on the floor where the first of the three punks had lain unconscious. He had no headache, strangely, but his head and face were crusty with blood, and his shirt spotted with stains.

The Front has a fart's chance in a hurricane of winning, he thought, if they can't even scare foreign journalists and torture dissidents properly.

It took him a half hour, but Hemingway managed to snap the oak spindles from the back of the chair that held him with the handcuffs and then to scoot his chained hands under his butt and over his curled legs. Then he stood, pulled his pants up, and refastened his belt.

On the street, *los Madrileños* eyed Hemingway, bloody and shuffling in two sets of handcuffs, as they might an escaped circus elephant lazily walking down the street. A few blocks away Hemingway had a stroke of luck, his first in a while: a blacksmithing shop. The owner inside was a gray-haired Corsican with forearms the size of maple trunks. Hemingway paid him several bills out of his pocket, and with a three-pound chisel sharp enough to cut skin the smith hammered through first the two chains and then, on the corner of an anvil, each of the steel cuffs. Then he wiped Hemingway down and rebandaged his head with real Red Cross gauze and strips of linen. They shared a homemade belt of brandy there in the iron dust and soot, after the sympathetic smith gave back the money, and Hemingway would later remember this moment of brotherliness and relief as his happiest moment in Spain.

# 22

Ignacio had lost track of Hemingway after he saw the American walking to lunch with the woman doctor the day before, and so today, April 21, 1937, Hemingway walked back south to the Hotel Florida alone, a stroll that took him a few hours because he kept stopping at any bar that had a sign and ordered a cocktail. It was rum if they had rum, gin if they didn't, and whiskey if all else failed. He always asked for fruit juice, knowing he needed vitamins, and sometimes got it.

When he reached the hotel, Hemingway found Ignacio and his cab loitering at curbside. The old Spaniard was apologetic, but Hemingway waved him off. The afternoon was waning already, and the sky over their heads was the color of salmon flesh.

"Ignacio, do you know of anyone who has a Bentley in Madrid?"

"*Un* Bentley! *Automobile, aqui?*" Shook his head grimly.

"I need a favor, *un favor,* but it could be dangerous. *Peligroso.*" The accumulation of drinks put his tongue in a straitjacket.

"*Si, señor, yo lo haré.*"

"Tomorrow, early, uh, before *el amanacer.*"

"*Si.*"

"OK, but *pronto,* I need a cop, *una policía,* who needs money. *Pobre y corruptos.*"

Ignacio's eyebrows. But after a moment the cabbie understood what Hemingway wanted despite his idiotic Spanish.

"*Un mercenario.*"

Hemingway winced, rocked a little on his feet. "Uh, well . . . *un hombre, un policia, desperado, y amoral.* A little. *Poco.* Not a criminal."

Ignacio nodded, thought, and looked up and down the street scratching his chin. "*Poco . . .*"

"And one that knows a little English, please."

"*Vamos.*"

They walked west, and turned a corner, a few blocks.

Ignacio led Hemingway into a threadbare house of flats, up the stairs to a room without a number, and knocked. A three-chinned, profoundly unkempt man in a sleeveless undershirt answered the door. The two spoke in Spanish. The fat man's eyes glanced at Hemingway, and then he shrugged, opening the door.

"You know no Spanish," he said, picking up a smoldering cigarette, gesturing that they sit down at his small kitchen table. Hemingway noted a Spanish policeman's shirt tossed on a chair back.

"No. Too little."

"OK, you're an American, you are wealthy, Ignacio says, and you want something done that is not exactly right. Legal? Legal."

Hemingway took a deep breath. "What I want is to get into the police offices, *la oficina de seguridad,* on Calle de las Huertas. Juan Posada's office."

The fat man didn't move a muscle; his half-lidded glower held like the horizon on a cold day.

"Get into."

"Yes. I need to look at files, his desk, whatever there is. But when no one is there, obviously."

"Obviously. *Por que.*"

"You don't need to know. But he did something very bad, I think, and I mean to set it straight. I hope you are not loyal to Señor Posada."

"Loyal? *Hijo de una puta.* I was once a deputy inspector, until I was caught selling English cigarettes to the black market. Posada demoted me to corporal."

"That's good."

"But his office, this is no small matter, if we are caught I'm a dead man, cut up and fed to pigs, you know?"

"Yes, I know."

"We break in, it is too risky."

"Can't you just lead us in, semi-officially?"

"Just walk right in? *Tú eres loco!*"

"Why not? Cuff me, I'll be someone you arrested."

The fat man paused. "I hate Posada, but I will not do this anyway, not unless you have a lot of money."

"How much do you make in a year."

"Eight thousand pesetas."

"I'll pay you eight thousand pesetas."

Hemingway finally went back to his hotel just as it was getting dark, drank cognac from the bottle and passed out, the day's head traumas finally catching up with him. He didn't see Franklin, which was good. He didn't want to involve the lug, not in this.

Ignacio went home, too, and returned to the Hotel Florida at 5 AM. He had the front desk rouse Hemingway, which had to be performed in person by a staff janitor, with an impatient series of shakings. Hemingway dressed in his bloodied shirt, and wore a large hat and blue-tinted sunglasses he'd bought at Piccadilly.

They met the fat man, who would not divulge his name, a block away in an alley still shadowed from the beginnings of dawn. Hemingway brought the money, in folded 10,000 Pts bills. The fat man cuffed Hemingway behind his back, a far from comforting circumstance after the previous day, and they all piled into the man's rusty police sedan. Hemingway was to be a drunk taken in for assault, Ignacio was the victim of said assault, and once in Posada's office the fat man would leave the two to read and translate, *try* to translate, with Ignacio's driblets of English, while he, the fat man, distracted the officers on patrol. This might buy fifteen minutes, maybe more, but maybe less. How exactly they'd leave without being questioned was a point the fat man said he'd figure out when they get there.

They drove over and west, as the dawn quickly lit the avenues up, turning into glare through the filthy windshield of the municipal jalopy. Hemingway sat back and tried to control his breathing, realizing that he'd managed to avoid doing anything technically criminal so far. So far—that's the end of *that,* he harrumphed to himself without a sound. Watch me end up in a Spanish jail, just as the war swells and then concludes and then either the Russians or the Fascists take over, doesn't matter which in this scenario, and find me and wonder why they don't just exterminate me like a roach, like the Front knocked off Robles. If there was a line to cross here, I've finally officially crossed it, and left a slug's trail behind me.

The *oficina* was an old manor house with marble columns out front, probably once a hot spot for debutante balls and spring galas. The floor of the lobby was white marble, too.

"You're *drunk*," the fat man hissed, grabbing Hemingway's shirt collar from behind and holding him up as if he were dragging the bloodied American in against his will.

Hemingway acted the role, as best he could, though he wished he'd had at least a few belts of port or something to loosen him up. He stumbled, squinted, and slurred, acted chastened, and avoided catching the eye of the two guards who sat at the front desk, which sat under a massive but mediocre portrait of Jaime, Duke of Madrid. Ignacio followed them at a few paces, trying his best to looked aggrieved.

The fat man blathered Spanish in a brusque and joking manner to the guards—Hemingway thought he was acting drunk, too, which given the state of Spanish law enforcement in those days might've merely been a stroke of insight—and he gesticulated with his head down the right hallway, extending to the back of the house. He waved a billy club in his right hand, and briefly made a demonstrative motion, as he jabbered uncomprehendingly to his comrades, of slugging Hemingway in the head with it, which only made Hemingway genuinely want to cry: Please, please don't hit me, not in the head, not again, my poor fucking head. I'll remember this entire visit to Spain as a photo-album series of skull injuries. But then the three men trotted on by, and in a tiny glance back Hemingway saw the guards had already gone back to dealing out a deck of cards, for a game of *Mus*.

The hallway's ceiling was high, and the building was stone quiet. It was still shy of 6 AM.

At the end, the fat policeman pointed his baton at an office door. As he uncuffed Hemingway, Ignacio tried the knob—locked.

"Of course," Hemingway said.

The fat man brushed them aside, took out a key ring thick with long keys, and singled out a piece of coping saw blade he had fastened to a piece of tied wire. He jiggled the lock, fished inside it for tumblers, and in a few seconds the door swung open.

The fat man took a step back into the hallway. Hemingway turned to him. "You're not going anywhere."

"I'm going out to the lobby, make sure those *policías* stay put."

"You won't strand us."

"Strand? No. If you're caught, I'm in more trouble than you."

Hemingway doubted that, but stepped into Posada's office, his eyes wide. It was a large space, a converted master suite, with fleur-de-lis crown molding fifteen feet up and tall windows that opened out onto a courtyard.

The office was pin-neat—Posada even lined up his pencils to the right of his blotter. There were file cabinets.

*"Lo que ahora,"* Ignacio whispered behind him. *Now what.*

"Uh, files, *archivos,* with Robles, José Robles, dated March or February, uh, *Marzo y Febrero*—"

*"Sí, sí, sí."* Ignacio understood; he went to one file cabinet behind the desk and Hemingway went to the other.

He knew it was sifting sand for a speck of diamond. But Posada *was* meticulous, and the files were perfectly organized, the Madrid *la seguridad y la delicuencia* files distinct from the Popular Front memo files and from the communiqués from Valencia and from Moscow, all of them apparently in scrupulous chronological order. Hemingway pulled the Front files from March and February and clicked with his cheek over to Ignacio as if the old Basque man were a horse, and they spread the fat file's content on the desk.

Ignacio began reading, but Hemingway scanned for Robles's name only, and began pulling pages and giving them to Ignacio to glance over, the two of them scurrying with eyes and hands like figures in a silent movie.

"Alright, alright, look, only March 10 to . . . March 21," he said, figuring that for Robles to have been arrested in Valencia it had to have been a weekend, and that whatever tripped the switch of Posada's cover-up may probably have been discovered by Robles during that week or the week before. Probably?

Hemingway found one sheet, an order for arrest, *detencion,* dated March 11, with Robles's initials signing off, indicating it had been translated and sent to Valencia and Moscow. The man arrested was named Jorge Polivados, he lived at 230 Calle de Sepulveda, he was an *anarquista* and an *usurpador.* Period. Hemingway immediately doubted that this Polivados guy had done anything wrong or "antirevolutionary," and found it amazing that Robles could sign off on this sort of thing, blithely, in the course of a work day. Such were the capabilities of the true idealist.

But then he realized, with an almost audible skidding: This Polivados, he was arrested officially, by policemen, by official order, and the paperwork went to multiple offices, and whomever ordered it, Posada or someone higher, everyone was informed of it. The memo would have been translated and disseminated and filed and initialed several times over. The policemen who performed the operation would report to work the next day, ready for another assignment. This was the Second Republic acting in its official capacity. No one hid anything. This is how it's done by the Popular Front, and the Comintern: If it's official, then it's unarguable and systemic and the will of Stalin. Polivados's family might not have been informed about specific charges and the man's eventual fate, just to keep them terrified, but sure as hell the men in power knew all about it. Blair said it: If anyone of stature is arrested by the Comintern and set up, it's done publicly, as a show.

It didn't happen this way with Robles. A band of larcenous *quinqui*-speaking mutts were promised a car to kill a man in the middle of the night, halfway across the country from where he could be found, prominently, most days of the week? And nothing but rumors floated around for weeks afterward, no definitive statement, no death certificate, no declaration of Robles's treasonous crimes and new identity as enemy of the state? No public purge?

Obviously there'd be no piece of paper to find attesting to or mentioning Robles's arrest.

Robles's was not an official execution. It was secret. Secret from the government.

Which meant that Posada—if he was indeed the Mussolini here, the big shot and widow-maker—if it was his Bentley, was not doing Popular Front business.

Which left two possibilities: that Posada was a serious criminal, a smuggler or embezzler, and Robles found him out.

Or he worked for Franco. A Nationalist spy. And Robles found him out. Robles was not, in turns out, a victim of his own revolutionary naïveté. He was killed in a cover-up of crimes *against* the Republic. Hemingway couldn't understand how he could have been so dim to have taken so long to come to this simple conclusion, and it chilled him, because his realization was sparked only by the three-line memo about Jorge Polivados, and because this made it glaringly obvious all over again how little Hemingway knew about the real politics of the shitstorm around him. How could he know enough when the lives of nations were decided by soulless espionage and pitless game playing?

Ignacio was still scanning the mid-March documents, putting some aside. Hemingway glanced at him and saw him notice a memo because it had a prominent burst of handwriting across its lower third. Ignacio went to place it with others, but then decided to look at it again, in a double take.

"Guernica," he said.

So? Ignacio's hometown. Hemingway took it. "Guernica," Ignacio repeated. *"Diecisiete de Marzo."*

It was written on the seventeenth. Hemingway couldn't recognize any Spanish easily, so Ignacio tried, in English. "From Juan Posada . . . to Aldo Gonzales, Mayor *de* Guernica . . . Army come . . . *yo no sé cómo decir* . . . moving . . . *antiaereo* . . . Uh, anti-aeroplane?"

"Antiaircraft? Guns?"

*"Si, canones* . . . to Madrid. *Pronto. Yo no sé cómo decir* . . . Signed, Juan Posada."

"OK. And the scrawl, there?" Hemingway could see it was Robles's initials underneath.

"Uh . . . *Alarma.* Alarm? He say, where order from? *Peligroso,* dangerous, will ask . . . Gorev?"

"Give me that." Hemingway folded it and stuffed it into his underwear. He had no idea what it meant, exactly, except this: Robles objected to something about the movement of guns around

Guernica—from Guernica, or back to it?—threatened to bring it to the mightiest military Soviet officer in the country, and then he became a bought corpse less than six days later.

Hemingway told Ignacio to look for other Robles initials on papers dated the eighteenth or later, but after several minutes they found none. Ignacio cocked a thumb at the other files, the municipal drawers, the Moscow folders, the drawers they didn't even open.

"No time." And they straightened the room up, putting the files back.

The fat man came back, told them in a hiss to hurry.

"How're we getting out of here."

"Through the front door. Sent those *hijos* out for *churros*. Come!"

They strode out the front door, and drove back to the Florida. The fat man barely slowed his car down to allow the other men to hit the sidewalk.

Up in 108, Hemingway immediately napped, like a fallen oak.

# 23

He was still dreaming, about the night road from Valencia and the overturned Ford in the rain, among other things, when he heard the pounding and hollering. In the dream, he stood on the dark road wondering where there was a door that someone could be slamming with a sledgehammer. Then he floated up out of the scene and woke up, still hearing it, and realized there was some kind of psychopath trying to break down his hotel room door.

Out of bed, naked, to the door—it was a man, yelling in Aragonese-inflected Spanish, and laying into the door of 108 with what sounded like the dull side of an axe. Hemingway figured it was a rifle butt.

*Fucking hell.* His adrenaline boosted and hit the top of his skull. He turned and looked around for escape routes—the window?

But if he were being grabbed by another gang of unwashed outlaws, they wouldn't make such a godawful ruckus in the hall. Would they?

Hemingway put his two hands up against the door, and

inhaled. "Hey! Who are you, what do you want? And you better know English!"

A pause, and an inhalation on the other side.

"*Yo soy* Teodoro Fajardo, *de* Zaragoza! *Yo*—"

"Who?! English, you psycho!"

"Teodoro! Fajardo! From Zaragoza! I have come to restore honor to my daughter, Ana Fajardo! You, Señor Hemingway, will pay for *arruinar su nombre y su honor!*"

"No! Look, I don't know what those fucking college kids told you, but I didn't fuck her or anything! I just gave her some wine!"

"You speak about my daughter this way?!" *Blam,* the rifle hit the door, and Hemingway heard the wood around the hinges crack.

"I'm sorry! But I didn't touch her! She's a good girl! She told me there'd be no way she'd sleep with me! She's pure!"

"*Que?!* You spoke with her about her own virginity?! You should prepare yourself, American, to die, for spoiling my family name!" *Blam.* "Open up, you Yankee *bastardo,* I will teach you manners among a Christian people!"

Then a gunshot thudded out in the hallway and brought a gust into the room—a foot-long splinter of door wood flew off the door past Hemingway's face, and the bullet crashed through the plaster wall across the room, beside the veranda doors, leaving a hole for light to come through.

*Jesus Christ.* Those friends of Ana's were right—her father was a straight-on crazy hot-blooded spit of trouble. Hemingway was already dressing in a blind panic, zipping his trousers even as he stumbled over to the veranda, figuring as he looked down, no, he couldn't jump, but to the side—could he escape jumping to the next veranda? From one low iron fence to the other had to be four feet. Hemingway would have to take a stretching step across the chasm, standing on the railing, with only a blank wall to hold onto.

And he *didn't* get to fuck that girl, that was the part that really irked him. Where was Sidney Franklin when you needed him? *Blam. "Abra!"*

Hemingway hoisted himself up onto his railing, leaning against the building's facade like a babe cowering against his mother's chest, and took a step out toward the other rail. There was no reaching it without shifting his center of balance forward, over the void, and just taking the leap. Which he would do. But he couldn't. Then his shoe slipped a touch on the rickety rail, and his heart rocketed into his throat.

He got down, stepped inside, wondered if he could take a door of the pantry off, and take it outside, and lay it down between two verandas—but then Fajardo landed a rifle butt to the door an inch to one side of the knob, and busted that side of the doorframe into splinters. The door flew open and in charged a short, wiry, white-haired, unshaven troll of a man, his eyes bloodshot and wet, with a rusted carbine gripped in his hands.

Hemingway's palms instinctively shot out, like a woman fending off a rapist. "Wait, wait, *espero!*"—but by that time Fajardo had spotted Hemingway's portable Royal typewriter on the table, and lifted his weapon to his eye.

*"American escrito!"* he spat, and shot, the low-carriage portable exploded into flying cast-iron shrapnel. Hemingway hated that, people calling him a writer as an insult. What do you say back? Well, so much for NANA. It was clear this crazy Aragonese codger came pickled to the gills.

Hemingway went to his knees, hands outstretched. He plastered a look of awed submissiveness across his face. "Señor, teach me the honor of Aragon, but first, you are my guest, and I have a rosé from Calatayud that I would like to share with you—you must be thirsty after your journey."

The old man practically licked his lips as he lowered the rifle a notch, and took a belabored breath. *"Si, claro,"* he said, *"un Catalayud sería bueno."*

Hemingway stood and went to the pantry, sensing Fajardo's slow eyes and rifle barrel following him, and pulled out a 1922 Aragonese rosé, banking on the old man's dry mouth and his tribal pride about anything from Zaragoza. He found two glasses in the bathroom and uncorked the bottle, sitting on his bed. By the time the wine was pouring, Fajardo had sat down in a chair close to the bed, the rifle laying across his lap, and eagerly accepted the wine. They drank—it was a strong, woody wine, and Hemingway was happy to have it, especially if he was on the verge of getting shot—so happy he filled his tumbler immediately again and quaffed like a man in the desert.

"*Tu es* . . . you are thirsty, also," Fajardo muttered.

"Dammit, I'm always thirsty."

Hemingway eyed the rifle, and Fajardo saw him. The Spaniard dropped his wine, stood, and pressed his gun barrel against Hemingway's forehead with a thud.

"Do not be sneaky, American, Hemingburg, I would shoot a sneaky man." He was wobbling, and Hemingway was already done kowtowing.

"Oh, fucking shoot, old man. For the love of God. At this point I'd love it. At least it'd be a way of getting out of this hellish country. I tell you, I've never before met so many obnoxious, obstinate, bellicose people on one patch of earth in my life. Each and every one of you, you're all evil under the skin, like you were bred in the cradle with scorpion bites. You look for any excuse to make trouble and spill blood. Do you know how many people have hit my head with hard objects in the last week with the serious intention of opening my skull? Look at you, Fajardo, uh? Your daughter drank some wine of mine and almost—*almost*—got sick at an outdoor café, and for this you're a homicidal menace. Honor! Are you understanding me? You're a dark-hearted idiot, just like the rest of the Spaniards I've met. Most of them. Alright, Ignacio is a stand-up man. But the rest of you. Oh, go ahead!"

Fajardo didn't move.

"Go ahead!" Hemingway shouted again, and Fajardo pulled the trigger.

With a shock Hemingway realized the hammer had come down on an empty chamber, and Fajardo jerked in surprise, shooting a look down, but Hemingway grabbed the rifle with both hands as he stood, a single movement, shoving the old man back down into his chair.

Hemingway stepped away and checked the magazine—empty.

"You came gunning for me with one friggin' bullet?"

Fajardo shrugged. "I shot at some crows yesterday . . . at the Jardin Botanico . . ."

"You must've been good and pie-eyed then, too."

He shrugged again.

Hemingway disengaged the magazine, eyed the clear chamber, pulled the trigger, and dropped the gun on the floor. The adrenaline spike had already begun to dissipate, and he took a deep breath.

"I ought to beat you like a rented mule," Hemingway said off-handedly, picking up the old man's glass. With a deliberate display of grace under gunfire, he poured more wine, in both glasses.

"*Si.* You have the right." Fajardo was very quickly a smaller man.

"Oh, shut up, you old coot," sitting down, "You know, in the America I come from, men who share a drink do not have to prove their honor or nobility to each other. They are brothers, and their bond sustains them in a world of raging armies and skittish women and poisonous fate. You are obviously a man of great character, an old-time man of the land, and you can obviously be trusted. This is something I value. Now, you will trust me, yes? I did not touch Ana, and we as men have reached an understanding. I think we should get seriously drunk."

"*Por favor,* call me Teo."

The two finished the bottle and then went out to the Gran Via where after sitting for a while Hemingway realized he had the crumpled memo from Posada's office stuffed into his trouser pocket, and he took it out and tried to smooth it on the table.

"Read this for me, Teo, *por favor,* in English."

Fajardo didn't blink, picked up the paper.

"'To Aldo Gonzales, Mayor of Guernica: Please be . . . adviced? . . . that, by order of the Republic, army contingents will come—will be coming—to Guernica by April 1 to remove the . . . *estacionario* . . . stationary? . . . antiaircraft guns, which are needed for defense purposes here in Madrid as soon as possible, and please extend all cooperations necessary. Yours in the Republic, Juan Posada.'"

"That's it? And the note?"

"Uh, 'Juan—I read this with alarm—where'd this order originate from? This is very dangerous—I will ask Gorev.'"

"Where'd you learn English?"

"Volunteered with the Gibraltar forces in the Great War. Fought at Ameins."

"Good man."

"This paper smells . . ." Fajardo was getting visibly woozy.

Hemingway took it back. "Why would Posada move guns out of Guernica? Where the fuck is Guernica, anyway?"

"North. Basque."

"Oh, that's right. But so? Why would Pepe get all apoplectic about it? Was he thinking there'd be another fucking terror bombing, like there was in Durango?"

"Who's Pepe?"

"Never mind—the guy with the sloppy handwriting. I'm not sure this means anything at all. I'm just chasing my tail. Maybe Posada's got nothing to do with all of this."

Fajardo wanted to ask what in heavens the *loco* American was talking about, but he couldn't find the energy. He slumped.

"Teo, I need to find a Bentley."

Fajardo was asleep on his own shoulder. Hemingway let him doze, sipped his brandy, and looked around: Quintinilla had his customary spot in the corner, urbanely sitting with a newspaper but really keeping his eye on the room, watching the foreigners and journalists come and go. The very fact, Hemingway thought, that Quintinilla is not on my ass like a snake on a fledgling makes it clear that the Front, and the Comintern, and their black operators, have not placed me on their radar. If this were typical Front business, Quintinilla would've taken me out by now, secretly.

He'd at least be watching me, threatening me, begging me then trying to terrorize me into going home. No, he doesn't know about D'Armoux or the Valencia escapade or the *quinquilleros* or even Mink. He is not a part of that thread. There is a secret government at work, one working silently beneath the real one. It may involve Posada, it may not, but it's not the official Communist machine at work. It is something else.

I need not fear Stalin or the Comintern, he thought. I need fear only what I do not know.

# 24

He slung the wiry little Zaragozan man over his shoulder and walked him back next door to the Florida, up the stairs, and down the hall. Fajardo was not heavy, and reminded Hemingway too acutely of the weight of Bumby in his arms when the boy was only four and had fallen asleep somewhere in their travels, on an Alpine train or hansom cab in Paris, and he'd had to spirit the boy out and home to bed. This before Hemingway was famous, when he was anonymous and free-floating and actually happy. Why couldn't I do that now? C'mon, because you wouldn't let yourself, you'd never relax knowing you could buy your way into a luxury hotel and a brace of whores at any moment. And who'd you go with? What woman, what innocent toddler? Who'd trust you?

The American writer laid Fajardo down on the bed, plopped down in the soft chair with his feet up, and fell asleep after three pages of a tattered British edition of *Typhoon*.

In the morning he fed Fajardo out of the pantry, canned peaches and pickled sausage, and offered him work: He'd pay him 500 pesetas to spend the day with him, searching for a particular car. Fajardo upped it to 750, which Hemingway accepted and offered as well to Ignacio once they'd gotten dressed and hit the front curb of the hotel. The crusty Aragonese and the affable old Basque got along immediately, as if they recognized each other's implicit history, reaching back to the coronation of Alfonso XII, as being intimately entwined.

First they had to return to *la oficina de seguridad,* on Calle de las Huertas, in Ignacio's crumbling taxi. Fajardo had to go in alone and connive the guarding officers there to give him the name and possible whereabouts of Señor Posada's chauffeur, because the chauffeur had left his wallet in a room on the whore-occupied third floor of *la* Hotel Florida, and he, Fajardo, was sent to return it as discreetly as possible. Apparently the guards all had a big laugh over this, and over the possibility of the story remaining "discreet," and they told the old fellow, who had a face and weather-beaten demeanor that every Spaniard naturally trusted, that the driver's name was Magnonia, and he should be with the cars around the corner off Plaza de Santa Ana.

Hemingway figured they'd better hurry, if for no better reason than Posada was at work in his office by now, and might find something amiss or call over for his car at any moment.

The three men strolled around the corner, where the Plaza opened up before them green and shaded by giant fig trees, except for the patches blackened and heaped by small shells that had fallen months before. A little reconnoitering, and they found the broad alley—a brick courtyard, really, but devoid of gardening—where several dozen large and expensive cars were parked. A guard sat on a stool by a hardwired battlefield phone, and various drivers could be seen flitting about, tinkering with their engines, smoking, and reading newspapers in their driver seats.

Following the plan, which no longer involved mentioning the whores of the Florida, Fajardo schmoozed with the guard, mentioning Magnonia's name, and soon turned and introduced Hemingway as Señor John Dos Passos, American journalist. They shook hands.

"Tell him I'm writing an article for American newspapers about the cars of the Republic!"

Fajardo translated, and the guard smiled, made a quick shrugging face—*what Americans will buy newspapers to read about, God only knows*—and walked with the men into the alley. Hemingway was introduced and shook the drivers' hands ("John Dos Passos, *mucho gusto*; John Dos Passos, *mucho gusto*—"), and Fajardo began asking in Spanish about the cars' vintages, and which bigwig, *un capo,* drove which vehicle. Hemingway acted interested, waiting for Fajardo's translations, and all the while scanned the place looking for something that might be a Bentley. He realized that outside of the double-*B* insignia on the keys he had no idea what a Bentley looked like.

Fajardo obviously enjoyed talking about cars, and the chauffeurs were proud of their charges. "This gentleman, Magnonia, says that a Russian colonel here named Tshukhmarev drives this one, which is a 1932 Alvis Speed Twenty, one of the first ever built, which is good because the Russian thinks the British are only good at beginning things, like empires, but not continuing them! And this is a 1929 Hispano-Suiza, still in brand-new condition, one of a few that were this color, which he said is *mora,* mulberry, and it is driven by the Republic ambassador to France, who only drives Spanish cars, even though he admits they're hardly ever worth the petrol you put into them! Ha! And this one is a Rolls-Royce—"

This went on for thirty solid minutes, during which time Fajardo quite obviously became completely distracted by the proximity of so many beautiful, impossibly expensive automobiles. Hemingway grew restive, but then a driver who'd been standing silently to his left piped up. "Señor Dos Passos, *por favor,* eh, I just want to say to you, I am a big supporter . . . uh, a fan?

Of *Manhattan Transfer*. I think it is the very greatest American book ever made."

"Really," Hemingway replied. He couldn't help himself. "Did you read it in Spanish?"

"No! I read English, uh, pretty good, better than I speak it. I learned in Barcelona, in school. I would never try to read your books translated! I think, there is no point, *si*? I feel that way, too, about others—I want to read James Joyce, but I cannot find a copy yet. It is too . . . scandalous. For Spain."

"For a lot of places."

"I must say, you look—more robust! Than in your jacket photo."

"Don't I? Thanks."

"I wanted to ask you, if New York is really like that, like in *Manhattan Transfer*. Because it is not like it is supposed to be like, from the way you hear about it in other books, or in movies . . ."

"Yeah? Uh, well, you know, it's actually not that bad."

"No? *Por que* did you write it like that?"

"The real city's sort of boring, honestly. I was sort of thinking about Dante, his journey through the Inferno . . . It was a way to be 'modern.' You know what I mean? All the writers in America are trying to be modern. You think that's pretentious?"

The driver was speechless for a moment. "Uh, pretentious? . . . No . . ."

"Do you still think it's the greatest American book ever made?"

"Well, *si,* but . . ."

"That's the thing you have to understand, my boy. We writers, with a few exceptions like that guy Hemingway, we just make stuff up as best we can, just to sell books. It's best not to get too excited by it all."

Fajardo and Ignacio had walked away from them, absorbed in car lore. The book-crazy chauffeur was almost sputtering.

"But you did not live that life in New York, you didn't see those things?"

"God, no. I was born wealthy, grew up in prep schools. I know Zurich better than New York. But if I did see that life in New York, just writing it wouldn't make me a great writer, would it? Why is that better than inventing it all?" Jeez, he was suddenly arguing for Dos Passos and against authentic experience.

"I don't know . . ."

"I think you're confusing the book you're reading with the life you're imagining the writer's had. Don't do that, it's a trap. Look only at the book. The writer doesn't exist. You think your life here in Spain, during a civil war, isn't exciting or meaningful enough? You must've noticed, or heard about, how many writers—me included!—have come here. Why, do you think? They want to be you, that's why, to write about *you*. Read the books, fine, but don't dream that being a writer makes someone special or makes their life blessed or thrilling."

"OK . . ."

"What's your second greatest American book ever?"

Thought for a moment, and snapped his fingers. *"Sister Carrie."*

"Have you tried any Hemingway?"

"I did, yes, once, *Farewell to Arms*, and I could not like it. It did not seem . . . very . . . *alive*. You know?"

"Sure, kid. I know exactly what you mean."

He looked up—Fajardo was gesturing "come on" with two fingers and wide-open eyes. Hemingway walked over.

Before them sat a Bentley, parked with its nose out, silver-blue, huge and long and dark, the chrome insignia rising from the grill edge like the prow of a schooner.

"Señor Dos Passos, this is Señor Posada's Bentley. The only Bentley here."

Hemingway looked over the shiny beast and nodded, fingering the keys in his pocket. That's almost a car worth killing for, he thought. He wasn't sure what the next step would be—do these uniformed yokels know anything about why this goddamn car has sat unused for over a month?

"They said this car is the biggest Bentley, a Litre 8, of which there were only one hundred made."

"Yes. I once met a man who wrecked one of them, and chuckled about it," he said. Fajardo translated, and the chauffeurs buzzed.

"They also said this is not the car Posada drives, that is the yellow Rolls-Royce over there. This one has sat silent for weeks and weeks. They said there have been rumors that it was promised to an agent, as reward for a very dangerous mission." Fajardo was looking at Hemingway with knowing apprehension. Ignacio stayed five paces behind everyone, ready to bolt for the street.

"They're correct," Hemingway said and took out the key, holding it up in front of him. The chauffeurs' eyes all went round. One chattered to Fajardo.

"They say, so you are no writer."

"Tell them I sure as shit am."

"They say they heard that the car was promised to an assassin."

"Tell them to shut up and never to speak of it again. Tell them John Dos Passos is not a man to be trifled with, he is a dangerous man, but he is no assassin."

Fajardo translated, and Hemingway made his way around to the driver's door and unlocked it. He sat inside and started her up. The engine roared like a tractor.

Another chauffeur chattered to Fajardo, who was following Hemingway's pointing finger: get in.

"He asks, what shall they tell Señor Posada?"

Hemingway looked through the grimy windshield: Ignacio had vanished. Probably hightailed it out to the street and ran full-out. Fajardo slid into the passenger's seat.

"Tell them to inform Señor Posada that the car has been redeemed. That's all."

And he drove off. First time driving a Bentley, or any European car of this caliber, and it was not a little like driving the landscape itself, impervious and heavy and endless. He sailed the car out of the alley and along the Plaza de Santa Ana, and realized he didn't really know where he was going or how in fact to drive on the right side of the road in a city as unplanned and self-entwined and hectic as Madrid. Plus, Spaniards drive like tequila-doused ten-year-olds, and he narrowly avoided a collision, in possibly the most expensive automobile on the Iberian Peninsula in 1937, nine separate times. Fajardo's arm remained bolted straight to the dashboard the whole trip.

Hemingway knew the drivers, busy hens that they were, would not leave it at "that's all," and would eagerly tell the story of an American named Dos Passos showing up with the keys to the mystery Bentley, and therein admitting, at least to the gossipers, that at least one body lay in his wake. Even if one book-crazed chauffeur actually knew who Dos Passos was, then everyone would soon know—the novelist who killed for the revolution! Dos is probably in America by now, so it can't hurt him, Hemingway hoped. There was, in any case, no controlling or second-guessing it now.

What was now unquestionable was the involvement of Posada himself. Suddenly there was no question about Posada's guilt, which was a relief and a haunting both. Nor would there be, of course, any ambiguity *for* Posada himself, that someone, Dos Passos or an American claiming to be, knows cold that he had in fact ordered and paid for the assassination of José Robles. And that American, not some cold-blooded *quinquillero* who'd happily hightail it back into the shadows, is driving around Madrid in a Bentley Litre 8.

Likely, George Mink would be sent, if Mink hadn't been eliminated himself by now for being such a rabid fuckup. Or someone else. Somebody would be sent. How long would it take? Posada must've learned by now that D'Armoux was dead, killed while trailing Hemingway into the black night of the low-lands. Maybe he's known for a while, and had been simply wait-ing for the last shoe to drop. Which, it turned out, was the Bentley.

Hemingway parked the Bentley behind the Florida, and paid the staff extra to keep mum about it. He and Fajardo found Igna-cio at the bar in the Gran Via, and he treated both old men to a large lunch, which featured fresh lamb and yellow rice and okra, and he let both of the underfed men order second plates. They drank riojas of various vintages, and Hemingway ordered the house's last bottle of amontillado.

The dark shapes in the doorway that Hemingway expected did not show up that day. He did not feel compelled to seek out any more information—he had his killer. He felt content, there in the shadows of the Gran Via, drinking with world-worn Spaniards who knew nothing of literature that wasn't Spanish and cared even less. If he survived to morning, then he would . . . what? Go to Posada? Yes, goddammit, why not? Bring Quintinilla with him, and see what the weasel has to say in the face of the Comin-tern's fearsome will.

He was too drunk in mid-afternoon to even try to answer the questions that inevitably arose: What exactly was Posada up to? *Why* was Robles killed? If it had to do with the Guernica guns, then, so? Perhaps the only way to find out, in the end, was to ask Posada himself.

He figured he'd get the chance, sooner or later.

It was later, slightly. They came to arrest him the next morn-ing, rather generously around 10 AM, after Hemingway had awo-ken, slammed a robust throatful of port behind some aspirin, and eaten three hard-boiled eggs Franklin had brought him from the third floor. Not long before the cops arrived, Fajardo, who had spent the night, hugged Hemingway, promised lifelong allegiance, and left to catch a train back to Zaragoza.

This arrest wasn't the shady, secret-service strong-arm garbage of Mink, but a small platoon of Madrileño police officers arriving in three cars in front of the hotel, announcing themselves to the front desk, and then marching, practically in formation, up the stairs and down the hall.

The pounding on the door of room 108 was loud and firm but not hostile. Hemingway knew the sound, heard the shuffle of boots outside. All very official. He decided he'd leave Liston Oak's gun in the pantry, hidden under sardines. The knock came again.

But then another noise, an explosion of body weight and breath—and Hemingway leaped at the door and opened it.

It was Franklin. He had heard the troops coming down the hall, had come crashing out of his room, and was now bum-rushing the policemen with his huge head down, like a bull, grabbing two around the waists with his arms and running over a third right in front of the doorway. Four others were trying to avoid being run over by the Sidney Express and trying to un-snap their billy clubs, but Franklin had knocked them off balance as well—all but one, who had actually leaped ten feet away and landed on his knees and tried to get up. Franklin, having a college football flashback or some such thing, had all seven officers off their feet in a matter of seconds. Hemingway jumped into the hallway, grabbing Franklin's shoulders and trying to pull him back, yelling, "*Sidney, fer Chrissake, you're just going to end up in a cell!*" By which time three of the policemen were scrambling away from Franklin, and he had dropped the Spaniard in his left arm and literally lifted the one gripped in his right arm up onto his shoulder and then with a step threw him down the hall, like one might throw a sack of rice onto a truck.

"*Shit, Sidney!*" Hemingway hollered, but the thrown policemen got right up and drew a gun that he didn't get to aim because Franklin had bulldozed the other young cops up to that point in the hall, only feet away from the stairwell where one policeman waited, and train-wrecked through the gun-holding cop, who fired once at the ceiling, fell, and dropped the weapon. The cops behind Franklin now pulled Hemingway off and jumped on the pile, and Hemingway went down on his rump. Franklin deliberately ran sideways into the wall at the top of the stairs, catching one policeman against it and crunching him, and then he tripped, in a split second, as Hemingway was getting from his knees to his feet, looking up, Franklin plummeted out of view down the stairs and took four Spanish policemen with him. The noise was quite like a bombing.

Hemingway ran to the stairwell, and all was still: Three policemen stood on their feet, gasping for breath, while four, with Franklin, lay sprawled down the length of the steps and onto the landing, moaning. Hemingway could see at least two limbs, one of them Franklin's right knee, that were bent in unnatural ways.

The nearest policemen looked to Hemingway, wiping his forehead. Hemingway shrugged.

"*Tu es* Señor Hemingway?"

Hemingway nodded.

The three officers arrested him without cuffs and took him into the patrol car, but it was almost fifteen minutes before a medic's team arrived to set and splint the seven bones that had been broken on the lobby stairs of the Florida. Once this was accomplished, Franklin was arrested, too.

# 25

The three policemen with Hemingway were laughing to each other about the debacle within minutes of leaving the curb. He gathered that one of the men immobilized by Franklin's attack was a captain everyone else hated.

They did not drive to Calle de las Huertas, and when Hemingway asked his escort where in hell they were going, they did not reply. He settled back, his jaw tightening, letting his worst fears run wild: The Ride to God Knows Where, the mystery ride so many have taken in the last few years, all over Europe, the ride that ends only at a place that has no name on a map, that no one can give directions to exactly, that no one frequents or owns, behind a hillock or deep in a forest otherwise taboo because of wolves.

But it was daylight, morning, and the officers had so far behaved with impeccable professionalism. Hemingway shifted in his seat.

A few blocks later he realized he was being shipped to Posada's penthouse, on the western flank of the city. It wasn't The Ride, but something more strategic, or, he hoped, diplomatic. That meant that Posada was still negotiating.

In short order he was escorted up—the elevator in this building worked—and entered the penthouse suite. It was familiar: the same posh '20s furniture right out of a French silent, the floor-to-ceiling windows, the veranda, the animal-pelt rugs over marble. Posada must have substantial side deals, he thought, to afford this. Why doesn't this building get bombed? And then he thought, It's becoming obvious why not, isn't it.

Juan Posada appeared, all silk business suit and glass of white.

"Ernest! You look horrible. I was hoping you'd join me for lunch."

"Juan, it's 10 AM."

"10:45."

"What're you drinking?"

"It's a 1924 Chablis, from Alella Vinícola."

"I don't know what that is. But it's probably good."

"Yes. It is good."

"Alright."

Posada shooed the policemen away. Hemingway thought this urbane banter routine, under the circumstances, was outrageous horseshit. But at the same time he enjoyed it, appreciated the wine, and understood that he might make it out with his hide intact if he played along.

Posada poured the glass and, as he went to the windows, let it sit on the table for Hemingway to come and pick up.

"So," Hemingway said into the glass. It was very, very good Chablis.

"So, Ernest, I understand you've been very busy, tangling with the lowest forms of life Spain has to offer, honestly, and—you have a new car."

"Yup. It's a beaut."

"I'm curious as to how you came to possess the keys." Posada's prep-school English was made even more elegant and suave by the Latin curves he put on it; Hemingway thought he more resembled an actor playing a cultured Spanish snake in the grass than the real deal.

"Well, that's a funny story, Juan, you see, the dunderpates you gave them to apparently dropped them in the foothills at night and couldn't find them. Not far from where they dropped Pepe. You couldn't even find half-wits, you had to go and hire the dumbest men on the Continent."

What, exactly, Hemingway was hoping to obtain by immediately showing every card he held escaped even him. Sometimes he felt like nothing more than a large and thoughtless mouth. Was he hoping Posada would get nervous, confess, give himself up? To whom, himself? Where was the endgame here? That was just the trouble, not knowing. All he knew was, this was where the dark road winds up, in an absurd penthouse with a heartless bureaucrat who had something to hide and all the reason in the world to extinguish Hemingway like gaslight. If he could—if he *thought* he could.

Posada took a moment, back turned.

". . . I think that's unfair," he said. "I've lost keys. So have you."

Hemingway wanted to play, swat the ball back, but he was starting to sweat.

"Oh, cut the shit, Juan. Do we have to dance around it?"

"I'd prefer we did, Ernest, frankly, because you have given me very few options, and none that aren't distasteful. You know, you could've left well enough alone—which is something I bet you were expecting me to say. But really, everyone else did. Even Dos Passos went home."

"I think he gave up on the revolution. Consider that your good work, too, comrade."

"Oh, that's the least of my sins, isn't it, Ernest. And it would be the least of yours, wouldn't it? How many men have you killed this month, Hemingway, in your spree?"

"My spree? I didn't kill anyone, you officious little asshole, not even D'Armoux. That's not my line of work."

"I'm not keeping score. I was just suggesting . . . a little ethical relativism."

"Relativism. Fuck you and your relativism. What, one man put down for the revolution is a pittance in a war, or fighting the Fascists, that's your rationale?"

"I think that's indisputable. Thanks for putting it so keenly."

"It's not only disputable, it's idiotic, especially since it's plain to a blind man that Pepe didn't die for the revolution, or even the Comintern's demented ideas of revolution or Communist necessity. He died for you, Juan, and it had nothing to do with Communism."

Hemingway refilled his glass—he was cooking but he wasn't thinking: It seemed to him that Posada was capable of being reasoned with. Which couldn't be true, this late in the game. The alcohol burned in his belly, but he had to remind himself, again, that Posada was no longer just an insultable weasel, but a bonafide mini-autocrat, with at least one killing notched on his belt and probably more than that. You may've been brought here to die, you idiot, he thought. You may never see Pauline, or Bumby, or Martha again. Or Key West, or Paris, or Africa.

Hallelujah? Wasn't he secretly hoping to fall under the wheels of the war, feed that ache finally? He would've, should've, let D'Armoux harvest him, if that was the case. But every time, Hemingway's instincts got the best of him, and besides, with his back up in the air, he bridled at the thought of someone else dictating the how and when and where and why. The *fuckers,* all of them. And Lord, did that include Posada.

Why doesn't he just corner Posada and spit in his eye and make the goddamn thing happen once and for all?

"What?" Posada was waiting.

"Robles wasn't a Popular Front matter, that's all. That traitor bullshit. C'mon."

". . . Really. You don't think so."

"Please. Just tell me why, Juan. What did Robles know? Was it Guernica?"

That did it. Posada finally turned, his right eye wide and a little shaky. The nerve had been found and poked. He paused, and Hemingway glanced toward the door.

". . . Ernest, this is what's going to happen. I'd like you to leave. The country."

"Ha! That's just what George Mink said."

"Yes, but I'd like to pay you to go. But you must leave now, today, before it's dark. This isn't your country. It's *my* country. There's no need for you to stay here. I'm asking, but I'm not, in actuality. I want you to go and I want you to take the Bentley with you. I don't know if you know how much it is worth."

"In dollars, no I guess I don't."

"It's a 1930, and it could easily fetch five thousand dollars."

"Really. For a car? Wowie-kazowie. So I shouldn't drive it off a Guadarrama cliff, you don't think?"

"I'm serious."

"Me, too, Juan, y'know why? Because the car's already mine, you can't use it to bribe me, and five grand ain't much more than a bale of hay to me these days, I've had a best seller or two, in case you haven't heard. Honestly, Juan, five grand? You must take me for some kind of cheap whore. Or one of your *quinquilleros*! Really, a Bentley was good enough for those illiterate blaggarts, so it's good enough for me? You've got your figures mixed up. Besides, what have you seen lately that gives you the idea I'm in Spain for the money?"

"You're getting paid well to write your little newspaper dispatches, aren't you? Propaganda."

"Why are we suddenly talking about me? Tell me about Guernica, Juan. I saw you, you flinched, you must lose so badly at poker. So you had antiaircraft guns moved out of Guernica, so what. Why did Pepe have a fit about it?"

Posada took a step, a small one as if he were conscious of not appearing to be disarmed, and sat down in a white lounge chair.

"I do not want to ask how you know about that, who you bribed, or what Republican officer you spoke to, because whoever he is, he's now a dead man."

Hemingway realized he had the stolen memo crumpled in his pocket. If Posada were to have him frisked, he'd probably be shot and hacked up right there in Posada's bathtub.

"I didn't speak to anyone, and I'm not the only one who knows. It's out there now, big boy. Don't go fishing for a fox in the henhouse, Juan. It's just me, a big, stupid American with a big mouth and a readership that stretches from Sacramento to Prague. You can't make me disappear, Juan, can you?, without creating a scandal that would use you up like dry brush in a fire. So, I'll just think out loud here"—Posada made no move to interject, avoided eye contact, and was getting redder on his forehead—"that if you wanted the guns out of Guernica, and Pepe thought that was screamingly wrong, and Pepe was not killed, as we both know, as an official act of government but as something illegal, something you arranged for reasons outside of government channels, then . . . the guns should've remained in Guernica. But you wanted them out. Why? What happened in Guernica?"

"Nothing," Posada muttered, his savoir faire slowed to a trickle. "These are government matters, Hemingway, they're none of your business. When you run a revolution of your own, there in Florida, you may understand. Why, exactly, cannot I make you disappear? You're imagining some kind of scandal? Have you forgotten where you are, you self-congratulating American?"

Hemingway watched the bureaucrat rise and pour more wine, straighten his tie. The few moments constituted a second wind. What was not said in the spacious room, what was uncertain and conjectural and presumptive, was voluminous, deafening, hot to the touch. Whatever the Spaniard was thinking, Hemingway couldn't let it alone. Maybe it was a day for dying.

"That's right, Juan, isn't it: Nothing's happened in Guernica. Not yet. I would've heard about it, and so would've a Basque fellow I know in town. But nothing. I assume that with Pepe out of the way the guns were shipped out, weeks ago. But that wouldn't be news. What reason did you give the Comintern for moving the guns? It had to be a lie, or there would have been no reason to have Pepe killed. . . . What's going to happen in Guernica, Juan? The Fascists aren't going to mow down Guernica like they decimated Durango in March, are they?"

The question hung and the tension in the room grew, Hemingway could almost hear it like tinnitus.

"Hemingway." Posada said it like he was standing at graveside. "I've brought you here to talk with you like a man, to give you options. But I see you do not desire options. You want only to throw your weight around, as if the whole world is merely just another barroom for you to lord over. But do not think this is like one of your stories. Whatever they're like—I do not read them. But you are not too famous to dispose of. Far from it. You would not be the first American to die here, nor would you be the first writer. Think about where you've been and what you've seen, and tell me why, even if I should let you go now, inside of an hour something shouldn't fall upon you with the decisiveness of a thunderbolt from Jehovah. You weren't difficult to find and arrest—Jesus, you announce yourself wherever you go. You're standing on your own front line, and if you caught a bullet in the skull no one, not even your mother, would be very surprised. Do you hear me? Who do you suppose will think twice about it, your Basque driver? Perhaps he will have to vanish as well. There are plenty of *arroyos* in the hills that aren't yet filled with troublesome bodies. You and your friend are merely more carrion. Aren't you?"

"Juan, but—" Hemingway fought for a word. He'd only

known danger as a fringe of Italian battlefield. This was not that. This was something else, something mundane and dreary. "You don't know that. I'm pretty famous. They'll come looking for me . . ."

"They may. I'm not certain of it."

"Look, Juan, don't underestimate—"

"Ernest, this is your last chance. Stop talking. For the love of Christ, stop talking. I will have you killed. Please believe me. I will have you killed. Today. I'm terribly afraid that you will force me to do it. Is that clear enough for you?"

Hemingway felt the debonair tough talk turn into humorless, desperate gravity, like he felt a shift in air pressure. He placed his wine glass down. It was clear. His fight-or-flight instincts finally smelled the mortal threat, and his stomach knotted. He glanced to the door again.

Ah, fuck this way of doing things, governments writing memos instead of real men facing each other with weapons. It galled him.

Posada was speaking quietly.

"But I'd rather pay you," he said, "a kind of gratuity for your good work for the Republic, and then you will leave for America. My officers will escort you to the airstrip in Toledo, and you will return home a hero and a rich man. Forget the Bentley. I'll have you leave with fifty thousand dollars in fresh banknotes. Just to go back to writing your books and leave the building of Spain to the Spaniards. The Republic would do better to have Ernest Hemingway alive and being Ernest Hemingway. You've done so much for the revolution already, we shouldn't let this little mess ruin that."

He paused. Hemingway could say nothing. Of course the offer was genuine, there was no reason for Posada to lie. But it wasn't an offer, either. It was a command.

"You understand," Posada said, "this is the most I can do for you. If you do not honor this arrangement, I cannot promise you a safe trip home. Or a safe stay in Spain. What do you say."

After a pause, during which he only looked down, Hemingway said, "Okay."

He tried to smile, tried to make the moment and the deal seem kosher to Posada, who was a little wracked with his own anxieties and hopefully didn't detect Hemingway's boiling rage and shame and distracted air, the latter of which he hoped to mask with a big gulp of wine, distracted by thinking about how exactly he'd dodge Posada's cops downstairs, and then find Quintinilla. As quickly as was humanly possible.

"Alright, Juan, whore me. Bend me over and pay me off. I'm through with this shit."

Without expression, Posada called downstairs for the policemen, and then went to a wall safe, behind a Goya original that frankly looked like a Goya knockoff, and took out stacks of peseta notes, placing them in a canvas satchel. He looked worn and saddened.

"I hope you are being sincere with me. This is two million, five-hundred thousand pesetas, which you should find will transact to the sum I mentioned when you land in New York. Even if Franco loses, a peseta is a peseta. Take it"—he snapped its clasp shut—"and be well . . ."

"Wait, Nationalist banknotes?" Christ, he was admitting outright that he was a Fascist agent.

"Yes, it's all I have right now. It's fine; no one will care what you say about me once you're in America."

"If I'm caught by Republicans or Russians carrying this . . ."

"You'd be in serious trouble, yes. Would they care where you got it, or simply condemn you as a Fascist? Don't get caught. If you don't take it, you know, your trouble will be not only worse but definitive, mortal. Have a good trip. Nobody will search your bags in Toledo."

"How do I know that?"

"Here, take my office number," he said, scrawling on an envelope, "have them phone me from the strip if there's any doubt. And rest assured, Ernest, what I do I do for my country—"

"You can eat that shit twice, Posada," taking the sack, "you're covering your ass and you know it. Spain's a woeful, trodden bitch by this point, and hardly stands a chance, whoever wins. And you're just a pilot fish, hanging on."

"You do mix your metaphors."

It occurred to Hemingway that this payoff was an attempt at something like a miniature show trial: create the chump's culpability, make him admit to it, bring him into the fold, lop his nuts off. Then, either put him to work or cut his throat.

He also supposed he'd never before met such a whole-hog four-flusher, not at the cellar card tables of Paris, nor the cock-fighting backyards of Chicago. How much soul-rending anxiety Posada's machinations had bought him had become crystal clear; the man was playing both sides, and only hoped he'd survive long enough to see one win. But there was no ambivalence about making others' lives pay for his wealth, his penthouse, his power. That was the difference, Hemingway figured, between the petty criminal, whose inflictions on others were singular and personal, and the dictator, who laid selfish waste to a society on a scale that'd make any ordinary man, even a hyena like D'Armoux, shrink with fear for his soul.

"One last thing," Posada said. "Your wallet." Hemingway handed him his wallet and watched the man rummage for a moment. Then he took out the NANA press pass and pocketed it. "You won't need this, and it'll stand as proof that I dotted the i's."

Hemingway said nothing more. Two policemen arrived, stone-faced with duty, and when Hemingway turned out of habit to bid *adios,* Posada was gone, retreated to some other corner of his ridiculous playboy flat.

The elevator.

In the lobby, Hemingway saw there was one more policeman,

just standing guard rather purposelessly, and, sitting in a chair, probably waiting to be summoned, was George Mink.

"*Señores,*" Hemingway said to his escort, "*un minuto.*"

Mink looked up, smiled. "Hemingway, you lucky sonofabitch, you—" But Hemingway hit him. Across the teeth with a closed fist, in a right hook that came from Portugal, and Mink's neck snapped to one side. Blood sprayed on the marble wall behind him, and a tooth clinked off the stone.

Mink gurgled some obscenity, but Hemingway looked at the policemen, who stood back and smiled big Spanish smiles, so he figured he had at least a few minutes liberty, and he put down the satchel of cash and he hit Mink again, same fist, down from above to the bridge of the nose, which creased. Mink's hands were up and trying to run interference, but he could barely open his eyes, and Hemingway hit him again, took a hold of his collar and pounded him like a heavy bag in a gym, and all you could hear besides the sound of dully smacking flesh was Mink grunting, the pitch of which got higher and more piteous as the hits rained down.

After a few moments Mink was practically blinded, but he still managed to reach inside his jacket below the blur of Hemingway's pistoning fist and take out a pistol, but for the half second he had he couldn't even aim it, he hardly knew up from down, and Hemingway slapped it away across the marble. One of the policemen picked it up, muttering in amusement, something about the brawl in the Florida and now this.

Hemingway felt in the beating at least one more tooth fold under his closed fist, and he knew Mink's nose was more than broken—it was kneaded flat.

When Hemingway's knuckles were skinned and bloody, he stopped, and Mink slumped to the floor, still conscious but limp like rags. His face was only beginning to swell.

Picking up the bag with his raw right hand, Hemingway turned to the cops, panting. "*Gracias,*" is all he said, and they all nodded, and with him the first two moved again to the front door. *"Mink necesario que,"* one said, and the other even patted Hemingway on the shoulder a little. He let out a little English: "Nice show."

On the sidewalk, Hemingway turned to them, bashfully friendly, squeezing the camaraderie. "Let me rest a minute, my friends, here," pulling a wad of Republican bills out of his pocket, waving it, "go get the car, I'll wait, whew!, and we can all have lunch—we'll toast the Republic with the Republic's money!"

The policeman laughed, translated for his cohort—who only saw the cash—and the two went to get the car. Hemingway affected a relaxed, fighter-between-rounds stance, dropping the satchel, taking deep breaths, not looking after the policemen. But the moment they disappeared around the corner he glanced at the third cop in the lobby, who was turned toward the still prone Mink, and he picked up the bag and ran.

He only had a vague notion of what direction he should be running in, and knew he only had a minute or so before they would come looking for him in their patrol car. And it's not likely they'd give up at all, despite their bonding over the beating of George Mink. Posada's urgency and despair had to ring in their ears just as it rang in his.

Running blindly through Spanish cities—Hemingway'd be glad to return home, eventually, to Key West where he knew every street and a twenty-minute walk in any direction led you to the sea.

He ducked into alleys, ran from shadow to shadow as if it were an active combat zone, past ordinary Madrileño bystanders on the sidewalks who knew a madman when they saw one. An hour passed this way, behind trash cans and under collapsing stairwells and lurking along building edges exposed and terrified that a police car would turn the corner. Hemingway confronted a litter of newborn kittens in a crumble of old newspaper, a sleeping hooker on a discarded mattress, a gang of five-year-old boys playing war with real but empty WWI handguns, a crystal chandelier tossed into an alley from what must've been a high window, and a dented tin bust of Kaiser Wilhelm II.

Eventually he recognized particular old buildings, and knew he was within a few miles of the Florida. They'd probably stake out the hotel, wouldn't they? Or could they, alone, instead of keeping up the search? Would the two cops dare to ask for reinforcements and admit they lost Hemingway, and 2.5 million Pts, almost before they'd actually left Posada's building?

In another half hour Hemingway skirted the avenue edges and made it to the Florida, which was not yet reaccosted by police.

He did not enter. With the bag in hand, he went instead into the Gran Via. It was midday, after the lunch crowd of foreign writers and vacationing Brigadesmen had thinned to a few stragglers, sleepers, and drunks. But in the corner, as he had hoped, sat Quintinilla, reading *Le Temps*.

Hemingway got a bottle of good Cockburn's at the bar first, and two glasses, and presented himself, the canvas bag dumped unceremoniously beside a chair. Quintinilla looked up with a start.

"Hemingway! *Mi amigo,* you look all beat up. Oh, port, yes, please." Hemingway sat down.

"Pepe, I've got a story for you." But he poured and they drank first, and had that absurd and happy moment men have when they share a drink. "Let me sit over here, if the cops come in I'll have to bolt."

"I heard about you, Ernest, you have been mucking about."

"What have you heard?"

"You beat up a bureaucrat in Valencia, in his own office, with his own gun!"

"Oh, Liston Oak."

"That's him. They were looking for you a while because of that. I gather they never found you."

"I don't know. Someone found me in Valencia, and cracked

my head open with a rifle butt. But I have no idea if they were angels of the Republic or not."

"Angels! But I'm sorry—was that your story? I didn't mean to stumble all over it."

"No, no, Pepe, there's more—"

"What are you carrying around in that bag?" Quintinilla could not see the bag from where he sat, and Hemingway thought he hadn't seen it at all.

"Laundry. Look, I have to tell you this thing, Pepe, have some more port, but I'm being dead serious, this isn't a sporting situation or anything."

"Come now. This is all sport."

"OK, maybe for you. But I need your oath of diligence as a Republican, as a soldier for the Popular Front. I know you as a sporting man and a comrade here at the Gran Via. But I know, too, you are a serious and deadly tool for the revolution. That is the real Quintinilla. That is the Pepe I need to speak to."

"I understand your meaning. There are not two, but I get you. . . . In other words, you are mixed up in state affairs?"

"Uh, not really. Or maybe I am. Listen, it's not really about me, it's about José Robles; remember I spoke about him? He was killed. I found out why."

"Does it matter why, to anyone but his widow?"

"It turns out, yes, it does. He was killed because he found out about something Juan Posada was doing, and Posada had him killed, illegally and covertly and by criminal gypsies in Valencia, who he was going to pay off with a Bentley, if you can believe that. They never got paid, I've got the Bentley. But the thing Robles found out, it had to do with Guernica."

"The town?"

"Yes. Posada had antiaircraft guns moved out of there weeks ago, in anticipation of something. Robles protested it, said he'd go to Gorev"—he took the crumbled memo out of his pocket and laid it out—"and within a week Robles was dead."

"Gorev is gone."

"I know."

Quintinilla eyed the page. "So what's it about? Nothing's happened in Guernica. You think Posada is a Fascist spy? You think he set Guernica up for an attack?"

"I don't know what, but look," and the bag came upon the table and was opened.

"*Mierda,* Hemingway, where did you get this."

"From Posada, just now. He's trying to get me out of the country, the cops are supposed to be escorting me to an airstrip in Toledo."

"A man carrying a bag full of Nationalist bills, this is a man the Comintern has condemned to die, Ernest."

"I know, Pepe"—Jesus Christ, he was sweating—"but come on, it's *me.* I'm telling you the truth. Here, take it, I don't want it. Here, he gave me this"—the envelope—"that's his office number, in his handwriting, in case I had trouble getting on the plane." Hemingway stuffed the envelope into the satchel. "Whatever it's about, he commissioned my friend's assassination, and he did it because he's getting paid by Franco. Full stop."

Quintinilla sat back and was quiet.

# 26

Hemingway finished the port alone.

Quintinilla didn't seem concerned or convinced about that Guernica business, but he trusted Hemingway, and saw clearly that Posada was indeed a mole for Franco, making threats and taking payments and maybe ordering assassinations, and that stopped him in mid-glass, and soon sent him off. "I have to talk to some people," is how he put it, but with a distinctly unurbane grimness that gave Hemingway a certain grave satisfaction.

So he drank alone, watching the door at the Gran Via, daring, in a way, the police to catch him as he leisurely finished his goddamn drink. Just for fifteen minutes or so, long enough for the afternoon to deepen and the air to begin to chill.

Then Hemingway snuck back into the Florida through the back entrance, past his Bentley. He knocked at the concierge's door, realizing he hadn't seen the man—an oily, lazy Barcelonan whom Hemingway guessed was interested in spying on clients and little else—since the first week of his stay at the hotel. The door opened, and Hemingway rushed in and shut the door behind him. The concierge had only a desk and chair and a file cabinet in the windowless room no bigger than a cheap boarding-house's WC. The man himself never raised his eyelids above half-mast, but he did shrug, before Hemingway even asked to use the phone. He wanted to call Guernica, anyone in the town, the mayor if possible, the police chief. But the concierge said nothing, simply picked up the receiver and tapped on the cradle and shrugged again. No phones.

Hemingway couldn't dare go out to the street now to find Ignacio and start driving north. He had to lay low.

He couldn't go to 108, so he loped upstairs to the third floor. The Burgundian woman, who might've been thirty-five but looked far older, whose eyes were still clear and cat-bright, took him in after opening her robe for him in the hall, seconds after he cleared the stairs. Her name, he remembered, was Anouk.

The door shut, he told her the basic facts: the police were look-ing for him, they wanted to deport him, there was a treasonous plan afoot, and he had to stay out of sight until the morning. Yes, he'd give her money to go buy wine, and money for sex besides. Just keep him hidden, at all costs. He spoke to her in French, be-cause he could.

"*Monsieur,* this is so tragic, so romantic—you are a freedom fighter, among freedom fighters!" Undressing.

"Don't get carried away, sweetheart. If I didn't have the money, you wouldn't be so smitten."

"You underestimate women, Ernest. I would harbor you if it cost me everything. Because it makes the hours count for some-thing real."

Evening began to rise. After a while, they were joined by the middle-age Basque woman named Oihana, whom Hemingway paid as well, and three had triangulated sex on and off for an hour, culminating in an orchestrated effort between Heming-way and Anouk, from beneath and above, to give Oihana an orgasm, because she said she hadn't mustered one since 1925, when her husband, a feverish Basque nationalist, was exiled by the Primo de Rivera dictatorship. He was sent to Morocco, and Oihana never heard from him again.

The police never came to the third floor, the door never opened, the three contemporaries never roused from bed. The night passed without a sound in the city, without a single explosive pop or thud, without a single siren.

At sunrise, having caught what he'd realized was a solid ten hours of sleep, Hemingway dressed and tipped the ladies. Oihana kissed him like a mother kissing a son leaving for the front, and took a single silk stocking off her leg, blessed it with a prayer, and jammed it into his pants pocket. Anouk pressed a flask into his hand, filled with *liqueur de poires*.

He snuck down to 108. The door was open and his things were strewn about the room, but it was clear the police were interested in nothing there except Hemingway himself, and perhaps the satchel of cash. The pantry was untouched. He threw it open and loaded up his duffel with dried food and wine and Oak's pistol, and the pages he'd written, slung the sack over a shoulder, and headed to the front desk.

In the lobby there was no one, and the desk clerk napped on the floor under the key boxes. Hemingway went outside, carefully looking up and down the street, but there was no one. If those two patrulleros are still on the case, he thought, and not shackled in a basement somewhere, they should be here soon.

Hemingway did not see Ignacio or his cab, and decided to drive to Guernica alone. He walked around the block, through the morning fog, to the back of the hotel and the Bentley, climbed in, and started her up. The gas gauge said nearly empty. He turned the car off, went inside, woke the desk clerk, and negotiated to buy gasoline from the hotel's backup generators. It came at an exorbitant price, and then took an agonizing half hour to procure, fill the cans, and so on. By the time he pulled the Bentley around the block, hiding behind the steering wheel but feeling as conspicuous as if he was driving a dinosaur out into an empty street, Ignacio was parked at curbside. Hemingway stopped, hired him for a few more days' work and a chance to go home. Ignacio locked his car and climbed in.

"*Peligroso,* maybe." A shilly-shally rocking of the hand. Hemingway still didn't have a solid idea what he'd find in Guernica, but he had to get there, to do whatever could be done. To stem the slouching toward mayhem and evil.

Ignacio shrugged. And smiled. And off they went, quickly finding the highway heading north to Burgos. Ignacio knew the way, and the back roads they could take to get off the main route whenever possible.

They talked, driving under the ripping Spanish sun, through the eastern hills of the Sierra de Guadarrama range. Hemingway sped as best he could, handling the hippo of a car on the shell-shocked and ill-kept Spanish outland roads.

"Not home in . . . seven years," Ignacio said.

"*Familia?*"

"*Si, mi madre, mi mujers, once sobrinas* . . . nieces."

"Eleven nieces? *Ay, caramba.* No wife?"

Ignacio shook his head, searched for English. "Left. For a French. After the war."

"No *muchachos?*"

"No. *Gracias a Dios.* Too poor. Too hungry."

They drove all day, pausing for lunch, keeping to the back roads, sometimes doubling back when a town intersection was crowded enough to suggest a checkpoint or roadblock. They drove fast, as if a speeding Bentley had less of a chance to be noticed than a slow-moving one.

"Ignacio," Hemingway asked at one point, "do you still stay out of the war? Picking sides?"

"*Si,* Ernest, what's the old saying, when elephants fight, it's the grass that hurts most. What I have seen—they are not so different. I am for your war."

"My war?"

"*Si.* This Posada . . . *mierda.* You look for the light, in *el oscuridad* . . . Darkness."

"Is that what I've been doing?"

Shrug. "You have not sold a friend. You have not betrayed."

"Well, you could say I betrayed Posada. Dealt him a black card."

"Posada! Ernest, he is *la sanguijuela.* No man cannot betray the Devil."

They traded turns in the driver's seat, Ignacio relishing the opportunity to drive a millionaire's car. When the Bentley began billowing steam and overheating somewhere in the sixth hour of driving and north of the mountains, and after Ignacio finally figured out the problem was not a leak but a snapped water pump belt, Hemingway took the stocking out of his pocket, braided it tightly, and tied it around the pulleys. They proceeded but drove more cautiously.

"Ignacio, you should come back with me to America. I can give you work, you will live better."

"*Gracias,* but no. Too far from Guernica."

Already evening came at them from their starboard side. They drove for hours more but then parked off-road, behind a copse of beech trees, and ate sardines and canned peaches and a box of stale Pennsylvania pretzels. They drank Anouk's *liqueur de poires,* which was very sweet and warming, and talked to each other in abbreviated sentences of both languages until Ignacio fell asleep in the driver's seat and then Hemingway curled up on the very broad, stunningly comfortable upholstery in the back.

The sunrise got them up and after a stretch they drove.

# 27

April 26. The Bentley passed through Burgos soon thereafter, and Ignacio steered the ship northeast, toward Bilbao, where they stopped and found coffee and pastries. Hemingway was by this point convinced that no one followed them, that they were journeying into Basque country on their own, come what may. Maybe the scattered Republican forces up north got a communiqué to watch out for a big, stupid British car, but maybe not—maybe other issues were more pressing. Who knows what a repercussive mess they left behind, for Posada or the cops Hemingway dodged, or anyone else. The driving had felt so endless Hemingway wondered if there wasn't a new push somewhere by the Nationalists, distracting everyone. Maybe the southern theater was where the action was, Málaga or Córdoba. Maybe Basqueland was exactly where nothing was happening at all, a sleepy little hunk of Iberia where nothing much had changed in half a millennium. Except in Durango, Hemingway guessed, where only a month earlier nuns had been strafed in the street by the Luftwaffe, and bombs had fallen onto the heads of Sunday morning churchgoers. Who had ever heard of such a wretched thing, for God's sake?

They arrived in Guernica before lunch, and drove the Bentley straight to the assembly house, beside the famous oak the Biscayan area holds sacred, a tree legend says is centuries old but is clearly, Hemingway thought, no more than fifty.

Ignacio led the charge, heading into the municipal house and enthusiastically trumpeting Basque to the clerk, who summoned the Biscayan mayor from a meeting of other local muckety-mucks, who all came to the front office and happily shook hands and whom Ignacio regaled with the story Hemingway had told him, using great sweeping arm movements. The speed and impenetrability of the language reminded Hemingway of a dozen medium-sized dogs barking, but in the end, the mayor shrugged. Ignacio tried again, but Hemingway assumed that the lack of military intelligence about the need for their errant antiaircraft artillery, and instead merely the paranoid hearsay coming out of a leathery old cabbie and a silent, round-faced American journalist, inspired little conviction. Hemingway heard Ignacio say "Durango" amid the Basque noise, and the mayor's face got a little steelier then, but the upshot was a reassuring pat on the back, *we'll look into it* is what he probably said, and then the bureaucrats returned to their business.

Out on the steps, gazing up at the oak just letting loose with its springtime spray of musty catkins, the men stood helplessly. But Hemingway looked at Ignacio, who was frustrated but also delighted to be home on such a sunny Sunday, a market day in Guernica, and he said, "Let's buy some wine and go to your mother's."

They did. The woman was ninety-two and liked wine, and then they walked to a run-down apartment house in town to see Ignacio's sisters and nieces, but only one sister and her two daughters were home. The rest, she said, had gone to Loiola by horse-cart to trade vegetables for flour and milk and candy, which they did every Sunday. She would've gone, too, but her two youngest had the croup. They stayed for coffee but Ignacio would not let his sister feed them lunch, lying to her by tapping his belly and telling her they'd already eaten. Hemingway just smiled through it all, not comprehending a word but understanding it from Ignacio later. Finally they said good-bye and practically ran to the nearest café in town where they ate pork and rice and beans, and had a pitcher of sangria with it. The town was lovely and the air was warm. And they had more sangria, this time with black xapata cherries because Ignacio asked, and more than an hour passed, waiting for the rest of Ignacio's sisters to return from the east. Hemingway told himself that even if he was wrong about Guernica and why Posada had killed Robles, the murder happened all the same, and so he shouldn't feel like a fool for hurtling to Basqueland in a desperate panic and finding only old ladies in wool shawls, ringing church bells, and new oak leaves.

Soon after that the planes came.

It was after 4 PM, and the sky was still bright. There was no noise, then the sound of engines. Ignacio knew the sound of incoming small shells, but he did not know this noise. Hemingway knew it right away, from the Great War, and shot to his feet.

*"Tu madre,"* he said.

First there was a German plane, a Dornier Do 17. It roared over the small town, and dropped bombs. The road into town erupted in a plume of sand and smoke and flame, and the church of San Juan caved in and burst into flames. Hemingway and Ignacio—like everyone, women and children and old men and dogs—ran wildly for cover and realized there was none, but once the plane passed the men ran full-out back to Ignacio's mother's house, which was far, too far away, a half mile or more as the seconds slowed as if they were caught in tar.

The next wave came, three black SM.79s, brand new and humpbacked and fast, soaring out of the distant sunshine and into the smoke, dropping dozens of heavy bombs each, and houses that had stood for 150 years were flattened in ten seconds, twelve, before you could form the question *what.* The ground shook under the men's running feet, and they landed on their faces, got up, ran, smelled fire, smelled the things that burned, wood and wool and gasoline and animal flesh and people, old ladies in their burning beds, children swept up in fire plumes, men who had run to help them. The dusty ground of Guernica was littered with burning boots still wrapped around their feet, arms, blown glass, pyramidical shards of stucco brick, whole bodies thrown or fallen and burned to charcoal.

Ignacio's mother's street had not been hit, and so the men managed to get her and Ignacio's sister and sick nieces out and into the Bentley, which Hemingway drove north to the bridge out of town, to find it obliterated, and then south, which is when the next wave came, looking to Hemingway like more Italian planes, the roads around the town were cratered and lifted into the sky as dust. Hemingway turned the Bentley around and drove it, with children crying in the backseat, to God knows where, he thought, but the planes had passed and were dropping their loads onto the town in front of them. There was hardly a building that didn't stretch fiery tongues and black clouds into the afternoon sky. Every second a new explosion, *boom boom boom,* throwing beds and iron stoves and entire limp corpses and vast bloody sections of horse and shattered furniture into the air, usually in an arc and landing dozens of yards away from where the bomb had landed.

There were two more waves of German planes to come over the next forty-five minutes. Hemingway could do nothing except drive blindly, yanking on the steering wheel like on the reins of a dray horse, out of what he guessed was their line of fire, and then he'd turn and drive back to where the planes came from, so the bombs would fall behind them. The sun was up but the sky was dark with smoke.

There was then a brief respite, in which Hemingway drove every way he could find out of town and found that none of the roads were passable. And then he tried to drive through a plowed field of young yams, and the heavy car got stuck in the muddy furrows, spinning its wheels, sitting out in the open.

And the next waves came, a crucifying barrage of swooping three-plane raids, four, five, six of them that Hemingway and Ignacio could see from the car windows, running from north to south, dropping more bombs, igniting the world at their tails, flattening everything that had not been flattened, punishing the defenseless town as if it were some kind of Sodom swept away by the old God. Hemingway felt as if he was dreaming, the kind of dream where you are chased but your feet are seemingly lodged in swamp mud, too heavy to lift for running. Some of the planes, Heinkel biplanes it looked like, with mounted machine guns, would circle around after their bombs had been dumped to strafe civilians trying to run out of town on foot—Hemingway could hear that happen but could not see it. From where Hemingway and Ignacio were they could no longer see flying bodies or body parts in the combustive clouds or what detritus of families' lives were torched and splintered in the streets or what grand century-old edifice was torn into gravel. They did see a horse run out of town, its mane on fire, its flanks ripped and bloody like butchered meat, out into the yam field some hundred yards away and eventually drop to its side in the soil.

When the last planes vanished, it was a natural assumption that there would be no more, because there was nothing left to bomb.

Hemingway knew the Nationalists would be moving in by morning, afternoon at the latest. He and Ignacio, as evening dropped, dug out under the Bentley's tires and eventually drove it backward, through its own tracks, back to the field's edge and into town. They tried to convince Ignacio's family to come back with them to Madrid, but the women wouldn't hear of it, especially once Ignacio's other sisters and nieces came home in the near-darkness and everyone sobbed in the rubble-filled street.

Let the Nationalists come, they cried. What is there for them to take now?

But Ignacio wanted out, and so he and Hemingway left. Drove south, stopped and bought gas, drove in silence. When they reached Madrid before dawn, Hemingway gave Ignacio the car, even if the old Basque could only keep it in a garage somewhere for now, until it was safe to either sell it or drive it.

# 28

Once Hemingway settled in the Hotel Florida again he quickly, in a white heat, wrote out seven lengthy NANA dispatches about Robles, about Posada, about George Mink, and about Guernica, on an ancient typewriter he borrowed from the hotel. He wrote them like they were real, breaking news, so they might have a better chance at being published. Then he rewrote all seven using his personal point-of-view, playing up his *mucho* macho spiel, in case *that* actually made them more marketable, and had the whole kaboodle all wired over. They were, he thought, some of the strongest and purest sentences he'd ever written. He'd tried to be neutral politically, acknowledging the soured ideals of the Popular Front as well as the crimes of the Nationalist spies. But none of the dispatches were ever published, or even acknowledged. Hemingway didn't know it then, but NANA took orders from the War Department, and in 1937 the federal, isolationist wind was blowing more against Communism than Fascism, and everyone knew that could change again, and so the word had been handed down to keep anything coming out of Spain as unpolitical, as uncommitted and uncontroversial, as possible.

Sidney Franklin met him for a late lunch that same day, for which Hemingway had whiskey, nothing but Irish whiskey.

"What happened, boss," Franklin was asking, but Hemingway only half listened. He thought he'd have a while before the smell of charred human tissue left his nostrils.

"It'll come out in a few days, probably. A town up north was bombed. Just to scare everyone. Hundreds and hundreds of Basques, dead in the street."

"Christ . . . What were you doing up there?"

"Nothing, really. I thought something was going to happen, but I wasn't sure. Wasn't sure enough. Nothing I could've done."

"This have anything to do with Robles? Because Posada's gone."

"Gone?"

"Word from del Vayo's office is that Posada was caught as a Nationalist agent, and he was being shipped out to Moscow for a trial, but as of this morning, del Vayo's adjutant told me nobody shipped out anybody, and that Posada's been . . . erased."

"Erased," he said. Quintinilla's good work, he thought. And mine. How many dead men were in the debit column now? "Good. Fuck that man."

They sat in silence.

"So you finally saw some war, then."

"Yeah, I guess I did."

That evening, Martha came back, by way of Marseilles and Barcelona, a trail of steamer trunks behind her, prepared to graciously receive a profusion of apologies, which she got and then some.

Hemingway made love, drank wine in bed, and ran his fingers up and down the skin along her spine.

He'd stay in Spain, he decided, for a while longer, because there didn't seem like there was anywhere else to go. This was still where the war was. His ambulances prowled the embattled city streets, his hotel still stood, his dispatches would still go out. Everywhere else was a sideshow.

"So," Martha said, smoking, looking up. "Are you going to write it?"

Not a chance. If he tried, he thought, it'd end up more like something Dos Passos or Blair would make, something *political*. It was too close, anyway, he could still smell the death, hear the guns, feel the rain on the night road.

Martha dozed off quickly, and Hemingway stared at the ceiling, remembering D'Armoux, how one time in Paris, maybe it was 1925, the two of them landed in a substreet brasserie after card gambling, and because Hemingway was literally penniless D'Armoux bought him a gin and patted him on the back, telling him in his marble-mouthed English, don't worry, you won't always be poor like this, I know, neither will I. Someday, he said, I will own those *batards*.

Who? Hemingway had asked.

Whoever it is that is keeping a boot on our throats, he'd said.

Hemingway remembered feeling grateful that night to have D'Armoux beside him. He remembered feeling as if he could've asked for anything, and it would've been given to him.

The next day he sat in the Gran Via writing—his notes were beginning to accumulate, and the paragraphs were getting as large as handprints. He drank and wrote his story in the gray sunlight coming in from the back for a few hours before Quintinilla came in, looming but quiet, and came over and silently sat across from him.

"Ernest," is all he said, and ordered a drink with a glance toward the bar.

"Pepe."

"You're working."

"Yes. Or rather I will again once you have your drink and leave. I'm not being rude."

"I know you're not."

"Good."

"I just wanted to let you know about Posada. Because you should know."

"I heard."

"That he's gone. But you need to know what happened. Because it is your kill, your victim. You asked for my help. I think it's proper."

"Proper. But I don't want to know."

Quintinilla's drink, a port in a short glass, came.

"That is irrelevant. I found him getting into his car, ready to go to the Palace. I took him to a place we use, an old butcher shop basement, and I tied him down. I had some fellows down there with me. We put a vice on Posada's temples, and beat his knees with piping. Until they were all broken up. I didn't want to waste time with any of those Soviet techniques that take days. He told us the truth about his informing for the Nationalists and manipulating the Guernica guns. We kept at him anyway, until he was unconscious and wouldn't come back. Then . . . the Russians have these big dogs, in a pen over on Calle de Belén, that eat anything . . . His bones we buried in the hills. Here, we saved this."

He slid Hemingway's press pass, unwrinkled and warm from his pocket, across the table. And downed his port.

"Be well, Ernest. Welcome to the war," he said. And left.

That assassin. I should be sickened or shocked, Hemingway thought. Demoralized, or haunted by images of suffering, of modern men doing things to each other, with tools, that you can read about in Dante.

But he wasn't, and he wasn't satisfied or anything like that, either. He was merely caught by the sentence he'd been writing, which was about killings and bad memories, and he could hear the hurt pulse of it better in his head now, better than before. Hemingway went back to it, pencil to paper, quickly, because he didn't want it to escape. When it rolled further on by its own steam, he smiled. Where he was in that sentence, it was vicious and dark, but it was better than where he was. It was safe, it had balance, and it was his.